Ellis Peters has gained universal acclaim for her crime novels, and in particular for *The Chronicles of Brother Cadfael*, now into their sixteenth volume.

City of Gold and Shadows

Ellis Peters

HEADLINE

First published in 1973
by Macmillan London Ltd

First published in paperback in 1989
by HEADLINE BOOK PUBLISHING PLC

10 9 8 7

ISBN 0 7472 3227 X

Typeset in 10/11 pt English Times
by Colset Pte Limited, Singapore

Printed and bound in Great Britain by
Collins, Glasgow

HEADLINE BOOK PUBLISHING PLC
Headline House
79 Great Titchfield Street
London W1P 7FN

City of Gold and Shadows

CHAPTER ONE

Mr Stanforth came from behind his desk to meet his visitor in person, and settle her with ceremony into the client's chair, though she was not a client, had no need whatever of a solicitor, and had come here in response to his telephoned request chiefly out of pure curiosity, of which she had a woman's proper share. Mr Stanforth was not entirely what she had expected, but neither, she deduced from the covert glances he was using upon her like measuring instruments, was she quite matching up to his preconceived picture of her. He was small and nimble and immaculate in fine grey mohair, with a clever, froggish, mildly mischievous face, like a very well-turned-out troll from under some Scandinavian mountain. But towards her he was being punctilious in a way which seemed slightly out of character, as though he did not quite know how to approach her, even though it was he who had brought her here.

Her part was easy. She had only to sit back with perfect composure – something at which she was adept – and wait for him to find his way through the necessary preliminaries to the real business of this meeting. After all, he had initiated it. He must have some need of her; she had none of him. This could not even be a matter of learning something to her advantage. Her mind – and she was well aware that it was an elastic and enterprising mind – was quite open.

Perhaps that was what baffled him about her. She should have been more concerned, more anxious to know what he had to confide, since he had invited her here for that very purpose.

'Mademoiselle Rossignol, it's very kind of you to spare me a little of your time . . .'

'Miss will do,' said Charlotte helpfully. 'I'm almost completely English, you know, apart from the name, although I've lived most of my life in France. My father walked out on my mother when I was seven, so the English influence came out on top from then on.' Her mother, flighty as a butterfly, had heaved a sigh of relief at getting rid of a whole entrenched family along with Maître Henri Rossignol, who still, perhaps, coloured Charlotte's image of the law, and made Mr Stanforth incongruous, with his pricked ears and his mild, perilous, goatish hazel eyes.

'That certainly makes things easier,' he said heartily, and leaned across the monumental desk to offer her a cigarette and a light. He was just warming up; she knew the signs, knowing quite accurately the effect her looks had on most males of most ages. What she had was not beauty, and she had learned that early, and come to terms with it, being of a practical mind. But there was something more adventurous than beauty in her, a tendency to surge forward into situations somewhat risky in their ambiguity, a taste for accepting any challenge that offered, and a manner and a gait to match the proclivity. Angels might well have feared to tread where Charlotte habitually planted her size four sandals with zest and aplomb.

'You must be wondering,' said Mr Stanforth, approaching by inches, 'why I asked you to come here like this. It was pure luck, my seeing that notice of your concert. There couldn't be many Charlotte Rossignols who happen also to play the oboe. So I made enquiries at the hall. It was an opportunity for me. I hope you didn't mind my asking you to come here. I would gladly have come to you, but I thought we could talk more freely here than in an hotel. Briefly, I need to ask you, my dear Miss Rossignol, if you have had any word within the last year from your great-uncle, Doctor Alan Morris.'

There was a moment of absolute silence and surprise. Her eyes had opened wide in wonder, and the light entered their long-lashed blackness and turned it to a dusky, flecked gold. Her small, delicate monkey-features quivered into childish candour, reassuring him that for all her formidable composure she was, indeed, no more than twenty-three. She had fine, white skin, not opaque and dull, but translucent and bright, with the vivid come-and-go of vibrant blood close beneath it; and she had beautiful hair, fine as an infant's and black as jet, curving but not curling about a very shapely head, and cropped cunningly to underline the subtlety of the shaping. Oh, yes, there was a great deal of France there, whether she knew it or not. And her lips, opening to reply to his question, were long and mobile, eloquent even before she spoke, though she might sometimes go on to contradict what they had intimated.

'Mr Stanforth,' she said now, 'I've never once in my life had any communication from my Great-Uncle Alan. I've never set eyes on him. I know quite a lot about his work and his reputation, and am quite proud of him, but I don't expect ever to exchange one word with him. My mother was his niece, and the only daughter of his only sister, but she was as foot-loose as he, and when she married into France she never kept in touch with her English connections at all. I grew up detached. I'm sorry if it seems almost unnatural. It wasn't out of any want of feeling. No, I've had no word ever from Doctor Morris. I should have been very astonished and concerned if I had. I should have taken it for granted there was something the matter.'

Mr Stanforth massaged his sharp jaw with one finger, and looked thoughtful.

'*Is* there?' asked Charlotte, making connections with her usual rash speed. 'Something the matter?'

'That's exactly the trouble, we don't really know. Naturally I hope not, and the probability is that we're exercising ourselves over nothing. But the fact remains, we can't be sure. I'm not surprised,' he agreed, 'that you've received no word from him, but it was just a chance.'

'I'm sorry to be a disappointment. Was that the only reason you asked me to come?' She was reasonably certain by then that it was merely a necessary preliminary to the real business he had with her.

'Hardly, or I could have asked it over the telephone, and avoided imposing upon you. No, circumstances make it very desirable that we should have this talk, and continue in close touch afterwards, if you're agreeable. I had better,' said Mr Stanforth, philosophically accepting the fact of her total ignorance, 'tell you exactly what the position is. I have acted for your great-uncle for more than twenty years now, and have often been left in charge of his affairs during his long absences abroad, on digs all over Europe and North Africa and the Middle East, everywhere that the Roman and Graeco-Roman power extended. You're familiar with his subject, you know he is an authority, internationally known and universally respected. So naturally he travels a great deal, and is in demand as a consultant wherever Roman sites are being excavated. A year ago last October he planned a year's tour in Turkey. It was approaching the end of the season, of course, but he intended to make a first flying visit to Aphrodisias, where some old friends of his were at work, and then to spend the winter on research in libraries and museums, and have the whole of the following summer for field work. He let his house in Chelsea furnished for the year, with the usual proviso that his own staff should remain to run it – he has a housekeeper who has been with him for years, and one daily maid. All quite in order, of course, he has done the same thing at least twice before. And of course no one expected to hear much from him during his sabbatical year, unless, as you say, something was wrong. But the trouble is that no one has heard anything from him even now that the year is over.'

'Nearly six months over,' Charlotte pointed out. 'Quite an edgy matter for his tenants.'

'Precisely! Finding accommodation in London is difficult in any circumstances, and this couple happen to be Australians who don't intend to stay permanently, but are anxious to see their daughter through her physiotherapy training here, and take her back with them afterwards. It would suit them very well to have the tenancy of the house for at least another year. But without any instructions from Doctor Morris it's difficult to know what to do.'

'And what,' she asked practically, 'have you done about them so far?'

'In the absence of any word from my client, I took the responsibility of renewing the tenancy for six months. They could hardly be expected to agree to less, and they're excellent tenants.'

'And now the six months is nearly up. And still no word! Yes, I see why I represented a last hope,' she said. 'Is this very unlike him?'

'Very. He is a man who has deliberately avoided certain responsibilities in his life, and certain involvements, but those business obligations which do unavoidably devolve upon him he has always observed punctiliously. There are money matters, investments, tax affairs to be considered. It is, one might say, a conscious part of his policy of personal detachment to have all his affairs in scrupulous order, and so obviate pursuit and inconvenience of any kind. To be slipshod is to be hounded, which is the last thing he wants. No, I must say that things have now gone so far as to justify me in feeling considerable uneasiness about his continued absence.'

She gazed back at him in thoughtful silence for a moment, and shook her head doubtfully. 'I don't know . . . he's a free agent, and he has confidence in you. At a pinch, he might very well feel safe enough in going ahead with what he's doing, and leaving all the rest to you. Supposing he got excited about some new discoveries, for instance . . .'

'During the winter months work would be at a standstill. In many places it couldn't open up again before June, late May at the earliest.'

'You ought, perhaps, to start official enquiries,' she suggested hesitantly.

'I already have, more than a month ago. I rather wish I'd taken the step earlier. The trail came to a dead end. One that might be perfectly normal, though it leaves us in complete uncertainty.'

'How much *do* we know? I mean really *know*? Do we even know that he ever reached Turkey? Exactly what did they find?'

'Oh, yes, he got to Istanbul, all right. He caught his flight from Heathrow on the 6th of October, the flight-list has been checked through. He claimed his reservation at the Hotel Gul Bejaze, and stayed there for three weeks. We even know just what he was doing, intensively, during that time. He took a piece of work with him to finish. He was commissioned to write one of a series of monographs on the settlements of Roman Britain, and he took the almost completed text with him when he left England. I knew of that from him before he left, for he was going to spend his last few days before the flight actually on the site, refreshing his memory on certain details. Well, he posted the finished text to his publishers from Istanbul about three weeks after he arrived there. The book has been out several months, of course, now. A few days after he mailed it, he telephoned his friend and colleague at Aphrodisias, in Anatolia, and called off his visit. He said he was afraid the delay over the book had lost him the opportunity of reaching the city in time to take part in any meaningful work, and promised to join the next summer's dig in June.'

'But he didn't.'

'He didn't. The day after that telephone call he paid his hotel bill and left by taxi for the main station. Attempts to trace one taxi in Istanbul, after a year and more, naturally fell flat. No one has heard from him since, no one knows where he is.'

It began to sound more serious than she had realised. 'Who undertook these enquiries?'

'The police, through their Turkish colleagues. Missing Persons has all the information available. But I'm afraid the trail was cold before I called them in, and we didn't take it the length of broadcasting or advertising. One doesn't want to set a public hue and cry in train after a perfectly rational and responsible person who knows very well what he's about.'

'He may still be that,' she said. 'There may be reasons for his silence, perfectly good reasons if we only knew them. And he may turn up at any moment with a simple explanation, and wonder what we've been worrying about.'

'So I think, too. Though let's admit that personal security has recently become distressingly tenuous all over the world, and the most innocent and uninvolved of people can still find himself made a pawn in all manner of dangerous games. And Turkey has its share of the modern virus. But urban guerillas don't kidnap distinguished foreigners only to keep their exploit secret, hijackers can hardly help becoming news on the instant, and here there has been profound silence. I tell myself that silence is more likely to be a personal choice than an imposed one.'

'There is such a thing as amnesia, I suppose,' Charlotte said dubiously. 'Illness or accident could have isolated him somewhere. I mean, if he did go off into the wilds of Anatolia, or somewhere remote like that – something might happen to him in some village, where he isn't known.'

'Villagers would be all the more anxious to get the responsibility for him off their hands. And there are quite a number of people in Turkey who do know him, people in his own field.'

They looked at each other for the first time with a long, speculative look, weighing up the possibilities honestly and in much the same terms. 'You think, then,' she said, 'that this disappearance is more likely to be voluntary on his part. But in that case, all we have to do is wait, and when he chooses, he'll reappear. And I take it the police still have his case more or less open, and will be looking out for news of him, in case there's something more in it. There isn't much more we can do, short of going off to Istanbul in person to try and find his tracks. And if, for some reason, he has really chosen to drop out for a while, he wouldn't be grateful for too much fuss, would he?'

'You state the position admirably. That's exactly how we are situated – you and I both.'

'I?' she said, drawing back slightly into her crystalline, black-and-white reserve, and becoming in a breath notably more French. 'I realise that I come into the picture as a relative, and I do feel natural interest and concern for my great-uncle. But I can't feel that I have any more positive standing than that in the matter.'

'You have a *very* positive standing, my dear young lady,' said Mr Stanforth patiently, and perhaps a little patronisingly, too, for this was where money entered into the reckoning, and very young concert artists and music teachers with a living to make must surely react to the alluring image. 'Let us suppose, just for one moment, that we are being over-optimistic, and that Doctor Morris will *not* reappear, as, of course, we hope and believe he will. If this situation goes on unchanged, then it may become necessary eventually, for legal reasons, to take steps to presume his death. That need not jeopardise his position if he should subsequently emerge from his limbo. But it would, meanwhile, regularise his affairs and ensure proper continuity, proper attention to investments, and so on. In short, Miss Rossignol, I've reached the point where I must have your approval and consent for whatever steps I take in protection of his financial affairs. Since your mother's death *you* are his only remaining relative, apart from some distant cousins in Canada, several times removed. And Doctor Morris – a remarkable quirk in his otherwise orderly character, I may say – has always stubbornly refused to make a will. There are people,' said the Norse troll, burning into sudden antagonistic fervour across his cavern-desk, 'who hypnotise themselves into believing that they are going to live for ever.' His client's optimism and appetites, with equal suddenness, burned clear in opposition, and Charlotte had a vision of two principles in headlong collision, and chose to ally herself with her own kinsman, by intuition and once for all. 'If we do not see him again – for we must take that possibility into account – you are his next of kin and his sole heiress. That is why I need to consult with you over anything I do, from now on, in his name.'

Charlotte had never in her life felt obliged to examine her relationships with anyone. Her mother, once rid of the armour-plated respectability of Maître Henri and his phalanx of parents, brothers and sisters, all devoted to the law, had married a happy-go-lucky literary exile from Leeds, as nearly as possible his opposite, and the half-English, half-French child had been absorbed into their slapdash household with the greatest enthusiasm and affection, and never given time to doubt or worry, surrounded as she was by joyous evidence of her own importance and value. There had never been too much money, but never less than enough. She had no vision of money as an independent power, or a formidable opponent. It was there to be used, insofar as you had it; and when you were short, you worked a little harder, and made good the deficiency. And foreseeing that necessity, you made sure that you knew something which could earn you money at need. It was as simple as that. She did not even know what it meant to adapt oneself to another person's requirements for the sake of self-interest. All she had, to enable her to visualise Mr Stanforth's view of her position, was a vivid imagination and a very acute intelligence. They helped her to understand him, and even, regretfully, to sympathise with him.

'If you're asking me,' she said carefully, 'to come into consultation and share responsibility for whatever decisions we have to make about Great-Uncle Alan's affairs, of course I will, though I don't claim to know anything about business and I probably shan't be much help to you. I can't even claim to know what he would want done, because I know almost nothing about him. But I don't at all mind saying what I think *I* should want done in the circumstances. I don't think, for instance, that I should want my death assumed and my property disposed of too soon, so we won't go into that part of the affair just now, if you don't mind. He'll probably live to be a hundred, and make a will leaving whatever he's got to his old college, and I shan't mind at all. But I quite see that you need someone to come in on a practical issue like what to do about his tenants. I think you should extend the tenancy for another full year, if that's what they would like. It would ensure the house being taken care of, and the staff maintained, since you say they're good tenants. And even if Uncle Alan turns up within a month or two, he can hardly complain. It's his own fault. And the inconvenience will be only slight, he can always take up residence at his college again until their time's up.'

She made it sound very simple, as young people do; and she hadn't yet considered the implications for herself, Mr Stanforth reflected cynically, or she would not so blithely dismiss the matter of the inheritance. It was not a fortune, but it was a respectable competence, thanks to royalties, which would continue for years yet, whether the doctor reappeared or remained in limbo. 'I'm gratified,' said Mr Stanforth, with only the mildest irony, 'that your judgement agrees with mine. That is indeed what I had intended suggesting to you, and it disposes of the immediate problem.'

'If you want me to keep in touch, and be available for consultation, of course I will.'

'Thank you, that will ease my position considerably. And as you say, all we can do is wait, and continue to expect Doctor Morris to turn up in his own good time. May I ask what your own plans are? Do you intend to stay some time in England?'

'I'm making my home here,' she said. 'I'm taking a teaching job in a new comprehensive school, but that won't begin until the September term. That's why I'm trying to fill

11

up the gap with a few concerts, but of course I'm not good enough for the big dates, it will be mostly provincial engagements. I'll let you have word of all my movements.'

'That would be most kind and helpful.'

The interview seemed to have reached its natural conclusion. She picked up her handbag, and he rose from behind his desk to take a relieved and ceremonious farewell. But before they had reached the doorway she hesitated and halted.

'You know what I would like? Could you let me have a list of all the books Uncle Alan's written? If I'm going to be a stand-in for him, even temporarily, like this, I really need to know more about him, and that seems as good a way as any. They must surely convey something about him.'

Strange, he thought resignedly, she's not at all interested in how much her kinsman's worth, only, rather suddenly and rather late, in what he's like. And at this stage, isn't that rather an academic consideration? But he said politely: 'Yes, of course. If you'll allow me, I'll have a few of his titles sent round to your hotel. This last one, the text he sent from Istanbul – the publishers took care of the proof-reading, of course – that one I believe I've got here. Take it with you, if you'd care to. Though it's hardly the most riveting of his works. He found Aurae Phiala, it seems, rather an over-rated site in revisiting it.'

There was a large bookcase in the corner of his office, stocked mainly with leather-bound volumes; but the end of the lowest shelf was brightened by the clear colours of a number of paperbacks. He plucked one of them from its place and brought it to her. 'The Roman Britain Library', the jacket told her, and in larger print: 'AURAE PHIALA', and Alan Morris's name, with a comet's-tail of letters after it.

The cover was a fine, delicately-composed, atmospheric

photograph of a shallow bowl of meadows beside the silver sweep of a river, the whole foreground patterned with a mesh of low walls in amber stone and rosy, fired brick and tile, with two broken pillars to carry the accented rhythms up into a sky feathered with light cloud. Charlotte gazed at it, fascinated. A landscape obviously planned, disciplined, tamed long, long since, and long since abandoned to the river, the seasons and the sky; and not a human soul in sight. A less cunning photographer might have felt the urge to place a single figure, perhaps close to the columns, to give life and scale. This one had understood that Aurae Phiala was dead, and immense, needing no meretricious human yardstick to give it proportion.

'But it's beautiful!' she said, and voice and accent had become wholly French for one moment. 'This is where he spent those last few days?' she said. 'Before he caught that flight into Turkey?'

'Yes. He knew the site from many previous visits, though I think he had never organised a dig there himself. The curator is an old friend of his, a fellow-student, I believe. But less distinguished.'

'So Uncle Alan would be with friends, when he stayed there? And he went straight from this place, to catch his plane?'

'So I understand. It is an attractive picture,' said Mr Stanforth, with patronising tolerance. 'Wonderful what a first rate photographer can do with even unpromising material. But you'll see what Doctor Morris has to say about the place.'

'Where is it?' she asked, still viewing the sunlit, fluted hollow with pleasure and wonder.

'Somewhere on the Welsh border, I believe. The text and maps will show you exactly where. The name means something like "the bowl of the gentle wind". Apparently an ideal climatic site. But you'll discover all about the place if you read it.'

Clearly he hardly believed that she would stay the course. She wondered if he himself had survived it. She closed the little book between her palms, and put it away in her handbag. 'Thank you,' she said. 'I look forward to setting foot in my uncle's field.'

She was not sure herself how much in earnest she was, at that stage; and if she had had any other agreeable reading matter to fill up her evening, she might never have started on *Aurae Phiala* at all. But she had no concert, and no engagement socially, since she knew hardly anyone in London, the small hotel in Earls Court was not productive of amusing company, and the television was surrounded by a handful of determined fans watching a very boring boxing match. Charlotte returned almost gladly to the recollection of her morning interview, and in retrospect it seemed to her far more strange and mysterious than while it was happening. She had never been brought face to face with her greatuncle, and never devoted any conscious thought to him. He became real and close only now that he had vanished.

Such a curious thing for an established and respected elderly gentleman to do, now that she came to consider it seriously. How old would he be now? Her grandmother, his elder sister, would have been seventy if she had been still living, and there were several years between them. Probably sixty-three or sixty-four, and according to the photographs she had seen in newspapers and geographical magazines, and his occasional appearances on television, he looked considerably younger than his age, and very fit indeed. Say a well-preserved sixty-four, highly sophisticated, speaking at least three languages, enough to get him out of trouble in most countries, and with a select if scattered network of friends and colleagues all across the Middle East, to lend him a hand if required. And on his last known move obviously still in full control of his actions. A taxi had dropped him and his luggage at the main railway station, he had walked in through the entrance with a porter in attendance; and that was that.

On the face of it, a man about whom the whole world knew, whose life was an open book – no, a succession of books. But what did she really know about him? She roamed back thoughtfully into childhood memories, hunting for the little clues her mother and grandmother had let fall about him, and the sum of them all was remarkably meagre. A handsome, confident man, who had managed to retain his friends without ever letting them get on to too intimate ground. No wife ever, and (as far as anyone knew!) no children anywhere, but all the same, his kinswomen had spoken of him tolerantly, even appreciatively, as an accomplished lady-killer, evading marriage adroitly but finding his fun wherever he went. An eye for the girls at sixty no less than at twenty; and silver-grey temples, blue eyes and a Turkish tan were even more dangerously attractive than youth. He played fair, though, her mother had said of him generously. Not with the husbands, perhaps, but with the ladies. They had to be more than willing, and as ready as he to part without hard feelings afterwards. Doubtful if he ever dented a heart; more than likely he gave quite a number of hearts a new lift after they'd imagined the ball was over for them.

It seemed she did, after all, know a few significant things about him. He lived as he chose, one foot in home comforts, the other shod for roaming. She understood now what Mr Stanforth had meant by describing him as a man who had deliberately evaded certain responsibilities and involvements, and even kept his affairs in scrupulous order mainly to avoid being badgered, or giving anyone a hold on him. And she thought suddenly, with a totally unexpected flash of dismay and sympathy: My God, you overdid it, didn't you? You were so successful at it that in the end you could vanish without leaving a soul behind sufficiently concerned about you to kick up a fuss – only a solicitor worried about the legal hang-ups, and especially the money!

Sympathy, of course, might be misapplied here. For all she knew, so far from being lonely and deprived at this moment, he might well be taking his mild pleasures in his usual fashion, with some lady chanced upon by pure luck in the wilds of Anatolia. In which case he would surface again when it suited him. All the same, the image of his isolation remained with her, and made her feel uneasy and even guilty towards him.

So it was partly out of an illogical sense of obligation that she began to read his book on Aurae Phiala. Eighty or so acres of Midshire by the river Comer, close by the border of Wales. A recreation city, apparently, for the officers of the garrison at Silcaster, and the legions tramping the long course of Watling Street. The account he gave of it was detailed, detached and distinctly unenthusiastic. A place of historical interest in its small way, especially for its sudden death at the end of the fourth century, after the legions that were its life and its protection had been withdrawn. But otherwise a site very unlikely to repay much further examination, and hardly worth spending money on, while so many more promising sites waited their turn to snatch a crumb of the meagre and grudging funds available. In plan after plan and page after page, Doctor Morris amended the estimates even he had given in articles previously published, and disputed various claims made for Aurae Phiala by other authorities. Their aerial photographs he subjected to destructive scrutiny, the light crop lines they detected under the unbroken fields he dated several centuries later than the sacking of Aurae Phiala, the dark crop marks emerging so strongly in contrast he refused to consider as early Roman military lines, but set well back into pre-Roman settlement. (A light, sandy sub-soil, Charlotte learned, provided a first-class ground for crop-marks, since crops growing over ancient foundations tend to ripen and show yellow while the rest of the field is still green. And the crop-marks that show dark instead of pale are likely to lie along the lines where timber walls stood, prior to the stone.)

In short, Doctor Morris was bored with Aurae Phiala, and succeeded in making it slightly boring for his readers. Charlotte found herself intrigued by his handling of some of his colleagues who took views different from his own. His deference, while he refuted their conclusions, was careful and considerate. Even, perhaps, a little cagey? She felt almost sorry for Professor M. L. Vaughan, who was obviously in the same rank as her self-confident great-uncle, and differed from him on almost every point.

She would have been completely convinced, but for that limpid, lovely photograph on the book's cover, so serene, and pure, and gracious in its emptiness of man, a tragic landscape recognised and captured.

It was one of those cosmic accidents which are no accident, that the next day, when she called in at a bookshop to look for some more Morris titles, she should find on the same shelf the total output of Professor M. L. Vaughan; and among the rest his: *Aurae Phiala: A Pleasure City of the Second Century A.D.* She took it down and opened it at random, and the prose caught her by its incandescent fervour. He was Welsh, of course, by his name; this frontier site might be expected to excite him. But he wrote like a sceptic captured and moved against his will.

She bought another of her uncle's books, but she bought, also, Professor Vaughan's; and his was the one she began to read, in the train to a modest concert engagement in Sussex.

Experts do differ, of course, even experts of equal eminence. And yet they were writing about the same place, and both of them knew it intimately, and had known it for years. Every indication Alan Morris rejected, Professor Vaughan accepted and expounded. He gave the city not eighty or so acres of ground, but more like two hundred and twenty, he burned to have the funds to take up lovingly every acre of those two hundred and twenty, and tenderly brush away the dust of centuries from every artifact he expected to recover; and his expectations were high. It was all very odd, very attractive, very mystifying.

Charlotte got back into London rather late that night, and rather tired, but hooked beyond redemption upon Aurae Phiala. It was the last preoccupation of her kinsman before his exit from England, and it was a strangely appealing bone of contention between him and several of his peers. Charlotte lay stretched upon her bed, waiting to relax enough for her bath, reviewing her evening's performance with merciless austerity – the oboe is a tyrannical instrument, and demands lofty standards – and confronting her odd, challenging, unknown English greatuncle, unexpectedly lost before she had ever become aware of him. He was beginning to threaten her personal security, her conviction of her own integrity. He was a ghost – a figure of speech, of course, she was in no doubt of his irrepressible re-emergence – whom she had to placate and exorcise.

She knew, then, that she was going to Aurae Phiala, to look at that charged, controversial, emotional ground-site for herself. It was a gesture without any wider significance, she knew that; she was exorcising and placating no one but herself. But at least she would be treading in his footsteps, and somewhere along the way a clearer picture of him might emerge. The move to Midshire even made economic sense; she had several modest school recitals in Birmingham and the Black Country during the next month, and it would be cheaper to move up there and find a furnished room somewhere, rather than spend the intervening time here in town.

She left by train for Comerbourne the next morning.

CHAPTER TWO

She paid her ten pence at the glass cage of the entrance booth, to a young man who could not possibly be the custodian, Great-Uncle Alan's contemporary, but was clearly something rather more scholarly than a mere gate-keeper. He had a long, agreeable, supercilious face, dark eyes which dwelt upon his latest customer appreciatively but not offensively, and a general style that hovered oddly between the fastidious and the casual. His long hair stopped neatly at the level where it curved most attractively, but his shave was indifferent. Either that, or he had only yesterday decided to bow to fashion and grow a beard. His slacks and sweater were well-styled and good, but he managed to wear them as if they were about to fall off him. His aim had been either hopelessly inaccurate, or else capricious of intent. He had a pile of books, two or three open, and a large loose-leaf notebook at his table in a corner of the booth. It was early in the season yet, and he probably had long periods of inactivity to fill up between visitors; but he was not going to be left at leisure for long this time, for in the gravelled car park outside the enclosure a large bus was just disgorging a load of loud and active schoolboys, shepherded by a frantic youth hardly older than the eldest of his charges. The schools were evidently back after Easter.

Charlotte took her ticket, and went on into the enclosure

of Aurae Phiala. Once round the low barrier of the gate-house and the prefabricated museum building, with her back turned on the plateau along which the road cruised towards distant Silcaster, the shallow, silver-green bowl of the book-jacket opened before her, wide and tranquil. There, even on this windy and showery day of late April, there was a stillness and a warmth, and in the flower-beds that had been laid out among the stretches of lush emerald turf the daffodils and narcissi were at least two weeks ahead of their fellows in the outer world. It was a naturally sheltered basin, a trick of the undulating meadows along the Comer. Narrow, gravelled paths led forward into the maze of low, broken stone walls, the pale ground-plan of a dead settlement. Delicately placed on a slight ridge, left-centre and midway between gatehouse and river, the surviving columns of the forum balanced, lifting the eyes to the exactly right focal point in a sky of scintillating, tearful blue feathered with airy clouds. Two groups of higher walls clustered below in the hollow of the bowl. And everywhere the orderly, skeletal bones of foundations, brittle and austere, patterned the brilliant grass.

The distant border of the enclosure was the river itself, sweeping in serpentine curves round the perimeter. From where she stood it shimmered in silver under a glancing sun, though upstream at the inn, where she had seen it close to, it rolled darkly brown and turgid, and laden with the debris of bushes, for the spring thaw had come late and violently, bringing down an immense weight of snow-water from the mountains of Wales. They were constructing a series of weirs upstream, so they had told her at 'The Salmon's Return', which would eventually control this annual predator, but for this year, at least, it surged down irresistibly as ever, biting acres out of its banks as it cornered, like a ferocious animal frustrated. Its wildness and this elegiac calm met, circled each other, and survived. The demon passed, not once for all, but constantly, and the dead turned over in their sleep, and went on dreaming.

From here, where she stood orientating herself to the unknown photographer's vision of Aurae Phiala, and sharing his revelation, even that violent force, at once protection and threat, seemed charmed into tameness, passing on tiptoe by this idyllic place.

'Idyllic! You're perfectly right,' said a voice just behind her shoulder; a male voice, pitched almost apologetically low, to make its uninvited approach respectable and respectful. And she was quite sure she had not said a word aloud! How did he know what she was thinking? It was a liberty. But wasn't it also a compliment? 'That's why they chose it,' the voice said, diverting her possible resentment before she could even be aware of it herself. 'It was a pleasure city, quite unreal like all its kind. And then it turned real – always the beginning of tragedy. People walked a tightrope here, in search of a secure living, just like today. And history walked out on them, and left them to die. It happens to most paradisal places. That's the irony.'

Many times during this pocket lecture she could have turned and looked at her instructor, and put him clean out of countenance merely by looking; but she had not done it because she was so sure that he was the young man from the entrance booth, a licensed enthusiast, and entitled to his brief moments of emotional escape. His bus-load of senior schoolboys were all over Aurae Phiala by this time, gushing downhill towards the river like streams in spate, and no doubt he was free for a minute or two to breathe again and care about his own theories and idylls. Besides, she liked his voice. It was low-pitched and reverentially modulated, a nice, crisp, modest baritone. And knowledgeable! She had a respect for people who knew their subject, and she was here to discover Aurae Phiala; he could be very useful to her.

'Are you doing research here?' she asked, and turned to face him.

Leaning over the glass counter of his booth, the young man in charge was deep in conversation with an elderly gentleman draped with cameras, and she was gazing into the face of quite a different person. The small shock of surprise disturbed her judgement for a moment, and the awareness of feeling and looking disconcerted inclined her to resent him, and to look for and find impudence in an approach which would have seemed perfectly excusable in a resident scholar. For that matter, she might not have been far out in thinking him impudent; his manner was innocence itself, his deference if anything delicately overdone, as though he were ready to come down off his high horse the moment she came down off hers, and didn't anticipate that the descent need be long delayed. He had the wit to keep talking.

'It began as a sort of rest-station and leave resort, as seasonal and artificial as a seaside fun-fair. And then it grew, and traders and service providers thought it worthwhile to settle here and go into business. They brought their families, some of them intermarried with time-expired soldiers who chose to settle here, too, and it grew into a real, life-and-death town, where everyone had a stake sunk so deep that when the legions started to leave, the locals still couldn't get out. Everything they had was here. No, I don't belong here, I'm only visiting,' he ended disarmingly, coming roundabout to the answer to her question. 'It's my subject, that's all. But I could see what you were thinking. It *is* a beautiful place.'

He was taller than she by only a few inches, and slenderly built, an athletic lightweight in a heather tweed sportscoat and grey cords. He had a thick crop of wiry hair the colour of good toffee, and heavy eyelashes many shades darker, as lavish as on a Jersey cow, fringing golden-brown eyes of such steady and limpid sincerity that she felt certain he could not possibly be just what he seemed. The face that confronted her with so much earnest goodwill and innocence, and with, she felt mistrustfully, such incalculable thoughts behind it, was square and brown, with a good deal of chin and nose to it, and an odd mouth with one corner higher than the other. He could have been anything from twenty-five to thirty, but not, she judged, beyond thirty. He did not look like a wolf, but he did look like a young man with an eye for a girl, and techniques that would bear watching.

'How kind of you,' she said, balancing nicely on the edge of irony, in case a few minutes more of this should see him running out of line to shoot, and make it desirable to jettison him, ' – how kind of you to tell me all about it!'

'Not at all!' he said, and had the grace to flush a little; she even had a fleeting suspicion that he enjoyed the ability to flush at will. 'How kind of *you* not to resent being told! I get carried away. Amateurs do. And this one I really like. Look at that hillscape over in Wales!' Fold on fold, rising gently from the water-meadows, the foothills receded in softening and paling shades of blue into the west. 'No wonder the men who'd served out their time put their savings into market stalls and little businesses, tanneries, dye-works, gardens. Nobody knew the risks better than they did. It was a brave gamble, and in the end they lost it. But it was a stake worth throwing for.'

'I should have thought,' said Charlotte, trapped into genuine interest and speculation, 'that they'd have built just a little further from the river. Weren't they for ever in danger of floods? Look at the height of the water now.'

'Ah, now, that's interesting. You see, the Comer has changed its course since the third century. Exactly when, we don't know, it may have been as late as the thirteenth century before it cut its way through. Come on down, and I'll show you.' And he actually took her arm, quite simply and confidently, and rushed her on the wings of his enthusiasm down through the green complexities of the bowl, between the crisp, serrated walls, across the fragments of tiled pavement, past the forum pillars, down to where the emerald turf sloped off under a token wire barrier to the riverside path and the waters of the Comer.

Here, at close quarters, the fitful, elusive silver congealed into the turgid brown flood she had seen upriver, a silent surge of water looking almost solid in its power, sweeping along leaves and branches and roots and swathes of weed in its eddies, gnawing away loose red layers of the soil along this near bank, and eating at the muddy rim of the path. The speed of its silent, thrusting passage dazzled her eyes as she stared into it. The snows in Wales had lain long, and the spring rains had been heavy and protracted; the Comer drank, and grew quietly mad.

'That's it!' she said, fascinated. 'That's what I meant. Would you choose to live close by that?'

'But look across the river there. You see how the level rises? Gently, but it rises, look right round where I'm pointing, and you'll see there's a whole oval island of higher ground. In Roman times the river flowed on the far side of that. Aurae Phiala was close enough for fishing, close to two good fords, in all but the flood months, and safe from actual flooding. In a broad valley like this you inevitably get these S-bends, and this was the biggest one. By the Middle Ages the river had gradually cut back through the neck of land at this side of the rise, until it cut right through to where it runs now. You can still trace the old course by the lush growth of bushes and trees. Look, a regular horse-shoe of them.'

She looked, and was impressed almost against her will, for everything was as he said. Alders and willows and rich grass and wild rose briars described a great, smooth horse-shoe shape that was still hollowed gently into the green earth, with such authority that it had been acknowledged in perpetuity as a natural boundary, and a single large field hemmed within it.

'Probably if they ever raise the funds to do a proper dig here, they'll find the town had a guard outpost on that hillock. Not that the tribesmen would attempt anything more than a quick raid by night, not until the legions were withdrawn. And if they ever did set out to open up this place,' he said consideringly, 'there are a dozen more important places to begin, of course.'

'Why haven't they ever? Labour isn't a problem, is it? I thought there were armies of students only too anxious to join digs in the long vacation.'

'It isn't the labour, it's the money. Excavation is a costly business, and Silcaster hasn't got enough money or enough interest.'

'Oh?' she said, surprised. 'I thought it was Ministry property.'

'No, it's privately owned. It belongs to Lord Silcaster. He keeps it up pretty decently, considering, but it's all done on a shoe-string, it has practically to pay for itself. The curator has a house downstream there, among the trees – you can see the red roof. And the only other staff seems to be that young fellow in the kiosk, and I rather think he's working for peanuts while he mugs up a thesis.'

'And a gardener-handyman,' said Charlotte, her eyes following the vigorous heave and surge of the mole-brown water as it tore down past them and ripped at the curve of the bank, lipping half across the trodden right of way. It had been higher still, probably some three or four days earlier, for it had bitten a great red hole in the shelving bank, like a long wound in the smooth turf, and left the traces of its attack in half-dried puddles of silky clay and a litter of sodden leaves and bushes. Round this broken area a big, blond young man in stained corduroys and a donkey jacket was busy erecting a system of iron posts striped in red and white, and stringing a rope from them to cordon off the slip.

'Hey, there's brickwork breaking through there!' Charlotte's companion said with quickening interest, and set off to have a closer look. The cordoned area was much bigger than they had realised, for several square yards of the level ground on top had subsided into ominous, shallow holes, here and there breaking the turf, and the slope down to the river path, once dropping gradually a matter of fifteen feet or so, now sagged in red rolls of soil and grass. The gardener had completed his magic circle, and was hanging three warning boards from the stanchions, with the legend boldly and hurriedly slashed in red paint: DANGER! KEEP CLEAR!

By a natural enough process, this injunction immediately attracted the most unruly fringe of the school party, straying from the group of their fellows in the forum. They came like flies to honey, not the heedless junior element, either, but a knot of budding sophisticates in their teens, led by a tall, slim sixteen-year-old on whose walk, manner and style all the rest appeared to be modelling themselves.

The young teacher, observing this deliberate defection, broke off his lecture to raise his voice, none too hopefully, after his strays. 'Boys, come back here at once! Come here and pay attention! Boden, do you hear?'

The boy who must be Boden heard very well. His

strolling gait became exaggeratedly languid and assured. One or two of his following hesitated, wavered and turned back. Most of the others hovered diplomatically to make it look as if they were about to turn back, while still edging gingerly forward. Boden advanced at an insolent saunter to the stretched rope. The gardener, suddenly aware of him, reared erect to his full impressive six-feet-two and stood still, narrowly observing this unchancy opponent. The boy gazed back sweetly, forbearing from touching anything, and daring anyone to challenge his intentions. He was a good-looking boy, and knew it. He was pushing manhood, and much too well aware of that, though he believed himself to be much nearer maturity than he actually was. Twice he advanced a hand with deliberate teasing towards the hook that sustained the rope on the posts, and twice diverted the gesture into something innocuous. The gardener narrowed long, grey-blue eyes and made never a move. The boy stretched out a foot under the rope, and prodded with the toe of a well-polished shoe at the edge of one of the ominous cracks in the grass. The gardener, with deliberation, put down the spade he held, and took one long step to circle the obstruction between them.

The boy gave an amused flick of his head, swung round unhurriedly – yet not too slowly, either – and sauntered away with a laugh, his admirers tittering after him. Distant across the grass, the young teacher, with opportunist alacrity, chose that moment to call: 'That's better, Boden! Come on, now, quickly, you're holding up the whole party.'

'The secret of success with performing fleas,' said Charlotte's self-constituted guide startlingly, diverted even from his Roman passion, 'is to synchronise your orders with their hops. Our unfortunate young friend seems to know the principle, whether he can make it work or not.'

The gardener stood a moment to make sure that his antagonist was really retiring, then turned back to complete his work. His eye met Charlotte's, and his face flashed into a sudden brief, almost reluctant smile. 'Flipping kids!' he said in a broad, deep country voice, with a hint of the singing eloquence of Wales.

'They give you much trouble normally?' asked the young man.

'What you'd expect. Not that much,' he allowed tolerently. 'But that one's a case.'

'You know him?' the young man asked sympathetically.

'Never seen him before. I know his sort, though, on sight.'

'Oh, I don't know . . . he's just flexing his muscles.' He looked over his shoulder, to where the youthful shepherd was fretfully hustling his flock from the forum into the skeleton entrance of the baths. 'He's got a teacher bossing him around who's about four years older than he is, if that, and a lot less self-confident, but holding all the aces. Not that he plays them all that well,' he admitted, thoughtfully watching the harried youngster trying to be as tall as his tallest and most formidable charge. 'And of course,' he said aside to Charlotte, with a devastating smile, 'having a girl like you around doesn't make their problem any easier for either of them.'

'I could go away,' Charlotte offered, between offence and gratification.

'Don't do that!' he said hastily. 'Each of them would blame the other. And you haven't seen half what's here to be seen yet.' He turned back to the gardener. 'When did this slip happen?'

'This morning. Water's been right up over the path two days or more, I reckon it's loosened part o' the foundations under here.' He stood at the edge of the slope, looking down the line of his cordon and into the turgid water. 'Who'd get the blame, I ask you, if some young big-head like him got larking about in that lot, and the whole thing caved in and buried him alive? I don't reckon they'd allow as a rope and three notices was enough. It'd be me for it, me and Mr Paviour and his lordship – ah, and in that order! But they expect us to keep the place open for 'em. We got stated hours, nobody lets us off because the Comer floods.'

His deep, warm western voice had risen into plangent eloquence, indignant and rapt. And Charlotte was suddenly aware of him as a person, and by no means an unintelligent person, either; but above all a vital presence, to be ignored only at the general peril. He was built rather heavily even for his height, a monumental creature admirably suited to these classic and heroic surroundings; and his face was a mask of antique beauty, but crudely cut out of a local stone. She could see him as a prototype for the border entrepreneur trapped here in the decline and fall of this precarious city, the market-stallholder, the baths attendant, the potter, the vegetable grower, any one of the native opportunists who had rallied to serve and exploit this hot-house community of time-expired settlers and pay-happy leave-men. He had a forehead and nose any Greek might have acknowledged with pride, and long, grey-blue eyes like slivers of self-illuminating stone, somewhere between lapis-lazuli and granite. His fairness inclined ever so slightly towards the Celtic red of parts of Wales, an alien colouring in both countries. He had a full, passionate, childlike mouth, generously shaped but brutally finished; and his cleanshaven cheeks and jaw were powerful and fleshless, pure, massive bone under the fine, fair skin. It was easy to see that his roots went down fathoms deep in this soil, and transplanting would have destroyed everything in him that was of quality. There was nowhere else he belonged.

Charlotte said, on an impulse she only partially understood: 'Don't worry about him. In an hour they'll be gone.' And just as impulsively she turned to check on the movements of that incalculable swarm of half-grown children who were causing him this natural anxiety. The boys and their uneasy pastor were moving tidily enough into the first green enclosure which must be the frigidarium of the baths, emerging in little, bulbous groups from between the broken walls of the entrance. She saw the stragglers gather, none too enthusiastically, but not unwillingly, either, and waited for the last-comers. Something was missing there. It took her a few minutes to realise what it was. The teacher, self-consciously gathering his chicks about him, was now the tallest person in sight. Where had the odious senior, Boden, gone, somewhere among those broken, enfolding walls? And how had he shed his train? The numbers there looked more or less complete. He was a natural stray, of course. He needed the minimum of cover to drop out of sight, whenever it suited him. But at least he was well away from here. No doubt something else had diverted his attention, and afforded him another cue to spread confusion everywhere around him.

'There's always closing-time.' said the gardener-handyman philosophically. He lifted one narrowed glance of blue-grey eyes, slanting from Charlotte to her escort and sharing a fleeting smile between them as recognised allies. He was gone, withdrawing rather like a mountain on the move, downriver where the water most encroached. He walked like a mountain should walk, too, striding without upheaval, drawing his roots with him.

'Come down to the path,' said the enthusiast, abruptly returning to his passion as soon as the distractions withdrew, 'and I'll show you something. Round this way it's not so steep. Here, let me go first.' He took possession of her hand with almost too much confidence, drawing her with him down the slippery slope of wet grass towards the waterside. Her smooth-soled court shoes glissaded in the glazed turf, and he stood solidly, large feet planted, and let her slide bodily against him. He looked willowy enough, but he felt like a rock. They blinked at each other for a moment at close quarters, wide-eyed and brow to brow.

'I ought to have introduced myself,' said the young man, as though prompted by this accidental intimacy, and gave her a dazzled smile. 'My name's Hambro – Augustus, of all the dirty tricks. My friends call me Gus.'

'I suspect,' she said, shifting a little to recover firmer standing, 'that should be Professor Hambro? And F.S.A. after it? At least!' But she did not respond with her own name. She was not yet ready to commit herself so far. And after all, this could be only a very passing encounter.

'Just an amateur,' he said modestly, evading questioning as adroitly as she. 'Hold tight . . . the gravel breaks through here, there's a better grip. Now, look what the river did to one bit of the baths.'

They stood on the landward edge of the riverside path, very close to the lipping water. Before them the bevelled slope, fifteen feet high, cut off from them the whole upper expanse of Aurae Phiala, with all its flower-beds and stone walls; and all its visitors had vanished with it. They were alone with the silently hurtling river and the great, gross wound it had made in this bank, curls of dark-red soil peeled back and rolling downhill, and a tangle of uprooted broom bushes. At a level slightly higher than their heads, and several yards within the cordon, this raw soil fell away from a dark hole like the mouth of a deep, narrow cave, large enough, perhaps, to admit a small child. The top of it was arched, and looked like brickwork, the pale amber brick of Aurae Phiala. Bushes sagged loosely beneath it; and the masonry at the crown of the arch showed paler than on either curve, as though it had been exposed to the air longer, perhaps concealed by the sheltering broom.

'You know,' said Gus, as proudly as if he had discovered it himself, 'what that is? It's the extreme corner of what must be one hell of a huge hypocaust.'

'Really?' she said cautiously, still not quite convinced that he was not shooting a shameless line in exploitation of her supposed ignorance. 'What's a hypocaust?'

'It's the system of brick flues that runs under the entire floor of the caldarium – the hot room of the baths – to circulate the hot air from the furnace. That's how they heated the place. Narrow passages like that one, built in a network right from here to about where the school party was standing a few minutes ago. They'd just come in, as it were, from the street, through the palaestra, the games courts and exercise ground, and into the cold room. The chaps who wanted the cold plunge would undress and leave their things in lockers there, and there were two small cold basins to swim in – two here, anyhow – one on either side. The sybarites who wanted the hot water bath or the hot air bath would pass through into the slightly heated room one stage farther in, and undress there, then go on in to whichever they fancied. The hypocaust ran under both. If you were fond of hot water, you wallowed in a sunken basin. If you favoured sweating it out, you sat around on tiered benches and chatted with your friends until you started dissolving into steam, and then got yourself scraped down by a slave with a sort of sickle thing called a strigil, and massaged, and oiled and perfumed, or if you were a real fanatic you probably went straight from the hot room to take a cold plunge, like sauna addicts rolling in the snow. And then you were considered in a fit state to go and eat your dinner.'

'By then,' she said demurely, 'I should think you'd want it.'

He eyed her with a suspicious but quite unabashed smile. 'You know all this, don't you? You've been reading this place up.'

'I could hardly read up this bit, could I? It only came to light today.' She strained her eyes into the broken circle of darkness, and a breath of ancient tension and fear seemed to issue chillingly from the hole the river had torn in history. 'But they're quite big, those flues, if that's their width. A man could creep through them.'

'They had to be cleaned periodically. These aren't unusual. But the size of the whole complex is, if I'm right about this.'

She let him help her back up the slope, round the other side of the danger area, and demonstrate by the skeletal walls where the various rooms of the baths lay, and their impressive extent.

She had no idea why she suddenly looked back, as they set off across the level turf that stretched above that mysterious underworld of brick-built labyrinths. The newness of the scar, the crudity of the glimpse it afforded into long-past prosperities and distresses, the very fact that no one, since this city was abandoned overnight, had threaded the maze below – a matter of fifteen centuries or more – drew her imagination almost against her will, and she turned her head in involuntary salute and promise, knowing she would come back again and again. Thus she saw, with surprise and disquiet, the young, dark head cautiously hoisted out of cover to peer after them. How could he be there? And why should he want to? The incalculable Boden had somehow worked his way round once again into forbidden territory, had been lurking somewhere in the bushes, waiting for them to leave. The twentieth century, inquisitive,

35

irreverent, quite without feeling for the past, homed in upon this ambiguous danger-zone with its life in its hand.

She clutched at her companion's arm, halting him in mid-spate and bringing his head round in respectful enquiry.

'That boy! He's there again – but inside the rope now! Why do they *have* to go where it says: Danger?'

Gus Hambro wheeled about with unexpectedly authoritative aplomb, just in time to see the well-groomed young head duck out of sight. He dropped Charlotte's hand, took three large strides back towards the crest, and launched a bellow of disapproval at least ten times as effective as the hapless teacher's appeals:

'Get out of that! Yes, *you*! Want me to come and fetch you? *And stay out!*'

He noted the rapid, undignified scramble by which the culprit extricated himself from the ropes on the river path, followed by ominous little trickles of loose earth; and the exaggerated dignity with which he compensated as soon as he was clear, his slender back turned upon the voice that blasted him out of danger, his crest self-consciously reared in affected disregard of sounds which could not possibly be directed at him.

'Those notices,' announced Gus clearly to the general air, but not so loudly as to reach unauthorised ears, 'mean exactly what they say. Anybody we have to dig out of there we're going to skin alive afterwards. So watch it!'

It was at that point that Charlotte began seriously to like her guide, and to respect his judgement. 'That's it,' he said, tolerantly watching the Boden boy's swaggering retreat towards the curator's house. 'He'll lay off now. His own shower weren't around to hear that, he'll be glad to get back to where he rates as a hero.'

She was not quite so sure, for some reason, but she didn't

say so. The tall, straight young back that sauntered away down-river, to come about in a wide circuit via the fence of the curator's garden, and the box hedge that continued its line, maintained too secure an assurance, and too secret a satisfaction of its own, in spite of the dexterity with which it had removed itself from censure. This Boden observed other people's taboos just so far as was necessary, but he went his own way, sure that no values were valid but his own. Still, he removed himself, if only as a gesture. That was something.

'You did that very nicely,' she said, surprising herself.

'I try my best,' he said, unsurprised. 'After all, I've been sixteen myself. I know it's some time ago, but I do remember, vaguely. And I'm not sure it isn't all your fault.'

She felt sure by then that it was not; she was completely irrelevant. But she did not say so. She was beginning to think that this Gus Hambro was a good deal more ingenuous than he supposed; but if so, it was an engaging disability in him.

'I was going to show you the laconicum,' he said, and he turned and snuffed like a hound across the green, open bowl, and set out on a selected trail, nose to scent, heading obliquely for the complex of standing walls where several rooms of the ancient baths converged. The amber brickwork and rosy layers of tile soared here into the complicated pattern of masonry against the pale azure sky.

'You see? That same floor we've been crossing reaches right to here, one great caldarium, with that hypocaust deployed underneath it all the way. And just here is the vent from the heating system, the column that brought the hot air directly up here into the room when required.'

It was merely a framework of broken, blonde walls, barely knee-high, like the shaft of a huge well, a shell withdrawn into a corner of the great room. Over the round vent a rough wooden cover, obviously modern, was laid. Gus put a hand to its edge and lifted, and the cover rose on its rim, and showed them a glimpse of a deep shaft dropping into darkness, partially silted up below with rubble.

'Yes – it would take some money and labour to dig that lot out! Wonder what happened to the original cover? It would be bronze, probably. Maybe it's in the museum, though I think some of the better finds went to the town museum in Silcaster.'

'This is what you call the laconicum?' she asked, drawing back rather dubiously from the dank breath that distilled out of the earth.

'That's it. Though you might, in some places, get the word laconia used for small hot-air rooms, too. They could send the temperature up quickly when required, by raising the cover – even admit the flames from the furnace if they wanted to. Come and have a look round the museum. If you've time? But perhaps you've got a long drive ahead,' he said, not so much hesitantly as enquiringly.

'I'm staying at "The Salmon's Return", just upstream,' she said. 'Ten minutes' walk, if that. Yes, let's see the museum, too.'

It was a square, prefabricated building, none too appropriate to the site, but banished to the least obtrusive position, behind the entrance kiosk. It was full of glass cases, blocks of stone bearing vestigial carving, some fragments of very beautiful lettering upon the remains of a stone tablet, chattering schoolboys prodding inquisitively everywhere, and the young teacher, perspiring freely now, delivering a lecture upon Samian ware. Boden was not among his listeners, nor anywhere in the three small, crowded rooms. By this time Charlotte would have felt a shock of surprise at ever finding that young man where he was supposed to be.

They made the round of the place. A great deal of red glaze pottery, some glass vessels, even one or two fragments of silver; tarnished mirrors, ivory pins, little bronze brooches, a ring or two. Gus, tepid about the collection in general, grew excited about one or two personal ornaments.

'See this little dragon brooch – there isn't a straight line in it, it's composed of a dozen quite unnecessarily complex curves. Can you think of anything less Roman? Yet it is Roman – interbred with Celtic. Like the mixed marriages that were general here. This kind of ornament, in a great many variations, you can locate all down this border. In the north, too, but they differ enough to be recognisable.'

She found the same curvilinear decoration in several other pieces, and delighted him by picking them out without hesitation from the precise and formal Roman artifacts round them.

'Anything that looks like a symbol for a labyrinth, odds on it's either Celtic or Norse.'

It was nearly closing time, and the school party, thankfully marshalled by its young leader, was pouring vociferously out into the chill of the early evening, and heading with released shouts for its waiting coach. The last and smallest darted back, self-importantly, to inscribe his name with care in the visitors' book, which lay open on a table by the door, before allowing himself to be shepherded after his companions. On impulse, Charlotte stopped to look at what he had added in the 'Remarks' column, and laughed. 'Veni, vidi, vici', announced the ball-pen scrawl.

'You should sign, too,' said Gus, at her shoulder.

She knew why, but by then it was almost over in any case, for when was she likely to see him again? So she signed 'Charlotte Rossignol', well aware that he was reading the letters as fast as she formed them.

'Now may I drive you back to the pub?' he said casually,

as they emerged into the open air, and found the studious young man of the kiosk waiting to see his last customers out, one finger still keeping his place in a book. 'I'm staying there, too. And as it happens, I didn't walk. I've got my car here.'

The car park was empty but for the elderly gentleman's massive Ford, which was just crunching over the gravel towards the road, an old but impressive bronze Aston Martin which Charlotte supposed must belong to Gus – it sent him up a couple of notches in her regard – and the school bus, still stationary, boiling over with bored boys, and emitting a plaintive chorus of: 'Why are we waiting?' The driver stood leaning negligently against a front wing, rolling himself a cigarette. Clearly he had long since trained himself to tune out all awareness of boys unless they menaced his engine or coachwork.

And why *were* they waiting? The noise they were making indicated that no teacher was present, and there could be only one explanation for his absence now.

'He's lost his stray again,' said Gus, halting with the car keys levelled in his hand.

'Here he comes now.' And so he did, puffing up out of the silvered, twilit bowl of Aurae Phiala, ominous at dusk under a low ceiling of dun cloud severed from the earth by a rim of lurid gold. A glass bowl of fragile relics closed with a pewter lid; and outside, the fires of ruin, like a momentary recollection of the night, how many centuries ago, when the Welsh tribesmen massed, raided, killed and burned, writing 'Finis' to the history of this haunted city.

'Poor boy!' said Charlotte, suddenly outraged by the weariness and exasperation of this ineffectual little man, worn out by a job he had probably chosen as the most profitable within his scope, and now found to be extending him far beyond the end of his tether. 'Whoever persuaded him ought to be a teacher?'

'He's not that far gone,' Gus assured her with unexpected shrewdness. 'He knows when to write off his losses.'

The young man came surging up to them, as the only other responsible people left around. 'I beg your pardon, but you haven't seen one of my senior pupils around anywhere, by any chance? A dark boy, nearly seventeen, answers – *when* he answers! – to the name of Gerry Boden. He's a professional absentee. Where we are, he is most likely not to be. Sometimes with escort – chorus, rather! This time, apparently, without, which must be by his own contriving. I'm missing just one boy – the magnate himself.'

Between them they supplied all they could remember of the encounter by the roped-off enclosure above the river.

'He never did come back to us,' said the young man positively. 'I always know whether he's there or not. Like a pain, if you know what I mean.' They knew what he meant. He shrugged, not merely helplessly, rather with malevolent acceptance. 'Well, I've looked everywhere. He does it on purpose, of course. This isn't the first time. He's nearly seventeen, he has plenty of money in his pockets, and he knows this district like the palm of his hand. We're no more than ten miles from home. He can get a bus or a taxi, and he knows very well where to get either. I don't know why I worry about him.'

'Having a conscience does complicate things,' said Gus with sympathy.

'It simplifies this one,' said the teacher grimly. 'I've got a conscience about all this lot, all of 'em younger than our Gerry. This time he can look out for himself, I'm going to get the rest home on time.'

He clambered aboard the coach, the juniors raised a brief, cheeky cheer, half mocking and half friendly, the driver hoisted himself imperturbably into his cab, and the coach started up and surged ponderously through the gates and away along the Silcaster road.

Charlotte turned, before getting into the car, and looked back once in a long, sweeping survey of the twilit bowl of turf and stone. Nothing moved there except the few black-headed gulls wheeling and crying above the river. A shadowy, elegiac beauty clothed Aurae Phiala, but there was nothing alive within it.

'When did it happen?' she asked. 'The attack from the west, the one that finally drove the survivors away?'

'Quite late, around the end of the fourth century. Most of the legions were gone long before that. Frantic appeals for help kept going out to Rome – Rome was still the patron, the protector, the fortress, even when she was falling to pieces herself. About twenty years after the sack of Aurae Phiala, Honorius finally issued an edict that recognised what had been true for nearly a century. He told the Britons they could look for nothing more, no money, no troops, no aid. From then on they had to shift for themselves.'

'And the Saxons moved in,' said Charlotte.

He smiled, holding the passenger door open for her. By this time he would not have been surprised if she had taken up the lecture and returned him a brief history of the next four centuries. 'Well, the Welsh, over this side. Death from the past, not the future. A couple of anachronisms fighting it out here while real life moved in on them from the east almost unnoticed. But their kin survived and intermarried. Nothing quite disappears in history.'

But she thought, looking back at that pewter sky and narrow saffron afterglow as the Aston Martin purred into life and shot away at speed: Yes, individuals do! Perversely, wilfully or haplessly, they do vanish. One elderly, raffish archaeologist in Turkey, one uneasy, spoiled adolescent here. But of course they'll both emerge somewhere. Probably the boy's halfway home by now, ahead of his party, probably he thumbed a lift the other way along this road as soon as he got intolerably bored. That would amuse him, the thought of the fuss and the delay and the inconvenience to everyone, while he rode home to wherever home is, in the cab of a friendly lorry.

And Doctor Alan Morris? He could be accounted for just as easily, and much more rationally. Total absorption in his passion could submerge him far below the surface of mere time. Somewhere in Anatolia, as yet unheralded, a major news story was surely brewing, to burst on the world presently in a rash of photographs, films, television interviews – some new discovery, one more Roman footprint in the east, stumbled on happily, and of such delirious interest that its discoverer forgot about the passing of the year, his minor responsibilities, and his fretful solicitor.

Over Aurae Phiala the April dusk closed very softly and calmly, like a hand crushing a silvery moth. But her back was turned on the dead city then, and she did not see.

CHAPTER THREE

'The Salmon's Return' lay a quarter of a mile up-river, and dated back to the early seventeenth century, a long, low, white-painted house on a terrace cunningly clear of the flood level of the Comer, and with ideal fishing water for some hundreds of yards on either side of it. It was small, and aware of the virtues of remaining small, lurking ambiguously between hotel and pub, and retaining its hold on the local bar custom while it lured in the fanatical fishermen from half the county for weekend indulgences and occasional contests. Its ceilings were low, and its corners many and intimate. And it belonged to a family, and reflected their stubborn conservative tastes, with a minimum of staff providing a maximum of service. The only relatively new thing about it was its romantic and truthful name, which someone in the family had thought up early in the nineteenth century as an improvement on 'The Leybourne Arms'; for the Leybourne family had been extinct since the fourteenth century, while salmon regularly did return several miles up-river from this house, and were regularly taken for a mile on either side. Downstream, the nearest weir was a tourist sight in the season, flashing with silvery leaps as the salmon climbed to their spawning-grounds.

From the narrow approach lane a gravel drive swung round to the side door of the inn, and then continued, dwindling, to the rear, where there was a brick garage and a half-grassy car park. Gus halted the Aston Martin at the doorway instead of driving straight on to the garage, and was out of the driving-seat like a greyhound out of a trap, to dart round to the passenger side and hand Charlotte out. His meticulous performance slightly surprised her; there had been moments when they seemed to have achieved a more casual contact, and he couldn't be still trying to impress. However, she allowed him to squire her to the desk, without comment and with a straight face, told him the number of her key, though keys were almost an affectation at 'The Salmon's Return', more for ornament than use, and let him take it down for her and escort her to the foot of the oak staircase, which wound in slightly drunken lurches about a narrow well, the polished treads hollowed by centuries of use.

He stood back then, and let her go, and she mounted the first flight, and the second, planting her fashionable square heels firmly on the beautiful old wood, which was austerely and very properly without covering, and recorded her movements accurately for anyone listening below. She didn't look back, and she didn't linger, but her ears were pricked at every step. She felt, rather than heard, how he turned smartly and loped back across the panelled hall towards the door, no doubt to drive the car round into the garage. No doubt! Except that he was in no hurry about starting it up. Its aristocratic note was not loud, but proudly characteristic. Though she had no car of her own just now, Charlotte had been driving, and driving well, for more than four years.

The second landing was carpeted, the wood of the flooring being slightly worn and hollowed. Her steps could no longer be heard below, once she reached the corridor. She did not even go as far as her room – the sound of the door being unlocked, opening and closing again should surely not carry down to the hall. She kicked off her shoes on the carpet, and slid back silently to listen down the well of the staircase; and picking up from this level only minor and ambiguous sounds, she went quickly down again one floor, to where she could lean cautiously over the glossy black banister, and train both eyes and ears upon any activity in the hall below. Visually, her range was limited. The acoustics were excellent.

She had no idea, until then, why she was acting as she was, or what she suspected, or why, indeed, she should suspect anything but a straight pick-up, and one so simply and attractively engineered as to be quite unalarming; a normal minor wolf on the prowl, with a long weekend to while away, and an eye cocked for congenial company, preferably intimate, but in any case gratifying. And yet she held her breath as she leaned out from the cover of the first-floor corridor, and hung cautiously over the oak rail.

Mrs Lane was there just below her; she could see the top of the round, erect, crisply waved head of iron-grey hair, and the bountiful bulges, fore and aft, of the pocket-clipper figure below. Mrs Lane was the miniature goddess who controlled her large, tolerant, good-humoured menfolk, and made this whole organisation work. And at this moment she had a finger threading the maze of the register, and one hand already vaguely gesturing towards the key-board.

'Well, yes,' said the comfortable border voice, pondering, 'I can give you a single room, but only for two nights, I'm afraid. Weekends we're usually booked up in advance, you see, even in the close season. There's a club meeting here for a social weekend – I think they like to keep their places warm here for when coarse fishing starts again. Number 12, if two nights is any good to you?'

'Better than nothing.' said Gus Hambro's voice heartily, but with circumspect quietness. 'I'll take it, and gratefully. This is a dream of a position you've got here, with the path down-river. You ought to keep rooms for archaeologists as well as fishermen.'

'They're not so predictable,' said Mrs Lane practically, 'and they do so tend to camp, you know. The fishermen are good men for their comforts, and then they do patronise the bar. After all, you need an audience when you talk about fish, and salmon especially. You don't fish yourself now, Mr Hambro?'

'I never really had time,' said the winning baritone voice. 'You might convert me, at that! Number 12, you said? And I can move my car round into the garage? Fine, I'll find my way. I'll sign in when I've put her away for the night.'

Charlotte withdrew into cover, and hoped no one on the upper deck had fallen over her discarded shoes. Gus was plunging away out of the door, contented with his dispositions, and Mrs Lane, apparently satisfied of his *bona fides* – and Mrs Lane had an inbuilt crystal globe, and took some satisfying – had subsided into her private enclosure and was lost to sight. Charlotte climbed the stairs to her own room, and let herself in silently, with considerable doubts about her own situation.

She sat on the edge of her bed and thought it out. It need not, after all, be so abstruse, or so deeply suspect. He was young, alert, very much aware of the opposite sex, and with a personal taste which apparently inclined strongly towards her type. When she had revealed that she was staying here, he had simply decided to hook up and join on. But no, that wouldn't do! She chilled, remembering. She had told him where she was booked, and at that stage he hadn't reacted at all. Not until she had signed her name in the book, at his request, and his long-sighted eyes had read it over her shoulder. Only after that had he said: 'Let me drive you back, I'm staying there, too'. As he had certainly not been, it seemed; not until now.

But what could her name mean to him? It wasn't Morris, it wasn't identifiable, even to a keen archaeologist – not unless he happened to be all too well informed about the experts who had interested themselves in Aurae Phiala, and even in their heirs and heiresses, down to herself.

But why? What could he be after, where could he fit in, if this was true? No, she was imagining things. He had simply hesitated to take the plunge and stake on a worthwhile weekend with her, and it was pure chance that he had made up his mind just after he had learned her name. Logic argued the case for this theory, but instinct rejected it. Unless she was much mistaken in that young man, pure chance played very little part in his proceedings. His manipulation of impudence and deference was too assured for that. Whatever he was about, there was method in his madness.

Well, she thought, it won't be difficult to judge how right I am, if I pay out a few yards of line for him. If he isn't just amusing himself, then I can expect total siege. And I shan't be making the mistake of attributing it to any charms of mine, either. And even if I'm wrong – well, I might find it quite amusing, too.

She had not intended changing for the evening, country inns being the right setting for good tweed suits; but now she took her time about dressing, and chose a very austere frock in a dark russet-orange shade that touched off the marmalade lights in her eyes. Why not use what armoury one has? If he was setting out to find out more about her, she could certainly do with knowing a little more about him, and her chances were at least as good as his.

He was sitting in the bar with a drink and the evening

paper when she came down, and though he appeared not to notice her quiet descent until she was at the foot of the stairs, she had seen him shift his weight some seconds before he looked up, ready to spring to his feet and intercept her. The look of admiration and pleasure, she hoped, was at any rate partly genuine.

'May I get you a drink? What would you like?' No doubt about it, he meant to corner her for the evening. If he had been simply playing the girl game, she reasoned, he would be getting steadily more intimate, and here he is reverting to deference. Because I'm Uncle Alan's niece? But she could not believe in him as that kind of reverent fan, whatever his enthusiasm for his subject.

'Since we're both alone here,' said Gus, coming back from the bar with her sherry, 'will you be kind enough to have dinner with me? It would be a pity to eat good food in silence, don't you think?'

'Thank you,' she said gravely, 'I'd like that very much.' Not that she intended accepting any favours from him, but she knew he was booked in for two nights, which gave her time to return his hospitality if she could not manipulate tonight into a Dutch treat.

'When you get bored with my conversation,' he said, 'I promise to shut up. There's even a telly tucked away somewhere.'

Boredom, thought Charlotte, as she made her way before him across the small panelled dining-room, is one thing I don't anticipate.

By the time they reached the coffee stage it had become clear that he was doing his best to pump her, though she hoped he had not yet realised how little result he was getting, or how assiduously she was trying, in her turn, to find out more about him. The process would have been entirely pleasant, if the puzzling implication had not lingered in her mind throughout, like a dark shadow without a substance. And his method had its own grace.

She saw fit to admit to her musical background. Why not, since some of her Midland concerts would be advertised in the local press, and inevitably come to his notice? 'I call that one of the supreme bits of luck in life,' he said warmly, 'to be able to make your living out of what you love doing.'

'So do I. One you enjoy, too, surely? Don't tell me you don't love your archaeology. But how does one make a living at it? Apart from teaching? Are you attached to one of the universities?' Her tone was one of friendly and candid interest, but she wasn't getting many bites, either. We should both make better fish than fishermen, she thought.

'There aren't enough places to go round,' he said ruefully, 'and I'm not that good. Some of us have to make do with jobs on the fringe.'

'Such as what? What *do* you do, exactly?' No need for her to be as subtle as he was being. She had, as far as he knew, no reason to be curious, and therefore no reason to dissemble her curiosity. It was an unfair advantage, though; it made it harder for him to evade answering.

'Such as acting as consultant and adviser on antiques generally – or in my case on one period. Valuer – research man – I even restore pieces sometimes.'

'Freelance? It sounds a little risky. Supposing there weren't enough clients?'

He smiled, rather engagingly, she admitted. 'I'm retained by quite a big outfit. And there's never any lack of clients.'

It was at that point that the stranger entered the dining-room, and stood for a moment looking round him as if in search of an acquaintance. Charlotte had seen him turn in the doorway to speak to Mrs Lane, whose placid smile indicated that she knew and welcomed him. He looked like a local man, at home and unobtrusive in this comfortable country room as he would have been in the border landscape outside. He was tall and thin, a leggy lightweight in a dark-grey suit, with a pleasant, long, cleanshaven face, and short hair greying at the temples and receding slightly from a weathered brown forehead. He was of an age to be able to wear his hair comfortably short and his chin shaven without eccentricity, probably around fifty. Middle age has its compensations.

There were only a few people left in the dining-room by that time, two elderly men earnestly swapping fishing stories over their brandy, a young couple holding hands fondly under the table, and a solitary ancient in a leather-elbowed tweed jacket, reading the evening paper. The new-comer scanned them all, and his glance settled upon Charlotte and her companion. He came threading his way between the tables, and halted beside them.

'I beg your pardon! Miss Rossignol? And Mr Hambro? I'm sorry to intrude on you at this hour, but if you can give me a few minutes of your time you may be able to help me, and I'll be very much obliged.'

Charlotte had assented to her name with a startled bow, but without words. Gus Hambro looked up with rounded brows and a good-natured smile, and said vaguely: 'Anything we can do, of course! But are you sure it's us you want? We're just visitors around here.'

The stranger smiled, still rather gravely but with a warmth that Charlotte found reassuring. 'If you weren't, you probably wouldn't come within my – strictly unofficial – brief. We locals don't frequent Aurae Phiala much, we've lived with it all our lives, it doesn't excite us. I gather from the visitors' book that you were both there this afternoon, that's the only reason for this visit. May I sit down?'

'Oh, please!' said Charlotte. 'Do excuse us, you took us so by surprise.'

'Thank you!' he said, and drew up a third chair. His voice was low, equable and leisurely; so much so that only afterwards did it dawn upon Charlotte how very few minutes the whole interview had occupied. 'My name is Felse. Detective Chief Inspector, Midshire C.I.D. – I mention it only by way of presenting credentials. Strictly speaking I'm not occupied on a case at the moment, and this is quite unofficial. If you were at Aurae Phiala this afternoon you probably saw something of a party of schoolboys going round the site with a teacher in charge. A coachload of them from Comerbourne.'

'We could hardly miss them,' said Gus. 'They were loading up to leave just when we came out.'

'Including a senior, a boy about seventeen, who was probably subjecting his teacher to a certain amount of needling?'

'Name of Boden,' said Gus. 'We had a modest brush with him ourselves. Incidentally, they'd lost him – the coach set off without him in the end.'

'Exactly the point,' said Chief Inspector Felse. 'He still hasn't come home.' He caught the surprised and doubtful glance they exchanged, and went on practically: 'I know! He's perfectly competent, well supplied with money always, and it's no more than a quarter past nine. Probably you'd already gathered that it isn't the first time he's played similar tricks, and that he's a law to himself, and comes and goes as he pleases. The simple fact remains, he's never yet been known to miss a meal. Suppose you tell me exactly where and how you last saw him.'

They did so, in detail, each supplementing the other's account and refreshing the other's memory.

'Odd as it seems, that's the latest mention of him I've got so far. He drew off and went back towards his party?'

'Not directly,' said Charlotte. 'I suppose we just took it that he would, and weren't surprised that he made a pretence of being unconcerned and going his own way about it. What he actually did was to stroll away down-river, right along the perimeter. I watched him as far as the corner of the curator's garden, and saw him turn in alongside the hedge. I didn't pay any attention afterwards. I just took it for granted he was on his way back to the group.'

'I've talked to his particular friends. None of them saw him again. He never rejoined his party.'

'Have his parents reported him missing?' asked Gus.

'No, not yet. His father happens to be a close neighbour of mine in the village of Comerford, that's all. Young Collins – he teaches Latin for his sins – reported to the Bodens when the coach got back to Comerbourne, not to complain of the kid, but so that they shouldn't be worried about his non-arrival. They know their son, and are more or less resigned to his caprices, but they know his consistencies, too. He likes his comforts and he likes his food. When he failed to show up by half past eight they did begin to wonder. I happen to be three doors away, and dropping it in my lap is a discreet step short of making an official report. Easier to back out of, and sometimes produces the same result. This isn't a case. And if it ever becomes one – God forbid! – it won't be my case. But the odds are Gerry's merely run into something more interesting than usual, worth being late for supper.'

'A girl?' suggested Gus dubiously.

'It happens. Though up to now he's been too much in love with himself,' said the chief inspector frankly, 'to show much interest in girls. He's not a bad kid, really. Just the only one, too spoiled, and too clever.' He rose, and restored his chair to its place at the neighbouring table. 'Thanks, anyhow, for pin-pointing the actual place and time. No one seems to have caught a glimpse of him since.'

'You don't think,' said Charlotte, suddenly uneasy, 'that he could possibly have missed his footing and slipped into the river? It's running so high, and so fast, even a good swimmer might not be able to get out if he once got caught in the current.'

'No, I don't. He *is* a good swimmer – quite good enough, and quite mature enough in that way, to respect flood water. And he wasn't attended by his admirers at that stage, so he had no inducement to show off by taking risks. No, I feel confident he absented himself deliberately, for some reason of his own.'

'Then he'll reappear,' she said, 'in his own good time.'

'In all probability he will. As soon as he begins to think pleasurably of his bed.' He smiled at her. 'Thank you, Miss Rossignol, and goodnight. Goodnight, Mr Hambro.'

He turned and left the room, threading his way between the deserted tables to vanish in the warm, wood-scented half-darkness of the hall. In a few moments they heard a car start up and drive away. Down-river, Charlotte thought. Perhaps he wasn't as completely convinced as he made out that a lost boy, however bright and confident, could not have ended in the Comer. And perhaps he wasn't going to wait until morning before launching a search.

Gus Hambro was sitting quite still, his brows drawn together in a tight and abstracted frown, and the focus of his eyes fixed far beyond the panelling of the dining-room.

'Of course he'll be all right,' said Charlotte, all the more firmly because she was not totally convinced.

Gus said: 'Of course!' in a slightly startled voice, and visibly withdrew his vision and his thoughts from some distant preoccupation in which she had no part. He looked vaguely at her, and quickly and intently at his watch; but at least he had returned to the consciousness that she was present. He even managed a perfunctory smile. 'He'll turn up when it suits him. Don't worry about him. What do you say, shall we see what's on television?'

Her thumbs pricked then. She let him accompany her into the small lounge where the set was kept in segregation from the vocal and gregarious fishermen, and settle her in a comfortable chair, cheek by jowl with a single elderly lady, who seemed pleased to have company, and disposed to conversation. That suited him very well. Charlotte was counting the seconds until he should extricate himself, and he did it in less time than she had expected, and without even the pretence of sitting down with her.

'You won't mind if I leave you to watch this without me? There's a letter I really ought to get written tonight – I hadn't realised it was quite so late, and I can get it off by first post if I do it now.'

'Of course!' she said. 'In any case, I shall be going to bed very soon, I am rather tired.'

'I'll say goodnight, then, if you'll excuse me.'

'Goodnight, Mr Hambro.'

It sounded absurdly false to her, as though they were playing a rather bald comedy for the benefit of the elderly lady, who was dividing her benign attention between them and a quivering travel film. He withdrew quickly and quietly, closing the door carefully after him. Charlotte strained her ears to hear whether he would slip out by the side door and make straight for the garage at the rear of the house for his car, but instead she heard the crisp, light rapping of his heels on the oak staircase. Room 12 was on the first floor. Arguably he must be bound there now, but almost certainly he had no intention of staying there.

'Oh, dear!' said Charlotte, groping in the depths of her

handbag, 'I seem to have left my lighter in the dining-room. So sorry to keep disturbing you like this, I must go and get it.'

She closed the door after her no less gently and purposefully than he had done, and snatching off her shoes, ran silently up the two flights of stairs to her own room. It was a risk, for she might well have run headlong into him on the first floor landing, but she had luck, and was round the next turn of the stairs when she checked and froze against the wall, hearing his rapid steps on the oak treads below her. Very light, very hurried steps, but the bare, glossy wood turned them into a muffled drum-roll. Down to the hall again, and across it to the front door. She had made no mistake; he had an errand somewhere that would not wait.

She ran to her own room, plunged frantically into her walking shoes, and dragged on a black coat. She had a small torch in her case, and spared the extra minute to find it and thrust it into her pocket. Even this brief delay meant that he would be out of sight and out of earshot, but did that matter at this stage? She knew, or she was persuaded that she knew, where he was bound. And he had gone out by the front door, presumably to present an appearance of normality if he should be seen by any of the family – a late evening stroll before bed being a simple enough amusement – while she could save the whole circuit of the house by using the back door close to the kitchen. At this moment she did not care at all whether she was observed, or what the observer might think of her. The curiosity which was quick in her had now a personal urgency about it. He had picked her up of intent, had followed her into this inn for some purpose of his own. And now for some purpose of his own he shook her off, and with almost insulting lack of finesse. Charlotte was not a commodity to be picked up and put down at will, and so he would find.

She saw no sequence in what was happening, and no coherence, but she knew it was there to be seen, if only she could achieve the right angle of vision.

Her walking shoes had formidable soles of thick, springy rubber composition, remarkably silent even on the staircase, and gifted with a firm grip even in wet river mud. The right footwear for venturing the riverside path, short of gumboots. She let herself out softly by the family door, and made for the silver glimmer of water in haste. The trees that sheltered the inn fell back from her gradually, and the vast, chill darkness of the sky mellowed by degrees into a soft, lambent un-darkness, moonless but starry, in which shapes existed, though without precision. By early habit she was a countrywoman, she could orientate herself by barely visible bulks and air currents and scents in the night, and she was not afraid to trust her feet in the irregularities of an unknown path. The torch she hardly used at all; only once or twice, shading it within her palm, she let it flash upon the paler gravel of the path, to align her passage alongside the faintly glowing water, and then snapped it out again quickly, to avoid reliance upon its light as much as to conceal her presence here.

She walked steadily, using all her senses to set her course accurately. And it was several minutes before her quick ears picked up, from somewhere well ahead of her, the snap of a broken branch under a trampling foot. A sharp, dry crack. Dead wood, brought down in the flood water and cast ashore perhaps two days ago. She eased her pace then, knowing he was there in front of her. She had no wish to overtake him, only to maintain her distance, and keep track of his movements if she could. He was on his way downriver, by the waterside path that enjoyed right of way through the enclosure at Aurae Phiala. Ten minutes' walk at most, by this route.

After that, she did not know. All she had to do was follow, and find out.

She knew, by the looming bulk of the bank on her right hand, when she reached the perimeter of the enclosure. To make sure, she risked using her torch, shielded by her body, and saw the single strand of wire, a mere symbol, that separated the path from the city site. Then, distant beyond the broad bowl full of skeleton walls, she saw the headlights of a car pass on the road to Silcaster, sweeping eerily across the filigree of stonework and grass, and vanishing again at the turn of the highway. Twice this random searchlight lit and abandoned the past, all in marvellous silence, for the trick of the ground siphoned off all sound. After every such lightning, darkness closed in more weightily. Then she went cautiously, losing ground but keeping her bearings. The river was dangerous here, still gnawing at the rim of the path. In the night its silence and its matt, pewter gleam were alike deceptive, suggesting languor and sleep, while she knew from her memories of day that it was rushing down its bed with a tigerish fury and force, so concentrated that it generated no ripples and no sibilance. One slip, and it would sweep you away without a murmur or a cry.

She had lost track of the movement ahead of her. It was vital here to pay proper attention to every step, or the river would claim forfeit. A mysterious line of pallor, the nearest thing here to a ripple, outlined the rim of the Comer as it lipped the gravel. She judged that she was somewhere very near to where the bank on her right had subsided, shattering the outer corner of the hypocaust. But so much of her attention was now centred on her own immediate steps that she had no leisure to orientate herself in a wider field. Curiously the darkness seemed to have become more dark. When she lifted her eyes, she was blind. Only when she looked down, fixing upon her own feet, had she at least the illusion of vision. A degree of light emanated from the silently hurtling water, which she felt as a force urging her forward, as though she were in its grip and swept along with it.

She was concentrating with exaggerated passion upon her own blind, sensitive footsteps when her instep caught in some solid, clinging mass, and threw her forward in a clumsy, crippling stumble, from which she recovered strongly, and kept her balance.

The block, whatever it was, lay still before her, lipped by the faintly phosphorescent rim of shallow water. All she saw was a rippling edge of pallor, but she felt the barrier as a solid ridge barricading the path. She fumbled for the torch, and thumbed over the button with a chilly hand, and the cone of light spilled over a man's body, face-down in the shallow water, glistening under the abrupt brightness in violent projections of black and white.

She turned and lunged into the crumbling bank with the torch until it lodged and held still, focused upon the motionless bulk below. Then she plunged forward with both hands, took fast hold of the thick tweed jacket, and dragged the inert body out of the river. He was a dead, limp weight, but the smooth mud greasing the path made her task easier. Clear of the encroaching water of the Comer, she collapsed across her salvaged man, and crouching on her knees beside him, turned up to the tight circle of light the wet, white face of Gus Hambro.

CHAPTER FOUR

She stooped with her ear against his lips, and could detect no sound of breathing, spread her fingers against his chest under the sodden jacket, and felt no faint rise and fall. Yet he could not have been long in the water. She had not been far behind him, and yet had heard no sound to prepare her for this. She felt nothing now but the urgency of her own role, and acted without thought or need for thought. She wound her arms about his knees and dragged him laboriously across the gravel into the safe, thick grass; his right cheek suffered, but he was hardly going to hold that against her if he survived. In the soft turf she turned his face to lie upon that grazed right cheek, and spread his arms above his head. Somewhere in the depths of her mind the fact was recorded, and later recalled, that from the shoulders down his back was dry, and even in front, from the knees down he was merely damp and muddy from the slime of the river bank. His head and his chest were soaked, and streaming water into the grass.

But at the time she had no awareness of any such details, though her senses missed none of them. She was entirely concentrated on the curved grip of her hands on his loins, and the rhythmic swing of her body as she leaned and relaxed, forcing the water out of him and dragging the air into him, and waited, holding her own breath, for the first rasping response out of his misused lungs. At first it was like leaning into a thick, inert sponge, and that seemed to go on for an age. Actually it was only a matter of perhaps fifty seconds before the first convulsive rattle of protest shook his ribs, and then she felt the first thread of breath drawn out long and fine under her coaxing fingers as she sat back from him. She dared not halt upon so tenuous a promise. She went on industriously compressing and releasing, but now she felt the breath of life responding to her touch, following the pressure of her hands in and out, lifting the body under her, until she was only orchestrating the performance, and signalling its progression by the measured touch of her palms and undulation of her body.

She ventured at last to sit back on her heels, let her hands lie in her lap, and listen. And palpably, audibly, he breathed. She heard him catch at air, and cough up the last slime of the river. Then he heaved in a breath that must have gone right down to his toes, and his whole body arched and stiffened, and then relaxed on as prolonged an exhalation. She waited, for a time renewing the light, guiding pressure on his back, afraid to leave all the labour to him. By then he was breathing so strongly and normally that she was able to extend her consciousness to details, every one of which was stunningly unexpected and astonishing, even the flickering yellow eye of the torch still beaming upon the recumbent body. She looked up, and became aware of the vault of faintly luminous sky over them, and the silence. An absolute silence.

She understood then that if she had had leisure to listen at the right moment, she might have heard the faint, suggestive sounds of a third presence. For men do not come out by night with the intention of lying down to drown in eight inches of water at the edge of a riverside path. Not cocky young men with roving eyes and a nice taste in girls. Now, of course, there was nothing to be heard at all, nothing to be seen but the sudden, wheeling pallor of one more set of headlights taking the curve in the Silcaster road, far beyond Aurae Phiala.

She leaned down to check closely upon the steady rise and fall of his chest, and the slight, rhythmic warmth of the air expelled from his lungs. The pulse in his wrist was vehement and strong. Cold, if he lay here too long, might be a greater enemy to him now than anything else. And if one thing was certain, it was that she could not get him from here alone. Probably he needed a doctor, but certainly he needed warmth and shelter and a bed. Twice she turned from him, and again turned back to make a double and treble check. The third time she clambered stiffly to her feet and looked about her, dazed by the darkness outside the closed circle of torchlight, and switched off the beam to acclimatise once again to the starry night. It was like enlarging herself ten-fold into a chill but resplendent vastness, like taking seisin of the night. She gave herself a full minute to find her bearings in this mute kingdom, and her senses made the adjustment gratefully. Gus Hambro – ridiculous name, she thought, with wonder, exasperation and affection, for he enjoyed it now by her grace – continued to breathe strongly and regularly in his oblivion. And she knew that she not only could, but must leave him.

Her memories of Aurae Phiala were sharp, but now she could not be sure how accurate. The entrance with its kiosk and museum was away at the far side, and not inhabited by night. But before her, downstream, was the hedge of the garden hemming the curator's villa. Gerry Boden, the lost boy, had made off in that direction when he was hunted out of the dangerous area. Somewhere along that hedge he had last been seen, and by her. By this time he was certainly in his own home, fed, unchastened, and ready for fresh mischief tomorrow. At this moment she did not believe in tragedies; she had just averted one.

She took the torch, using it freely now because speed was of the first importance, and stealth of none at all, and went on down the slippery path towards the thick box hedge, behind which the invisible red roof hung, representing help and companionship. There was a narrow gate opening on the pathway, as she had expected there would be. Within it, the curator's garden climbed in three steep terraces, concrete steps lifting the level at each stage. The house loomed undefined, a large bulk between her and the milky sky. She found herself facing a glass-panelled door, with the luminous dot of a bell set in its frame. She pressed the spark, and seemed to feel a warmth in it. There were people on the other side of that door. She was not accustomed to wanting people, but she wanted them now.

She seemed to wait a long time before she heard footsteps within, and then a light sprang up beyond the frosted glass. There was an interval of clashing bolts and keys turning – she had to remind herself that it must be nearly eleven by this time, and that this was an isolated spot – before the door opened. But at least it opened fully and vehemently, offering every hope of a welcome within. Somehow she had expected six inches of semi-darkness, and half a face enquiring suspiciously what her business might be at this hour.

This was not the front door, but a garden way to the river. She saw a white conservatory full of plants, soft light filling it, a few flowers making knots of dazzling colour; and at the door, casting a spidery shadow, a long, meagre but erect man, all angles, like a lesser Don Quixote put together out of scrap iron. A well-shaped grey head leaned to peer at her out of concerned hollow eyes, whose colour she could not determine. By this light they had no colour, only an engraved darkness in his ivory face. He had a small, pointed, elusive beard like the Don, and wispy grey moustaches drooping to join it.

'I'm so sorry,' said a high tenor voice, soft and mild in surprise, and apologising even for the surprise, 'but we don't normally use this door, and especially at night. I hope I didn't keep you waiting.'

With distant astonishment at her own efficiency, she heard her voice saying very clearly and reasonably: 'I do beg your pardon, but I came to you as the nearest house. I've just pulled a man out of the river, two hundred yards or so upstream. I've been giving him artificial respiration, and I think he's going to be all right, but we ought to get him into shelter as quickly as we can. Can you help me? Could we bring him here?'

After one stunned instant, for which she could hardly blame him, he reacted with admirable promptitude. The door opened wider than ever. 'Come inside!' he said. 'I'll call my colleague, and we'll get the poor chap indoors at once.'

'I could help you carry him in,' she said. 'We ought not to lose any time.'

'Don't worry, Lawrence is only a couple of minutes away. He has a scooter, he'll be here in no time. You sit down by the fire, you're wet and cold. I'll be back directly.' And he thrust her briskly into a small, book-lined room, and himself went on along a passage to the hall and the telephone, leaving the door open between them. She heard him dial, and speak briefly and drily, almost as though similar rescue operations landed on his doorstep every night. It might not be the first occurrence, she realised. People who live beside flood rivers are liable to be recruited from time to time. Certainly he wasted no time in calling up his reserves. After the click of the hand-set as the connection was cut, she heard him dial and speak once more.

When he came back into the doorway of the room where she waited, he had a duffle coat over his arm, and was carrying a folding garden-bed with a rigid aluminium frame and a patterned canvas cover printed with brilliant sunflowers. Incongruously festive for a stretcher, but she saw that it would serve the purpose very well.

'If you wouldn't mind coming along to light us on the way back? I've got a coach-lantern here in the garden room. I called the police, as well,' he explained. 'You may not know, but we had an officer here looking for a missing boy, earlier this evening. I hope you may have found him for them.'

'No,' said Charlotte quickly, 'this isn't the boy. I do know about that, but this is someone else, a man I know slightly. He's staying at "The Salmon's Return", like me.'

'Oh . . . I see! A pity . . . I called the number the chief inspector gave me, I felt sure . . . Well, never mind, here's Lawrence! Let's get this one in, at any rate.'

The busy sputter of a Vespa came rocking round the bulk of the house, and the young man of the custodian's box put his head in at the open door, gave Charlotte a brief, blank glance, and asked briskly: 'Where is he?'

'By the path, just upstream. Here, take this! I'll lead. And mind how you go,' he said, heading rapidly out through the garden, the lantern held out beside him to light the steps for Charlotte. 'That path's in a very dangerous state until it dries out properly. What was he doing taking a night walk there? A stupid thing to do!'

His voice was detached and impersonal, but she heard very clearly the implication: And what were *you* doing taking a night walk there? 'Lucky for him you came along,' he said, almost as if he had recognised the implication, too, and was making a token apology for it.

'Listen!' said the young man named Lawrence suddenly, and checked to strain his ears for the small, recurrent sound that had reached him. 'Someone else out late, too. This place is getting like Brighton beach.'

They had reached the gate in the box hedge, and froze in the grass for an instant to listen. Slow, irregular footsteps, audible only by reason of the slight sucking of soft mud at the heels of someone's shoes as he approached along the path.

'I called the chief inspector,' said the curator, advancing again to meet the sound. 'I thought it likely this might be the young fellow he was looking for. But he couldn't be here yet.'

'He wouldn't be coming along here, anyhow. He'll be driving. Mrs Paviour surely wouldn't walk this way in the dark, would she?'

'Lesley's home, twenty minutes ago, and gone to bed. I hope she's sleeping through this disturbance.'

They walked towards the unsteady steps, and a figure took shape out of the darkness, weaving as it came and blinking dazedly as the lantern was lifted to illuminate its face. Wet and muddy, but moving doggedly under his own steam, Gus Hambro lurched into the circle of his would-be rescuers, braced his rubbery legs well apart, and stood dazzled, holding his head together with both hands.

'It's him!' said Charlotte, humanly indifferent to grammar at this crisis. 'He's walking . . . he's all right!'

The young man named Lawrence put her aside kindly but firmly, and took over in her place, drawing Gus's left arm about his shoulders. 'Man!' he said admiringly. 'Are you the tough one! Here, girl, cop hold of this thing, we don't need a stretcher for types like this.'

The curator moved to the other side, encircled Gus competently but aloofly, and handed over the lantern. It was Charlotte who led the way back slowly and carefully through the garden. Mounting steps was what Gus found most bewildering at this stage; his feet made manful efforts, but tended to trail, and he was half-carried the last few yards to the door. And yet he had come to himself unaided, clambered to his feet without even the support of a fence to lean on, and made his way some two hundred yards towards the single light of the curator's open door. A tough one, as Lawrence had observed. Or else his handicap had been rather less than she had reckoned. She was tired by this time, and unsure of her judgement: of stresses, of odds, even of personalities.

'I'm sorry,' said Gus, quite distinctly but as if from a great distance. 'I seem to be causing a lot of trouble.'

'Not to worry, chum!' said the Lawrence youth benignly, puffing a little on the steps but indestructibly cool and amiable. 'See that nice, bright hole in the wall? Aim for that, and you're home and dry!'

The nice, bright hole in the wall stood wide, as they had left it, gleaming with the reflections of white paint within. They bore steadily down upon it. And suddenly the oblong of light was inhabited. A shadowy silhouette materialised, rather than stepped, into the frame, and stood leaning forward slightly, peering understandably into the dimness outside, and curious about the massed group of figures converging upon the doorway. There was an outside light which no one, so far, had thought to switch on. The girl in the conservatory reached out a hand and flicked the switch, lighting them the last few yards, and floodlighting herself at the same time. Appearing magically out of shadow, suddenly she shone there before them, the focus of light and warmth and refuge. She had not the least idea what was going on, and she was smiling into the night in enquiry and wonder, her brows arched halfway to laughter, her lips parted in a whimsical welcome to whatever might be pending.

There was one brief moment while she stood illuminated thus theatrically, and still not at all comprehending that the group which confronted her had had a close brush with tragedy. She had a heart-shaped face, of striking, creamy smoothness, and broader than its length from brow to chin, like the bright, intelligent countenance of a young cat, innocent, assured and inquisitive. Her eyes were so wide-set and widely-opened that they consumed half her face in a dazzling pool of greenish-blue radiance. Her nose was neat, small and short, and her mouth full-lipped and firmly formed above a tapered but resolute chin. She had a cloud of short hair curving in clinging waves about her head, the colour of barley silk, and under the feathery fringe her forehead bulged childishly, with room in it for a notable brain, the one thing about her that was not suavely curved and ivory-smooth.

The details sounded like a collection of attractive oddities. The sum total was a quite arresting beauty. And the most jolting fact about her emerged only by implication. In a nylon jersey house-gown of peacock pattern and iridescent colouring, which clung like a silk glove, she could not possibly be anyone but Mrs Paviour, that same Lesley who walked when the fit took her, last thing at night, and had been home twenty minutes when Charlotte rang the door-bell. Ergo, the wife of this elderly Don Quixote, Great-Uncle Alan's colleague and contemporary, who must be well into his sixties at the very least, and slightly arid and passé even at that. How old was the girl in the doorway? Not a day over twenty-five, Charlotte reckoned – hardly two years senior to herself. Perhaps even less. What an extraordinary mis-match! And not just

69

because of the tale of years involved. The old man was a cracked leather bottle trying to contain quicksilver. She *could not* feel anything for him! It made no sense. And yet she had not the look of a woman cramped or dissatisfied. She glowed with ease and wellbeing.

At sight of her Gus, stiffening into startled consciousness between his supporters, set foot of his own volition on the last step, and his soiled eyebrows soared into his muddy hair, in reflection of the apparition before him. Very faintly but quite clearly he said: 'Good God!' and seemed to have no breath left for anything more explicit.

The moment of charmed stillness collapsed – or more properly exploded – into motion and exclamation. The girl in the Chinese house-coat narrowed her eyes upon the central figure in the tableau before her, and the supple lines of her face sharpened into crystal, and lost their smiling gaiety.

'My God!' she said, in the softest of dismayed voices. 'What's been happening, Steve?' And she went on briskly, springing into instant and efficient comprehension: 'Well, come on, bring him in to the fire, quickly! I'll get brandy.'

She turned in a swirl of nylon jersey, and flung wide the door to the study, where the subsiding glow of the fire still burned. Her movements, as she receded rapidly along the passage beyond, were silent and violent, a force of nature in action. Only gradually did it emerge that she was rather a miniature whirlwind, perhaps an inch shorter even than Charlotte, but so slender that she escaped looking like a pocket edition. When she came back, with a tray in her hands, they had installed their patient by the fire in a deep chair, and peeled the soggy, wet jacket from him. They were five people in one small room, and hardly a word was said between them until Gus Hambro had a large brandy under his belt, and was visibly returning into circulation. His still dazed eyes followed his astonishing hostess around, measuring, weighing and wondering, in forgetfulness of his own predicament. He said nothing at all, as yet, but very eloquently. Charlotte hung back in a corner of the room, and let them encircle him with their attentions. So far he had not even registered her presence, and she was in no particular hurry to enlighten him.

'He should have a doctor,' said Paviour anxiously, standing over him with the empty brandy glass.

'I don't want a doctor,' protested the patient, weakly but decidedly. 'What could he do for me that you're not doing? All I've got is a headache.' He looked round him doubtfully, winced abruptly back to his original position, and clapped a surprised hand behind his right ear. 'What happened?' he asked blankly.

'You fell in the river,' said Paviour patiently. 'I shouldn't worry about remembering, if I were you. The main thing is, you're here, and you're going to be all right.'

'Fell in the river?' repeated Gus like an indignant echo, and stared at the smear of blood staining his muddy fingers. 'I never did! I was keeping well on the landward side of the path, on the grass. And that's where I was lying when I came round just now. All I've got is a welt on the head here. Somebody jumped me from behind and knocked me out.' He looked from face to face, questioning and wondering. 'If I was in the river,' he said reasonably, 'what am I doing here now?'

'This lady,' said Paviour, stepping aside to allow him to follow the mild gesture that indicated Charlotte, 'pulled you out. Not only that, she administered artificial respiration and brought you round, and then came here to get help. Why did you suppose we were setting off with a stretcher and torches, at this time of night?'

'I didn't know . . . I never realised . . .' He sat forward, staring in outraged recognition at Charlotte. 'You mean *you* . . . it was *you* who . . .' He shut his mouth and swallowed hard, and in the space of about two seconds she saw a whole kaleidoscope of emotions flash in succession through his mind. If she's here, if she found me, it's because she followed me! If she followed me, it's because she doesn't trust me, and if she doesn't trust me it's because she knows something, or has found out something. So far she was sure of her ground. And what followed was neither surprise nor mystery to her. For suddenly Gus Hambro performed a minor miracle, by producing a fiery blush that made itself visible in waves of dubious gratitude and indubitable mortification even through the layers of river mud that still decorated his face. Tales of gallant rescues ought not to go into reverse, and cast the lady as hero and the man as helpless victim. Especially when, whatever other circumstances may hold good, the man has been exerting himself to make an impression on the lady in question. Fate, thought Charlotte, gazing innocently back into his admiring, devoted, humiliated and furious face, has certainly given me the upper hand of you, my boy!

'The kiss of life, I hope?' said the young man Lawrence, putting a deliberate finger through the slight tension which was palpably building up within the room.

'Schafer,' said Charlotte shortly. 'The only method I know.'

Gus did not sound at all like a man recently revived from drowning as he said with sharp disquiet: 'Right, that disposes of how I got out, and I'm duly grateful, believe me. But now will somebody please explain to me *how the hell I ever got in*?'

They were all staring at him in speculative silence when the sound of a car's engine circled the house, coming to rest in the arc of gravel before the door. After it died, the silence was absolute for a few moments. Then incongruous suburban chimes jangled from the front porch.

'That must be the police inspector,' said Paviour. 'Will you let him in, dear?'

His wife turned without a word, and went to open the door; and presently ushered in Detective Chief Inspector George Felse, mild, grey-haired and ordinary, a tired middle-aged man who would have been inconspicuous and among his peers almost anywhere he cared to materialise.

'I got a message,' he said, 'that you wanted me here.'

He looked round them all as though none of them afforded him any surprise, though two of them did not belong here, and to his certain knowledge had been elsewhere only a short time ago. So short a time, Charlotte realised with a shock, that he could not possibly have returned home in the meantime, since he was a close neighbour of the Bodens, who lived ten miles from Aurae Phiala. The relayed message must have found him somewhere not far from this house. Somewhere by the river, she thought, downstream. Whatever went into the flooded Comer here would fetch up at one of several spots, no doubt well known to the police, where curves and currents tended to land what they had carried down. The chief inspector had just come, case or no case, from setting a close watch on those spots, in expectation – in foreboding, rather – that the flood would bring some unusual freight aground very shortly.

Only then did she fully realise that if she had been five minutes later the watchers keeping a lookout for a stray boy might, tomorrow, have been hauling ashore the sodden body of Gus Hambro.

Washed, warmed, with a shaven patch and an adhesive dressing behind his right ear and a second large brandy nursed gratefully in his hands, Gus told his story; though not, perhaps, quite ingenuously.

'All I did was come out for a walk before going to bed, and I was about by that place where the bank's caved in, when somebody jumped me from behind. I never heard a thing until maybe the last two steps he took, I never had time to turn. Something hit me on the back of the head, here, and I went out like a light. I remember dropping. I never felt the ground hit me. But I do know *where* I was when I fell – in the belt of grass under the bank, and facing straight ahead the way I was walking. And when I came round I was in the same place. I took it for granted I'd just been lying there since I went out, and whoever had jumped me had made off and left me there. When I could make it, I got up and made for the nearest shelter. There was a lighted doorway here, I steered for that. And just outside the garden I ran into this rescue party coming out to find me. Now they tell me,' he said flatly, 'that I was in the river, drowning, and Charlotte here pulled me out and brought me round.' He had used her Christian name without even realising it, so intent was he on pinning down the details of his own remembrance.

'When I found him,' said Charlotte, 'he was lying right across the path.'

'*Across* the path?'

'*Across* the path,' she said firmly, 'with his feet just touching the grass on the landward side, and his head and shoulders in the river. His face was completely under water.'

She felt them all stiffen in instinctive resistance, not wanting their routine existence to be invaded by anything as bizarre as this.

'There may be a simple explanation for this discrepancy,' ventured Paviour hopefully. 'If there was a fresh fall of earth there – the bank is quite high, and we've seen that there's brickwork exposed there . . . Perhaps it wasn't a deliberate attack at all, just a further slip that struck him and swept him across the path. After all, we didn't go along to have a look at the place.'

'*I* was there,' said Gus drily. 'There wasn't any fall.'

'I was there, too,' said Charlotte. 'There's something else. When you get a blow on the head and fall forward, whether it's flying stones or a blackjack, you may fall heavily, but even so I don't think you'd embed yourself as deeply in the mud as Mr Hambro was embedded.'

Chief Inspector Felse sat steadily watching her, and said nothing. It was Paviour who stirred again in uneasy protest. 'My dear girl, are you sure you're not recalling rather more than happened? After stresses like that, the imagination may very easily begin to add details.'

'I'm recognising things I did see, and never had time to recognise then. But the other thing is a good deal more conclusive . . .'

George Felse asked quietly: 'How were his arms?'

'Yes, that's it!' she said. 'How did you know? When you fall forward, fully conscious or not, you put out your hands to break your fall. His arms were down at his sides. Nobody falls like that. Even if you were out on your feet, and fell as a dead weight, your arms wouldn't drop tidily by your sides. And that's how his were.'

She was watching the chief inspector's face as she said it, and she knew that he believed her, and accepted her as a good witness. Both the Paviours were stiffening in appalled disbelief, even young Lawrence had drawn a hissing breath of doubt. Probably Gus himself found it hard to swallow, and would have preferred not to accept it, the implications being too unpleasant to contemplate. But George Felse had come halfway to meet her.

'But, good God,' objected Stephen Paviour faintly, 'do you realise what you're suggesting?'

'Not suggesting. Stating. I'm saying that someone, having knocked Mr Hambro cold, dragged him across the path to the water, and shoved him firmly into the soft mud with his face under water, to die.'

In the stunned silence George Felse got up, without speaking, and crossed the room to where Gus's jacket hung on the back of a chair, turned towards the replenished fire, and steamed gently as it dried. He slid his hands into the sleeves, and lifted it to turn the back to the light, and for a few minutes stood studying it closely.

'The back,' said Charlotte, watching, 'was dry as high as the shoulder-blades. Except that I probably made some damp patches, handling him after I got him out.'

'Quite a difference from actually lying in the river.' He spread the jacket between his hands, holding it out for them to see. 'Look in the middle of the back, here, from just above the waist upwards. What do you see?' He turned to look at Gus, with a faintly challenging smile.

'A moist patch – sizeable. Two patches, rather, but practically joined in one.' The warm, heathery colours of the tweed darkened there into a duller, peaty shade, two irregular, fading patches, with a vague dry line between. A thin rim of encrusted mud, drying off now, helped to outline the marks, but even so they were elusive enough until pointed out.

'Well? What do you make of it? You tell me!'

'It's a footmark,' said Gus, and licked lips suddenly dry and stiff with retrospective fear. 'I know what to make of it, all right! It means some bastard not only laid me out cold, and stuck me face-down in the Comer, but even rammed me well down into the mud with a foot in the small of my back to make dead sure of me, before he lit out and left me there to drown.'

CHAPTER FIVE

They were too numbed by then, and too tired, to do much exclaiming, however their orderly minds rebelled at believing in mayhem and murder at Aurae Phiala. They stared in fascination at the imperfect outline which did indeed look more and more like the print of a shoe the longer they gazed. Lawrence said hesitantly, with almost exaggerated care to sound reasonable and calm: 'But why? Why should anyone want to . . . to kill him?' It took quite a lot of resolution to utter it at all. 'Just a visitor here like anyone else. There couldn't be any personal reason.'

'I think,' said Lesley sensibly, 'I'll make some coffee. We could all do with some.' And she walked out of the room with something of the same wary insistence on normality. It was then still some twenty minutes short of midnight, though they seemed to have devoured the greater part of the night already in this improbable interview.

'Someone,' said Gus, 'didn't want me around, that's certain. But wasn't he still taking rather a chance, if it was all that important to him that I shouldn't survive? I might have revived enough to struggle out, once he was gone.'

'So you might,' George agreed. 'With a river handy, and you past resistance, why not do the obvious thing, and shove you far enough in to make sure the current took you? Even a swimmer with all his wits about him might well be in trouble down those reaches at this time of year. Out cold, you wouldn't have a dog's chance.'

'You comfort me,' said Gus grimly, 'you really do. Go on, tell me, why didn't he?'

'Pretty obviously that's what he intended. He simply didn't have time.'

'Because he heard me coming,' said Charlotte.

'I think so. He needed no more than one extra minute, or two, but he didn't have it. He heard you, and he preferred to run for it. He dropped Mr Hambro where he was, in the edge of the water, and planted a foot between his shoulders to drive him in deeper before he made off.'

'But without reason!' protested Paviour. 'Surely no one but a madman . . .'

'The procedure would appear to be far from mad – quite coldly methodical. And since, as Mr Lawrence says, there could hardly be anything personal in the attack, we're left with the probability that *anyone* who had happened along at that moment would have been dealt with in the same way. You were suspected, in fact, of having blundered head-on into something no one was supposed to see.'

'I didn't see a thing,' Gus said bitterly. 'Not a thing! He needn't have bothered scragging me, if that was his trouble.'

'He could hardly ask you, and take your word for it, could he? Obviously he thought you'd witnessed something you shouldn't have. At best he was afraid you *might* have, and that was enough. But Miss Rossignol was some way behind, and advancing without stealth.' He cast one brief glance at Charlotte, caught her large, clear, self-possessed eye, and one conspiratorial spark of laughter passed between them. He knew she had been exercising what stealth she was capable of, and he knew why, but that was purely between the two of them. 'There was no need to think she'd noticed anything, and whoever he was, he wasn't mad enough to go looking for extra murders. He took a chance – admittedly an almost negligible one – on you, and slipped away to avoid her.'

Lesley brought in a laden tray, set it down on a side-table, and distributed cups in silence.

'In view of the apparent urgency of getting rid of you,' said George Felse, stirring his coffee, 'it might be an idea if you tried to recall what, if anything, you *did* see.'

Gus held his head, and pondered. 'Well, of course there's always some reflected light, once your eyes get used to being out at night. But I didn't meet anyone, I didn't hear anyone. Oh, yes, after I got to the perimeter of Aurae Phiala, where you can see clean across the bowl to the road the other side, I did see cars pass there a couple of times. You get a sort of lighthouse flash from the headlights, as they swing round the curve there and out of sight. The lights cross the bowl gradually, and out again, and then the dip in the road cuts them off. Yes, and the second time that happened it swept across the standing walls there, and in the near end of the caldarium there was somebody standing by the wall. No, not moving, quite still. It was only a glimpse. The light swerves off in an instant, and it's darker than ever. But he was there, all right.'

'*He*?' said George.

'Oh, yes, it was a he. The whole cut of him,' he said, imprecisely but comprehensively. 'No doubt about it.'

'But nothing more detailed? Clothing? Build?'

'Oh, for God's sake!' said Gus irritably. 'One flash of light, and gone. Just a mass, like a Henry Moore figure. He didn't have any clothing, just a shape. All I know is, it was a he, and he was there.'

'And how long was this before you were attacked?'

'I'd say about three full minutes, maybe even four,

before I was hit. I didn't think anything of it. He had as much right to be out walking as I had.'

'Not in Aurae Phiala,' said Stephen Paviour, in tones of quiet outrage. 'Not at that hour. Our gates are closed at six – seven in summer. He had no right inside the enclave, whoever he was.'

'No, true enough. But the path along the river is a right of way, and there's only a token wire in between. Anyone could walk up into the enclosure. You'd have a job to stop them.'

'You know,' said Lesley, busy at the coffee-tray, 'I must have been out there about the same time. Oh, no, I wasn't down by the river, I was over on the side next to the road. I often have a little walk along the new plantation there. That's what cuts off the headlights, you see. The site is very exposed on that side, in Roman times there was a woodland there, so it was sheltered. Now we're trying to replace it, to reproduce the same conditions. I was home well before ten, though. I never noticed the exact time, but I was in the bath when I heard the stir down here.'

'You didn't see anything of this man in the caldarium?' George asked.

'No, I didn't. Though I must have been around just at that time, I think. I do remember seeing two – maybe three – cars pass on the Silcaster road, but I didn't notice anything shown up in their headlights.' She hesitated for a moment, poised vulnerably with the coffee-pot in one hand, and the jug of hot milk in the other. 'You know . . . please don't think I'm being funny! – maybe Mr Hambro saw the Aurae Phiala ghost. And don't think I'm crazy, either,' she appealed warmly. 'Look, it's only half a joke. You go and ask in the village. People *have* seen things! You don't have to take my word for it, they'll talk about it quite freely, they're not ashamed or afraid of it.'

'My dear, this is frivolous,' her husband said with frowning disapproval. 'Mere local superstition. We're concerned with realities, unfortunately.'

'*Are* there such stories?' George asked mildly.

'Can you imagine such a place as Aurae Phiala existing without giving rise to its own legends? I have heard loose talk of people seeing things here by night, but I've never paid the least attention, so I can't tell you what they claim.'

'I'm not being frivolous,' Lesley declared firmly, 'and these *are* realities. I don't mean helmeted sentries literally do patrol the walls by night, I don't mean even that anything's actually been seen, but the things that go on in people's minds *are* realities, and *do* influence events. It hardly matters whether there's a ghost there to be seen or not – what matters is whether someone is convinced he saw it. Besides, what's a ghost, anyhow? I'm not a convinced believer, I just don't find it difficult to credit that in these very ancient sites of occupation, where such emotional things are known to have happened, people should develop special sensitivities, racial memories, hypernormal sympathies, whatever you like to call them. I don't see anything supernatural about it, just rather outside most people's range of knowledge. The test of that is, that the local people treat the experiences they claim to have had as perfectly acceptable – almost take them for granted. They don't go challenging them, they respect them, take what's offered but don't go probing any farther. A thoroughly healthy attitude, I call it. Look at Orrie,' she appealed to her husband. 'He's seen the sentry twice. He doesn't run away, or hang out crosses or wreaths of parsley, or ring up the local press, he merely mentions it to his friends in passing, and gets on with his work. And you couldn't find anyone more down-to-earth than Orrie.'

'Orrie?' George enquired.

'Our gardener. He's local stock from way back. They had the same site, even bits of the same cottage, in the sixteenth century.' She laughed suddenly, the evening's first genuinely gay sound. 'You wouldn't credit what the Orrie's short for! Orlando! Orlando Benyon! The name's been in the family for generations, too.'

'And Orrie's seen the Roman sentry?'

'Listen!' she said, abruptly grave again. 'I've seen him myself, or else hearing about it has put me in a special state of mind, and all the other factors have come up right, atmospheric conditions, combinations of light and dark, what you like, and made me create what I believed I was seeing. Twice! A figure in a bronze helmet, both times a good way off, and both times close to the standing walls. I didn't find anything very strange in it, either. In its last years Aurae Phiala surely did mount a watch every night. Just such a sentry must have been the first to die, the night the Welsh came.'

Paviour's uneasiness and distaste had grown so palpable by this time that his rigid bones looked tensed to breaking point. He said with nervous acidity: 'We're not dealing with atmospheric hallucinations here, but with an attempt at murder. When violence breaks in, something a good deal more material than imagination is indicated.'

She agreed, with an unabashed smile. '*And* when ordinary mundane light like a car's headlights starts making the immaterial perceptible. Now that would be supernatural! I paint a bit for fun,' she said, with a grimace of deprecation for the unsatisfactory results. 'I do know about masses and light, even if I can never get them right. No, this person you saw was a pretty solid kind of reality.'

'And he wasn't wearing a helmet,' said Gus.

'Tonight's haunting was for a pretty compelling reason,' said George. 'But what you've told us is very interesting,

Mrs Paviour. We'll see what the village has to add.' He put down his coffee-cup in the tray with a sigh. 'You've been very kind to put up with us all for so long, I'm most grateful. But now I think there's nothing more we can do here, and it's time we left you to get some rest. If you feel fit to go back to the inn, Mr Hambro, I'll be glad to drive you and Miss Rossignol round there.'

Lesley had begun to gather up the remaining cups, but at the mention of Charlotte's name she put down the tray abruptly, and turned with a startled smile. 'Rossignol? You're not *Charlotte* Rossignol? Steve, did you hear that? There can't be two – not two and both connected with Roman antiquities! You must be the niece Doctor Morris mentioned. He told us once his sister's girl had married a Frenchman.'

Charlotte admitted to her identity with some surprise. 'I didn't think he took so much interest in me. We've always been a rather loosely-knit family, and I've never seen him.'

'It's true he didn't often talk about his family, but I couldn't forget your lovely name, I liked it so much. You know Steve is an old fellow-student of his, and a close friend? Isn't it wonderful, darling, Miss Rossignol turning up like this?'

His face was grey and drawn, Charlotte thought, perhaps with pure fatigue, for after all, he was an old man. He favoured her with a slightly haggard smile, but his voice was dry and laboured as he said: 'I'm delighted to meet my old friend's niece. I'm only sorry it had to be in such circumstances of stress. I hope you'll give us the opportunity of getting to know you better, on some happier occasion.' His lips were stiff, the words of goodwill could hardly get past them.

'I'm not quite such a coincidence as I seem,' she said, 'I've just been reading my uncle's book on Aurae Phiala, that's why I came to have a look at the place for myself. He didn't really do it justice, did he? I find it beautiful.'

'Stephen doesn't agree with him, either,' said Lesley, smiling, 'but of course Aurae Phiala is our life. Are you going to stay a little while, now you're here? You should!'

'I have a few concerts in the Midlands, and I thought I'd make my base somewhere close by until they're over. Yes, I think I shall stay on for a few days here.'

'But not at the "Salmon"! Oh, no, you can't! Anyone belonging to Alan Morris has a home here, of course. You must come to us. Look at all the rooms we have, the house is much too big for two. Do come! Stay tonight, too, I can find you everything you need overnight, and we'll fetch your things from the pub tomorrow.'

Confronted by sudden and eager invitations from strangers, Charlotte's normal reaction was one of recoil, not out of insecurity, but to maintain her independence and integrity. She was never afterwards quite sure why she side-stepped only partially and temporarily on this occasion. There existed a whole tangle of possible reasons. She was in search of a closer knowledge of her great-uncle, and here were informed friends of his, one of them of long standing, who could surely tell her a great part of what she wanted to know. She was attracted by this place, and here was her opportunity of remaining. She was held by the disturbing events of the night, and here was her chance to wait out a better understanding of them on the spot. And also there was something in Lesley's appeal that engaged her sympathy in a way she hesitated to analyse. Here was this young creature, beautiful and restless, married to a man almost old enough to be her grandfather, and apparently setting out to make the very best of it, too, with no signs of regret or self-pity; but the prospect of having a girl of her own age in the house, even for a few days, might well matter to her a great deal more than the extension and acceptance of a mere conventional politeness. And Charlotte heard herself saying quickly:

'That's awfully kind of you, and I should love to come for a couple of days, if I may. But I'd like to go back with Mr Hambro to the "Salmon" now, if you don't mind. If I may come tomorrow?'

She had not looked at Paviour until then. Lesley had issued her fiat with such confidence that she had taken his compliance for granted. His long, lean, lugubrious face was dry and rigid as carved teak, and his eyes, sunken between veined lids and deep in cavernous hollows of bone, looked like roundels of cloudy glass with no light behind them. With all the grace and spontaneity of a wooden puppet, but in the most civil and soft of voices, he said: 'We shall both be delighted if you will. We have the highest regard for Doctor Morris, and of course his niece is most welcome. And Lesley will enjoy your company so much,' he added, and the sudden faint note of hope and warmth sounded almost as though he was issuing comfort to himself, looking on the single bright side. No doubt, she thought, a visitor might be a very unwelcome distraction in his entrenched life.

But it was done now, there was no way of backing out. And she need not, after all, stay long. After two days it would be easy enough to extricate herself.

During the short drive back to the inn they were all three monosyllabic, suddenly isolated in private cells of weariness and preoccupation. The occasional remark passing seemed to come from an infinite distance, and be answered after a prolonged interval.

'I hope Mrs Lane won't have locked you out. We should have given her a call.'

'I've got a key,' said Gus, and lapsed into silence again. He made no comment on Lesley's invitation and Charlotte's acceptance of it, none on the curious complexities which had confounded their own relationship since they left 'The Salmon's Return' two hours and more ago. No one said a word about Doctor Alan Morris, and the charged significance of Charlotte's name. There were things all three of them knew, and things all three of them were wondering, but no one cared to question or acknowledge at this hour. Silence, if not golden, was at least more comfortable than speech.

Only as the car was crunching softly to a halt in the gravel of the yard did Charlotte ask suddenly, but in a tone so subdued as to suggest that she had been contemplating the question for some time, and refrained from asking it only for fear of the answer:

'You haven't found him yet?'

The engine fell silent, and there was a brief and pregnant pause. Then: 'No,' said George Felse, equally carefully and constrainedly, 'we haven't found him.'

In the first chilly greyness of dawn, before the sun rose, Sergeant Comstock, of the uniformed branch, who came of a long line of native fishermen, not to say poachers, and knew his river as he knew the palm of his own hand, thankfully abandoned what he had always known was a useless patrol of the left bank downstream, and on his own responsibility borrowed one of his many nephews, and embarked with him in the coracle which was his natural means of personal transport on the Comer. They put out in this feather-light saucer of a boat from his nephew's yard only just below the limits of Aurae Phiala, transport downstream in the spate being rapid and easy – for experts, at least – and the return journey much simpler by portage.

This consideration had dictated his choice of nephew. Dick was the one he would really have preferred, but Dick lived well downstream. Jack was not only in the right spot, and the family coracle-builder, but a bachelor into the bargain, so that there was no protesting wife to contend with.

The sergeant had already mapped out in his own mind, with an eye to the wind, the speed of the flow and the amount of debris being brought down, the procession of spits, shoals, curves and pools where a heavy piece of flotsam would be likely to cast up, beginning immediately below the village of Moulden, which lay just below the Aurae Phiala enclosure. Cottages dotted the waterside through the village; and anything which had gone into the water some hours ago must, in any case, either have been brought ashore there already or long since have passed through, before the general alarm went out.

From there they went darting across the boiling surface like a dragon-fly, skimming with the currents where the banks were swept too open and smooth to hold flotsam, swinging aside round the sergeant's paddle in the marked spots; round the shovel-shaped end of Eel Island, which had scooped up a full load of branches, twigs, uprooted grass, and even more curious trophies, but not what they were seeking; a little way down the sluggish backwater beyond, until motion ceased in stagnant shallows, and still there was nothing; out into the flood again, hopping back on to the current as on to a moving belt that whisked them away; revolving out of the race again where the trees leaned down into the water at the curve by the Lacey farm, acting like a great, living grille to filter out debris; clean across the width of the river at the next coil, to where the long, sandy shallow ran out and encircled a miniature beach. Every junk-heap of the Comer on this stretch they touched at and ransacked. It was a game they could win only by losing;

every possibility checked and found empty was a point gained, and with every one discarded their spirits rose towards optimism.

The sun was up, and they were a mile or more downriver, in wider and less turgid reaches, where some of the best fishing pools deepened under the right bank.

'Looks like we've had our trouble for nothing,' Jack said, with appropriate satisfaction. 'Anything that's run that gauntlet without getting hooked has got to be brother to an eel.'

It was one more case of famous last words. In the first dark pool under the hollowed bank the steady, rolling eddies went placidly round and round, smooth as cream, their tension dimpling the centre into a slow, minor whirlpool. And in the middle of the slanting span, circling upon a radius of about three yards, and light enough to maintain its place a foot or so below the surface, something pale and oval went monotonously round and round. First oval and single, then weaving as it spun, like a water-lily on a stem, then suddenly seen as articulate in separate petals, a limp magnolia flower.

'Why don't you keep your mouth shut?' said Sergeant Comstock, with deep and bitter resignation, and reached for the boat-hook they'd brought with them. His third nephew Ted had made it to family specifications in his forge in the village of Moulden. 'Cop hold of this paddle, and move us in slow. And hold us clear of him, or he'll go down.'

There was a second drifting flower now, deep below, and greenish brown with the tint of the water between. And presently, as Jack held the paddle like a brake and let them in by inches, a third, without petals, a pale disc trailing tendrils of weed. A spreading darkness wove lazily beneath it, keeping it afloat.

The boat-hook reached overside gently, felt its way under the leaves of dark material, was lifted delicately into their folds, and held fast. The three submerged flowers lost their rhythm, jerked into stillness, and hung quivering. A palpable bulk aligned itself beneath them, a fish on a line, but a fish without fight.

'I've got him,' said Sergeant Comstock gruffly. 'Better take us down a piece, where the bank levels out. We can get him ashore there.'

The fish floated uncomplainingly with them, down to the gentle slope of grass fifty yards downstream. There they brought the coracle ashore lightly, and drew in, with reluctance and the reverence of finality, what they had been hunting with such assiduity, and so persistently hoped they would not find. To have settled something is always an achievement and, of sorts, a satisfaction. This they would rather not have settled, and yet there was a kind of relief in it.

The body came ashore into the grass with monstrous and majestic indifference, for the first time caring nothing at all what impression it made. A long, young body in correct school uniform, black blazer, white shirt, black tie, dark grey slacks. Very like its living counterpart still, because it had not been in the river very long. The Comer had not managed to loosen the knot of the tie, though its ends floated wide, or to hoist off one of the regulation black shoes. He even had a ball-point pen still firmly clipped to the top of his breast pocket.

'That's him,' said Sergeant Comstock, looking down at the slow rivulets of storm-water trickling down out of clothing and hair to wind their way thankfully through the grass back to the river. 'Hang on here, Jackie, while I cut up to the farm and 'phone.'

CHAPTER SIX

George Felse telephoned his wife from the Sallows farm somewhat after eight o'clock in the morning. By that time he had not only set in motion all the police retinue that attends on sudden and unexplained death, but also attended their ministrations throughout, seen the body examined, photographed, cased in its plastic shell and removed by ambulance to the forensic laboratory, delegated certain necessary duties, placated the police doctor and the pathologist, come to terms with the inevitable grief and rage which do not reach the headlines, and made dispositions within his own mind for the retribution which is so often aborted.

'We found him,' he said. She, after all, had been left holding up the universe over the parents, and in all probability, whatever strict injunctions he issued now, she would, by the time he rejoined her, have relieved him of the most dreadful of all the duties his office laid on him, and somehow, with sense, sedatives and sturdy, unpretending sympathy, have gone part-way towards reconciling the bereaved to their bereavement. 'Dead, of course,' he said. 'Some hours, according to preliminary guesses. Yes, in the river. Drowned? Well, provisionally, yes. Personally, I wonder. Don't tell them that. They're almost prepared for the other. I'll tell them later – when we know.'

'It's all right,' said Bunty Felse. It wasn't, but he would know what she meant. 'I was half expecting it. So are they, I know. When will you be home?'

He had been up half the previous night upon a quite different case, and all this night upon this, which had only just become a case, and his, after all.

'As soon as I can, but it may be three hours or so. I shall take time out to call at Aurae Phiala. They won't have heard officially. I want to be the one to bring the news. I've got to see their faces.'

'Not the Rossignol girl,' said Bunty. It was a little less than half enquiry, and a little more than half assertion. He had called her shortly after midnight, she already knew something of the personalities involved.

'I want to see her face, too. But no – you're right, not the Rossignol girl. On present form,' he said, his voice warming wearily into a semblance of the voice she knew best, 'she only pulls people out.'

His timing was good, though it was determined mainly by the exigencies of the situation. When he drove down the gravelled road along the edge of the site to the curator's house, at half past nine, he found the bronze Aston Martin parked in front of the doorway, and Gus Hambro just handing out Charlotte's suitcases. Both the Paviours had come out to greet their guest, Stephen Paviour long and sad and constrained as ever, Lesley eager and young and welcoming. Her movements as she ran down the steps had an overflowing grace of energy. Behind her Bill Lawrence appeared in the doorway. So much the better. One was apt to overlook Bill Lawrence, who nevertheless was there on the spot like all the rest, and able to move even more privately, since he lived alone in the lodge cottage, further along the Silcaster road. Probably he rode over here for his meals on most occasions. The Vespa was a handy transport for the mere quarter of a mile involved. He wore his usual air of meticulously contrived casualness, and the shadow of beard round his by no means negligible jaw was a shade more perceptible than on the previous day. Apparently he was setting out to grow whiskers of the latest fashion, for his lips were carefully shaved. Probably he knew and cared, in spite of his cultivated disdain for appearances, that he had a very well-cut and intelligent mouth, too good to be hidden. His lazy, supercilious eyes, too, managed their affectation of aloofness without actually missing a trick. It might be a great mistake to overlook Mr Lawrence.

He had been the first to hear the sound of the car approaching, and the quickest to identify it, for he was the only one who looked completely unsurprised as it rolled gently alongside the Aston Martin, while all the rest had checked momentarily and turned to gaze. Recognition halted their breath for an instant. He was there with intent. With news or with questions.

Lesley came towards him, veering from the advance she had been making upon Charlotte. 'Chief Inspector Felse! We didn't expect to see you so early. Is there any news?' The intense blue of her eyes shaded away into a translucent green in a bright light, burning into emerald in her moments of laughter or animation, clouding over into a ferny darkness when she was grave. She gazed into his face, and they darkened. Unexpectedly but very simply she said, with concern: 'You haven't had any sleep!'

'I'll catch up on that soon.' He turned from her to look at Paviour. To him the light was not kind. The contrast with his radiant, vital young wife was blatant almost to embarrassment.

'You wanted to see us? – some one or more of us,' he said. 'If we can help you at all . . .'

'Thank you, but this time I needn't keep you more than a minute. I thought that as I'd involved you all, to some extent, in the enquiries that were launched yesterday, I ought to inform you of the results of our search for the boy, Gerry Boden . . .'

He was listening very carefully, for any exclamation, any indrawn breath, even, that would single out one person among these five; but they remained anonymous in their concern and foreboding. The issue, after all, was fairly plain. No one is that much of an optimist.

'One of our sergeants took him out of the river about six o'clock this morning, a mile and a half downstream from here. Dead.'

They stood frozen, all transfixed by the same small, chill frisson of shock, but no one exclaimed. He looked round all their sobered, pitying faces, and registered what was there to be registered, but it was not much; nothing more than was due to any boy of sixteen, suddenly wiped out for no good reason. No use looking for the one who felt no surprise, for after the gradual attrition of hour after hour without word they could none of them feel very much.

'How awful!' said Lesley in a resigned whisper. 'Terrible for his parents. I'm so sorry.'

'The poor fool kid!' said Gus. 'I wish to God now I'd lugged him back to his chain gang by the ear. Can't say we didn't half expect it, I suppose, by this time. It began to look . . . But there's always the odd chance.'

'Which in this case didn't come up. I thought you should be told. Sorry to have ruined your day.'

Paviour moistened his pale lips. 'Do you think it was here, on our premises, that he fell into the river? I feel to blame. But the path is a right of way, we couldn't stop it if we tried.'

'It's too early yet,' said George with deliberation, 'to say where and how he entered the water. The forensic laboratory has a good deal of work to do on his clothes, and the contents of his pockets. And of course there'll be a post-mortem.'

'A post-mortem?' The meagre, gallant Don Quixote beard quivered and jutted as though every individual hair had suddenly stiffened to the clenched tension of Paviour's jaw. He relaxed the convulsive pressure of his teeth cautiously, and drew breath deeply before he resumed with arduous reasonableness: 'Is that really necessary, in a case like this, I know you have to be thorough, but the distress to the parents . . . And surely the cause of death isn't in doubt? A clear case of drowning . . . ?'

'It would seem so,' George agreed gently. 'But double-checking does no harm, and as you say, we try to be thorough. I doubt if it's an issue that will affect the parents' distress one way or the other.' He was turning back towards his car when he looked back with a casual afterthought. 'By the way, you won't be surprised or disturbed if you find some of our people patrolling the riverside path or inspecting that slip, will you? A routine precaution, that's all.'

He did not look back again, except in the rear-view mirror as he drove away. They were grouped just as he had left them, all looking warily after him. And if he had got little enough out of that interview, at least he had lobbed one small, accurate pebble into the middle of the pool of their tranquillity, and its ripples were already beginning to spread outwards.

A young giant working on the flower-beds along the drive straightened his long, lithe back to watch the car go by, without curiosity though with fixed, methodical attention, his senses turned outwards for relaxation while he took a breather. The reddish-fair head, Celtic-Roman, with chiselled features and long, indifferent lapis eyes, belonged to a statue rather than a man. George knew the type locally, a pocket of fossils preserved among these border valleys, though this superlative specimen was not personally known to him. Orrie Benyon, of course. Orlando, who admitted his ghostly ancestors ungrudgingly into his territory by night. Those cropped military curls, that monumental neck and straight nose, would have looked well in a bronze helmet; no doubt he recognised his own kind, and was at home with them. And indeed his stock might well go back to just such stubborn settlers, survivors after the death of this city, the offspring of time-expired legionaries and the daughters of enterprising local middlemen. Deprived of their urban background, they had rooted into the valley earth and turned to stock and crops for a living. And survived. Tenacious and long-memoried, they had not allowed themselves to be uprooted or changed a second time.

George stopped the car at the edge of the drive, and walked back. He stood watching beside the flower-beds; and after a long minute of uninterrupted work, Orrie straightened his long, athlete's back again, and turned towards his audience the massive, stony beauty of his face, flushed with exertion. At this range the flaws that reduced him to humanity, and a fairly limited humanity at that, were plain to be seen: the stubble of coarse reddish beard he hadn't bothered to shave, the roughness of his weathered skin over the immaculate but brutal bones, the inlaid indifference of the blue eyes.

'Good morning!' said George. 'Nice show of bulbs you've got coming along.'

'Not bad, I reckon,' the gardener admitted. 'Be some tulips out by now if it'd bin a bit warmer. You come round in three weeks or so, they'll be a show worth seeing.'

George offered his cigarette case and a light. Both were

accepted tacitly but promptly. 'You take care of all this place single-handed? That's a lot of work for one.'

'I manage,' said Orrie, and looked with quickening curiosity through the smoke of his cigarette into George's face. 'You're police, aren't you? I saw you once when you picked up that chap who was firing ricks, up the valley.'

'That's right. My name's Felse. You'll have heard we fished a young fellow out of the Comer this morning?' Everyone with an ear to the ground in Moulden had heard the news before ever the police surgeon reached the spot. 'He was here with a visiting school party yesterday. You had to chase him off from where you were cordoning off the slip. That was the last you saw of him?'

'Last I *saw*, yes,' said Orrie, with a long, narrowed glance. 'I finish here half past four, Wednesdays, I do a bit at the vicarage that night. I was gone before closing time – the vicar'll tell you where I was. I told your chap, the one who came after me up home, 'bout nine that'd be. Seems there was some others saw him after I did, monkeying about by that cave-in again. But I tell you what,' he said confidentially, 'I reckon I know one place he's been since then. If he hasn't, someone else has. In my back shed. Not the tool-shed where I keep the mower and all that – the one down behind the orchard. I got a little work-bench in there, and me stores of sprays and weed-killers and potting compost. And I can tell when somebody's bin moving me stuff around.'

There were interesting implications here, if Orrie wasn't imagining the prying fingers; as why should he? He wasn't the imaginative kind, and a man does know how he puts down his own tools. The orchard lay well back from the riverside, and the wealth of old and well-grown trees between isolated it from the house. Gerry Boden had last been seen alive strolling negligently along the garden hedge, and somewhere along the course of that hedge he had vanished. Now if there should be a hole, or a thin place, inviting him through into the plenteous cover of the orchard, and the solitary shed in its far corner . . .

'You don't lock that shed?'

'It's got no lock. I keep thinking I'll put a padlock on, but I never get round to it. Him,' he said, with a jerk of his head towards Paviour's house, 'he's always scared of having things pinched, but the stuff in there's mine, no skin off his nose. Folks are pretty honest round here, I'm not worried. I do me own repairs – make me own spares when I need 'em.'

'And there's nothing missing this time?'

'Not a thing, far's I can see. Just somebody was in there, poking around, shifting things, passing the time nosing into everything, and thinking he'd put it all back the way it was before. Which you can't do. Not to kid the one who uses the place regularly.'

'You didn't say anything about this to Detective-Sergeant Price.'

'I didn't know, did I? I hadn't been back here. I only went into the place twenty minutes ago.'

'Fair enough,' said George. 'How about coming down there with me now? No need to disturb the household, if we can come round to it from the other side.'

There was a navigable track that circled the perimeter, and brought the car round to the other side of the curator's house and garden by inconspicuous ways. The shed was of wood, a compact, dark, creosoted building tucked into the corner of the shrubbery. Inside it smelled of timber and peat and wood-shavings. Various small packets and bottles and tins lay neatly but grimily along shelves on one side, folded sacks were piled in a corner, and full sacks stacked along the base of the wall. Under the single window was

Orrie's work-bench, a vice clamped to the edge of it, and a rack of tools arranged under the window-sill. He was comprehensively equipped – power drill, sets of spanners, sets of screwdrivers, planes, even a small modern lathe. In the fine litter of sawdust and shavings under the bench the morning light found a few abrupt blue glitters of metal.

George advanced only just within the doorway, and looked round him. There was dust and litter enough on the concreted floor to have preserved the latest traces of feet, though it was clearly swept reasonably often. And if Orrie had not already tramped all over it this morning, since his discovery, nosing out the signs of trespass, there just might be something to be found.

'Did you move about much in here when you came in and realised you'd had an intruder?'

'Didn't have time. I never went no further than you are now, all I come for was my little secateurs, and they were on the shelf here inside the door. I reckoned I'd come back midday and have a look over everything, but I don't think there'll be anything missing. Yes, I did go a bit towards the window and had a quick glance round. That's all.'

'Then what made you so sure somebody'd been in? You were talking about something more than just a feeling.'

'That!' said Orrie succinctly, and pointed a large brown forefinger at the top right corner of the window, where his periodic cleaning had not bothered to extend its sweep.

He wasn't clairvoyant, after all; he hadn't even needed the tidy workman's hypersensitive unease over his tools. In the small triangle of dust the tip of a finger had written plainly GB, and jabbed a plump round fullstop after the letters. The human instinct to perpetuate one's own name at every opportunity, whenever more urgent occupation is wanting, had made use even of this mere three square inches of dusty glass. The act cast a sharp sidelight of acute intelligence upon Orrie's remark about passing the time.

'There's the way things are lying, too,' conceded Orrie, 'but that was what took my eye right off.'

What had taken George's eye was that splendidly defined fullstop. With the morning light slanting in here, and showing up every mote of dust and grain of wood-powder, the individual nodules of that fingertip showed even to the naked eye. Almost certainly the right forefinger, unless Gerry Boden happened to be a southpaw. And he had impressed that print with careful precision – he or whoever it was. It wouldn't take Sergeant Noble very long to find out.

'Do any of the others ever come here?' George asked. 'Legitimately?'

'Could happen,' allowed Orrie indifferently, and shrugged. 'Not often. Not lately. What for?'

'Good! Then stay away from here today. Can you do that? If there's anything you want, take it now.'

'There's nothing I want,' said Orrie. 'It's all yours.'

George made two or three telephone calls from the nearest box, handed over the minute inspection of Orlando Benyon's shed to the appropriate people, made contact with the police pathologist and his own chief at C.I.D. headquarters, left strict instructions about what news and reports should be channelled to his home number immediately, and what could wait, and drove with the exaggerated care and deliberation of sleeplessness back towards the village of Comerford, uncomfortably in transition to a suburban area, where he, and the unhappy parents of the boy Boden, lived within three doors of each other. One more hurdle, the highest, and then he could sleep. Whether the Bodens would be able to sleep was another matter. With sedatives, maybe. But not everyone responds to sedatives.

Some people feel them as a kind of outrage and violation, and Boden was a strong-minded and passionate man. George was not looking forward to that interview. On the other hand, he would not for any money have delegated it to anyone else.

'I hope you didn't mind,' said Lesley Paviour blithely, swinging the wheel of the old Morris nonchalantly as they negotiated the sharp turn by the downstream bend of the Comer, not very far from where Gerry Boden's body had been towed ashore. 'I had to get away from there for a few hours. Normally I can ride it. I mean, for God's sake, I took it on, didn't I? I don't welch on my bargains, I really don't! But under pressure, I tell you, it gets tight. But *tight*!' She sat back in the driving seat, a neat, competent figure in a deep green spring suit as modest and suave as her own creamy countenance. 'I'm a placid person,' she said deprecatingly, 'I have to be. But I've got my limits. I know when to duck out for a breather. Trouble is, I don't always get such a marvellous excuse. So I know you won't mind being made use of. Am I making you nervous? Driving, I mean?'

'Not in the least. You drive well.' And so she did, with verve and judgement, and certainly with decision. She smiled with quick pleasure at being praised.

'If I had your friend's Aston Martin, now, instead of this old thing!'

Charlotte declined to rise to this fly. They had seen nothing of Gus since he had withdrawn, she suspected with reluctance, after delivering her and her luggage at Paviour's house. He had strung out the conversation, after the chief inspector's departure, or made an attempt to, but without much backing from anyone else, and failing to get any invitation to remain, had finally taken himself off.

'He seems to be a gentleman of leisure, that young man,' Lesley continued thoughtfully. 'Whatever can he do for a living, if he's free to ramble about in the middle of the working week in April? Have you known him long?'

'I don't know him at all, really,' said Charlotte. 'We only met walking round Aurae Phiala yesterday, and then found we were both staying at the same pub. I gathered he's some sort of adviser on Roman antiques – I'm a little vague about details. Maybe to museums? Or collectors.' Those things she knew about Gus Hambro which did not fit into this picture, such as his manipulations over the room at the inn, she did not care to mention to anyone until she herself understood them better. 'He seems to know his subject,' she said. 'At least, *I* couldn't fault him, but of course I'm only a beginner.'

'In spite of having Alan Morris in the family,' Lesley said, and smiled as she drew into the left traffic lane at the lights on the outskirts of Comerbourne. 'Have you really never met him? Oh, you must! You don't know what you've been missing.'

'Nobody's finding it very easy to meet him at the moment,' said Charlotte. 'He seems to have gone off into the wilds of Turkey on some dig or other, and got so interested that he forgot to come back. Nobody's heard from him for more than a year. As a matter of fact, his solicitor is getting a bit worried about his silence.' She did not care to make the point any more strongly, or to admit any anxiety on her own part, not even to this impulsively talkative companion whose goodwill and sympathy were already taken for granted. 'Tell me about him,' she said. 'What is he really like?'

Lesley turned smartly left as the lights changed, and wound her way by back-streets to the parking-ground on the edge of the shopping centre, a multi-storey monstrosity of raw concrete, at which she gazed with resigned distaste as she crept slowly up to the barrier and drove in to the second tier. 'Brutal, isn't it? In a nice Tudor-cum-Georgian town like this, I ask you! Doctor Morris? Well, I suppose I do know him fairly well, he's stayed with us a couple of times. But of course Stephen knows him much better, he was at college with him, and they've always kept in touch, in a fairly loose sort of way. Don't think I'm being bitchy if I say that Stephen probably resents him as much as he admires him. They began more or less level, you see, and then the one went on forging right to the top, and the other came labouring along always further and further in the rear. They never were less than friends, though, so admiration must have kept on winning out.'

The car slid neatly into its slot, and she cut the engine and opened her door. 'Grab the shopping bag, would you mind? – it's slid over your side. Let's go and have coffee first, and then I've got to call at the bank to get some cash, and dump that package, before we start shopping.'

Charlotte lifted out a large bag of pale, soft leather, so limp as to seem empty, and lifted her eyebrows in surprise at the weight of the small, brown-paper-wrapped box that dragged down one corner of it. And Lesley laughed.

'Yes, that's why I want to get rid of it first. It's something of Orrie's, actually. Country people are odd! He claims he doesn't trust banks, he refuses to open an account, yet he doesn't see anything illogical in asking me or Stephen to put things in our safe-deposit box to keep for him. He's not so dumb, you know. Quite sharp enough to know all about dodging income tax on the odd jobs he does in his spare time. Cash payments and no account books! And every now and again he probably gets a shade nervous at keeping cash under the floor-boards or wherever he puts it, and starts spreading the load.'

Now that she was away from Aurae Phiala, Lesley had flamed into an almost delirious fluency and radiance, she who was bright enough to dazzle even in her chosen prison. She talked incessantly and joyously over coffee in the feminine precincts of the main dress shop: about Aurae Phiala itself, about Orrie, and the village community of Moulden, about Bill Lawrence and his aspirations. She rejoiced in being free from the place, but she talked of it with comprehension and critical affection. Perhaps she needed this interlude only as the lover needs a rest from loving.

'Poor Bill, he has ambitions towards scholarship. I mean the real thing. I could be wrong, but I don't think he has the real thing in him. He's doing a big thesis on the border sites, that's why he's working at our place for a year or so. It doesn't pay much, so you can imagine he's in earnest about his aspirations. He's a nice boy,' she said tolerantly, and a shade absurdly in view of the fact that she was perhaps two years his senior, 'but somehow I don't see him making it to the top. He prowls about the place, you know, on his own, and dreams of springing a dazzling surprise on the archaeological world some day. I don't know! I see him ending up pretty much like Stephen, half-fulfilled and half-frustrated – a third-rater,' she said, candidly and regretfully, 'and knowing it.'

She talked of the limitations of her husband and her acquaintances in a perfectly detached way, quite without personal venom and certainly without any delusions. Charlotte could imagine her discussing her own imperfections, if the subject should arise, with the same critical precision.

The bank was directly across the street from the shop. Lesley rummaged in the depths of her calf handbag for a matching key-case as they crossed at the lights, and flicked out the smallest of the keys on the bunch it contained. 'You won't mind waiting a minute for me? They make a thing of this strong-box business, but ours mostly has rather dull securities and family papers in it. And Stephen's will, I suspect. Not that he ever mentions it, or that I've ever asked him, but he's the type to consider it a sacred duty to have everything in order for every emergency.'

'It could be a virtue,' said Charlotte rather drily, reminded of the unimaginably sudden aspect death sometimes assumes.

'It *is* a virtue. One I envy but am never likely to possess. I'm an improviser, he's a method man.'

She disposed of her errand, and armed herself with cash, and they went to shop, the usual duty shopping for the household, the more esoteric lines which were not stocked and delivered locally; and a few items for her own pleasure. Then they loaded the purchases into the car, and went with free hands to view the delectable older parts of Comerbourne. Lesley set herself to be the most enlightening and intelligent of guides. Her knowledge was wide, and her taste was decisive and good.

'I was born here,' she said, sensing the question Charlotte had not asked. 'Not here in the town, but only about four miles away, in a village. I used to be a typist in Lord Silcaster's estate office. Not a very good one. That's how I got to know Stephen. We used to do any typing that was needed for the Aurae Phiala publications, and for the few little books and articles Stephen occasionally produced. I was the one who mucked up his texts worse than any of the others, that's what made him notice me in the first place.'

'It sounds highly improbable,' Charlotte said frankly. They were leaning side by side on the stone parapet of the oldest bridge over the Comer, and the same river that scoured so savagely at its banks upstream flowed beneath them here full, strong and smooth, partially tamed by two weirs in between. A few black-headed gulls wheeled headily above the water.

'No, honestly I wasn't much good. I wasn't interested enough. And as I had this urge to correct manuscripts as I went along, and couldn't read his handwriting, and didn't know the first thing about Roman Britain, you can imagine he felt obliged to educate me. Looks like being a life-work, doesn't it?'

There was no being certain how serious she was, or how flippant. Her lips were curved slightly in a mild, private smile. But she did not elaborate anything or withdraw anything, then. She took Charlotte companionably by the arm, and they turned back together towards the car park, and the Morris, and home. Not until they were drawing near to Moulden did she suddenly reopen, more gently and more directly, the subject of herself.

'You're wondering about Stephen and me,' she said; a statement, not a question, and with nothing defiant or defensive about it. 'Impossible not to wonder, isn't it?' And that was a question, and required an answer.

'Quite impossible,' said Charlotte, 'since you ask me.' It was difficult to feel any tension or embarrassment while Lesley felt none. 'I do it regularly, about all the interesting people I meet.'

'Good! So do I. But I know we're a rather special case. For one thing, you have to realise that even three years ago Stephen was rather a different person – to look at, I mean, and to be with, and all that. Growing and ageing don't work in a smooth, regular sort of way. A stunted little boy suddenly starts to shoot up like a weed, a plain adolescent turns into a beauty overnight, and well-preserved middle-aged men who reach sixty still looking forty-five suddenly make up the deficit and more than overtake their age, all in a few months. For no good reason that I can see. And for another thing, he began to take an interest in me just when I was on the rebound from a very unhappy love affair – the kind of let-down that alters not just your life but even your nature. He was kind, and attentive, and soothing. And I'd gone off passion. I married for safety, and comfort, and consideration. Not to be alone, and not to be vulnerable any more. Maybe a little for reputation, too,' she said, with a serene air of examining her own motives in the light of a new discovery, and finding them credible, reasonably creditable, and slightly amusing. 'My own family was pretty undistinguished, and Stephen had at any rate a respectable reputation in his own field – though I probably overvalued it at the time. So I married him. I think it was just as big a gamble for him, perhaps bigger.'

They had reached the rising curve in the road, where the plantation of young trees came into view, fringing Aurae Phiala with delicate pales of green.

'Insecure young girls,' said Lesley seriously, 'are often happiest with much older men. They feel safe.' And suddenly she laughed, a gay peal, refreshed by a whole day of escape from her selected cage. 'Doesn't always work out that way, though. Yes, you really must make the acquaintance of your great-uncle. Now there's a handsome old dog! He knows it, too! He must have put in some agile footwork at times, to get this far through his life still single, and yet have all the fun he's had.'

'I've been hearing about his reputation as a lady-killer,' Charlotte admitted. 'Everyone tells the same tale about him, so it must be true.'

'I speak,' said Lesley feelingly, 'as one of the many at whom he made charming and – relatively! – harmless passes.'

'I thought you might!'

'But unfortunately – I suppose it isn't surprising in the circumstances – Stephen is almost pathologically jealous of me, so it wasn't much fun. It was pretty innocuous play, but I had to discourage it. Absurd, but even so it could have been dangerous.'

'I suppose,' said Charlotte casually, 'you haven't heard from him since he left for Turkey? He went straight from here to the airport, I was told.'

'That's right, he did. No, I haven't had any word. He knew it wouldn't be a good idea, you know. Neither has Stephen, I'm sure. But in the ordinary way we shouldn't expect to, of course, he isn't a writing man. Only books! And they've been friends long enough to take each other for granted, turn up when they feel like it, and shut up when they're busy. They always get on well, except that they never can agree about Aurae Phiala. After all,' she said simply, 'it's all Stephen has, and he's never going to excavate it, not really, nobody's ever going to put up the money. But he lives on the hope, and that's enough.'

The Morris rolled briskly through the carriage gates, and down the gravelled drive towards the house.

'And you've never had any regrets?' Charlotte asked.

'Me?' said Lesley, opening her wide eyes even wider in amused surprise. 'I never regret anything.'

CHAPTER SEVEN

George slept until six o'clock, and was then awakened by the telephone. Sergeant Noble had a comprehensive report to make, the day's summary of his own activities and those of several others.

'Got a preliminary estimate for you from Goodwin, but he's not through yet, he'll be on the line again later this evening.' The pathologist attached to Comerbourne General Hospital enjoyed Home Office recognition in this region, and he was an old friend, and amenable. 'It confirms what Braby suggested, but we'll have to wait until he's finished the post-mortem. Yes, the father showed up to identify. Very composed, considering. Shall I read it out?'

He did so. Doctor Braby, hard-worked GP and police surgeon to the district, had done more than confirm the fact of death on this occasion, he had called immediate attention to certain peculiarities about the body, and boldly essayed a guess at the length of time it had actually been in the water. A very suggestive guess, too, but there was no acting on it until Dr Reece Goodwin had made a more detailed examination and confirmed or corrected Braby's estimate. Noble's matter-of-fact voice made short work of the interim report.

'And this shed of Benyon's. We've about mapped it, took us most of the day. He was there, all right. We got a set of his prints from the body. The letters on the glass are drawn, of course, but you were right about the dot. Right forefinger tip – a beauty. But besides that, we've collected half a dozen more, various but his, from all round the place. And as good as a complete set off the vice – the metal had the thinnest possible film of oil. He was there, and there for some time, poking into everything. No damage, no mischief, just having a look. Like you and Benyon put it – passing the time.'

'So, alone,' said George.

'That's how it looks. Nearly all the other prints we lifted are Benyon's, naturally. One or two of someone else, probably Paviour himself, but of course we haven't got him on file, and these are where you'd expect 'em, on the door, where you might well finger it if you just looked in to have a word with the incumbent, so to speak.'

'So young Boden spent some time alone in there, alive and active. What about getting in there, considering where he was last noticed?'

'Easy! The box hedge is solid as a wall as far as the corner, but just round there it ends, and that short side is privet, and there's a place in it where an old wicket's been taken out, and the gap hasn't grown in completely yet. Not much doubt he slipped in there and went to earth in the shed, for some purpose of his own. Otherwise *someone* would have seen him again.'

'And waited. For what, I wonder? I can't think he had any date to meet somebody there. He came with the party, and halfway through the visit he was still showing off for his fans and being mildly provocative towards all authority. He wasn't doing any showing off when he slipped quietly away into Orrie's shed. Something happened, something came into his mind, while he was there at Aurae Phiala, that prompted him to disappear and let the party leave without him.'

'He may not have expected them to do that,' objected

Noble reasonably. 'They never had before. Maybe he just wanted to make 'em hunt and fret a bit.'

'Look, Orrie's shed isn't any special joy, and this was a boy who liked his comfort, and company, and adulation. He might sit it out ten minutes just to annoy, but not the time it took him to fidget all round the place as he seems to have done. He'd have to have a much more compelling reason than that. It looks to me more as if he wanted them to push off and abandon him. For his own reasons. And that means a reason right there on the spot, otherwise, once out of sight, he'd simply have made off for wherever it was he wanted to be. But he didn't. Where he wanted to be was right there, but unobserved. He camped out and waited. For what?'

'Closing time,' said Noble. 'For everyone to go away.'

'You're not far off target, either, but it's no answer. Look, there wasn't any sign in there of a scuffle of any kind? Even tidied up afterwards?'

'Not a thing. The dust lay peacefully, except where he'd actually trodden or pawed. Nobody'd been fighting in there, take it from me.'

'Then nothing to suggest that – granted he walked in of his own will – he didn't walk out the same way?'

'I was coming to that,' said Sergeant Noble with satisfaction. 'He walked out, all right. I don't know if you noticed, but just outside the door, where the ground's trodden, the grass thins, and there's a slight hollow that obviously holds water every time it rains, and only dries out gradually in between – nice smooth black mud like double-cream. It's in first-class shape just now. I've got two and a half beautiful prints in that layer of mud, heading *out* of the shed. I haven't got the shoes he was wearing, but I have got his spare school pair. They're his prints, all right. If there was any doubt, there's one very nice curl of metal swarf, shed from the shoe, bang in the middle of one of those prints. I've got the whole piece of turf under plastic. It looks like the same sort of swarf that's lying under Orrie's bench. I reckon when we get the actual shoes we may find some more. That stuff works into composition soles like nails knocked into wood. He walked in, and he walked out – alive, in case you were wondering . . .'

'For a while,' George conceded, 'I was. It was just a possibility. Knowing what we know.'

'Yes, granted. But there it is. He went out of there alive and alone, after a fairly lengthy stay. And where do we go from here?'

'Home to bed,' said George, 'in your case, and leave me the file. In my case – back to Aurae Phiala.'

It was after nine o'clock, however, by the time he got there, since his route was complicated, and involved calls at the mortuary of the General Hospital, at police headquarters, and a telephone call to the forensic laboratory. He collected the full list of the contents of the dead boy's pockets, and one unexpected item in the collection sent him out of his way to pay a visit to 'The Salmon's Return' before he finally reached Paviour's house.

'Why, Mr Felse!' said Lesley, opening the door to him, and blessedly forgetting to think of him first by his rank and office. 'Do come in! Do you want Stephen, or all of us?'

He said that he didn't mind who was present, that he had something to communicate which might slightly affect the convenience of everyone in residence here, and therefore could be stated in everyone's presence. And he hoped it wouldn't inhibit the activities of anybody here. Anybody, of course, with an easy conscience.

'I don't promise anything,' said Lesley serenely, 'about anybody's conscience except mine. But I don't anticipate any real onslaught from you, somehow. Come along in!'

They were all there, opportunely including Bill Lawrence. Paviour greeted the visitor with immaculate politeness, but a certain air of acid disapproval which might well have stemmed from nothing more than nervousness. 'I thought,' he said, in withdrawn enquiry, 'that we had answered all the relevant questions already. Your men have had access wherever they wished. Is there anything more we can do?'

'No questioning is entailed tonight,' said George. 'I called to tell you that we find it necessary to remain on your grounds for a day or two. It might – it's for you to decide – be preferable to close Aurae Phiala to the public for some days. No doubt you'll consult Lord Silcaster about that. We're prepared to cordon off our section if you see fit to continue admitting the public. I'm sorry to put you to any inconvenience, but it can't be helped. What we intend is to take up the area of ground you now have roped off, or a part of it – the broken corner of the hypocaust.'

Paviour shot up out of his chair, for once jerked erect to his full gangling height, which was impressive. He looked more than ever like Don Quixote confronting the most formidable of spectral windmills; and his tenor voice blazed from a reed to a trumpet in his indignation.

'You can't do such a thing! You've no right! Can you imagine the harm you might do? Uninformed digging is disastrous. Lord Silcaster will never tolerate it.'

'Lord Silcaster has already given his permission. On the grounds set before him.'

'I can't believe it! Grounds? What grounds? I quite understand that where there's some reasonable connection, some prospect of information to be gained . . . But surely here, tragic though the circumstances may be, there's no question of a crime? This poor boy fell into the river –'

'I'm afraid your information is not quite complete,' George said equably. 'Gerry Boden did not simply fall into the river and drown. He was knocked on the head, just as Mr Hambro was last night, and *put* into the river.'

Paviour stood rigid, frozen into silence like the rest.

'Put into the river,' said George, studying the circle of shocked faces, 'somewhere on these premises. He showed particular interest in that subsidence, it's reasonable to assume that his object was to return to it at a time when there would be no one around to interfere with him. I can also tell you, roughly, at any rate, the time when he entered the water. It was somewhere around ten o'clock. And you won't need reminding what happened here at very much the same time last night.'

No, they needed no reminding. Charlotte had been the first to make the connection; her eyes lit with a spark of alert intelligence which was meant as a communication, and as briefly acknowledged by a warning flicker of George's glance in her direction. She said nothing. Paviour was the last to understand. His habitual greyness faded into a bleached and waxen pallor.

'We were concerned last night,' said George, 'with the question of what Mr Hambro could possibly have blundered into, to make it essential that he should not survive to talk about it. Now we needn't wonder about that any longer.'

When he left the house, he went down to the riverside, and spent some time considering the extent of the job they were about to tackle, the resources they were going to need, and the best way of setting about it. He came back to his car, parked inconspicuously on the grass by the privet hedge, shortly before half past ten. From the darkness where the thicker growth of box began, a shadowy figure slipped out

114

to join him, and he saw the oval of a girl's face as a paler gleam above her dark coat.

'Miss Rossignol! What are you doing here?'

'I had to speak to you,' she said in a hurried whisper. 'It's all right, they won't miss me. I think they were glad to have a little time to themselves. I said I'd like to walk a little way with Bill Lawrence when he left. I had a sudden thought, when you mentioned the timing. One I don't much like, and can't quite believe in, but it's there.'

'What is it? What's on your mind?'

'I was pretty close behind Gus Hambro last night. I know you realised I was following him. And it was a quiet night, no noise from wind or leaves. Look, I'm no expert at that sort of thing. I was as quiet as I could be, but all the same, I can't help wondering if at some stage he realised I was on his heels. There *is* something curious about him, you know. The way he shook me off, as soon as you left us, and hurried off down the river like that. And even his *being* there at the inn. He pretended to me that he was already booked in there, but he wasn't – I heard him ask for the room afterwards. When he knew who I was.'

'You think that's significant?' George asked, and drew her a step deeper into the darkness of the hedge.

'I think it ought not to be,' she said earnestly. 'But yes, I think it is. So it adds up to something ambivalent about him, so much so that I *have* to wonder. Was he genuinely attacked, because he blundered into murder? That's what the timing suggests, but that's not the only thing it could suggest. The other is that he heard me following, and staged the attack on himself, with the help of some accomplice unknown – for it couldn't have been done alone, could it? – to put himself in the clear, and immobilise me long enough for the other person to get away, and the body to be well downstream. Maybe someone bold enough to improvise like that would even take the risk of getting himself really knocked out and dropped in the water, knowing I couldn't fail to find him in a few minutes.'

'And knowing you,' George added. She sensed that he was smiling, and was a little disconcerted. 'Enough to estimate your capabilities, at any rate. In the circumstances you outline, I agree I'd rather take a chance on you than on most people.'

'Thank you,' she said, 'but I think you're laughing at me.'

'I assure you I'm not. But I'd still be a bit wary of taking a risk like that. Even on you.'

'It would be a pretty desperate choice, though, wouldn't it? It isn't a thought I like, myself,' she admitted. 'But I *know* he isn't what he seems to be. He isn't here by accident, and your news about an unofficial hunt being launched for the boy sent him off in a hurry to this place.'

'As it well might,' said George, interpreting, 'if the boy was already dead, and concealed somewhere here, and Hambro had guilty knowledge of it. The news that the police were interested made it imperative to get the body away at once – and the river was the obvious ally. Is that what you think happened?'

'I hadn't thought as far as that,' she said, quivering. 'It simply seemed a possibility that he was somehow involved.'

'That isn't what I asked you.'

Now it was she who was invisibly smiling, oddly encouraged and reassured. 'No,' she said, 'it isn't what I think. I *don't* think it. But I could be wrong, too, that's why I had to hand it over to you.' And abruptly reverting to painful gravity: '*Was* the boy already dead?'

'It isn't certain yet. We shall get the pathologist's report tomorrow. But yes, I think he was.'

'Not drowned, then?'

'In confidence, though again we haven't yet got the word officially – no, not drowned. I'm trusting you with some part of the background. I'm afraid you saw the beginning of it. This boy had found something very intriguing and exciting here at Aurae Phiala yesterday afternoon. I rather think he must just have picked it up when Mr Hambro chased him away from the cave-in. He didn't dare attempt to go back again until the coast was clear, so he hid himself until everyone was gone. Not until dark, since his intention was to search that patch of ground thoroughly. But he may have waited until it began to be dusk. And someone – someone from close by, someone on or near this site – caught him in the act, and took drastic action. Whoever it was didn't go through his pockets. His find was still there when they stripped him at the mortuary.'

In a whisper she asked: 'What was it?'

'A single gold coin. An aureus of Commodus – that's round about the end of the second century AD.'

'But you couldn't!' she said just audibly. 'You couldn't kill somebody for one gold coin. It isn't possible!'

'People have been killed for less, even taking it at its face value, though its actual value is very much greater. But no, he wasn't killed for that, or it wouldn't have been still on him. No, whoever caught him hunting for more knew that there was more there to be found – knew it because he himself had come out as soon as he dared, to remove whatever was there to a place of greater safety. Don't forget the landslip had taken place only that morning, Orrie Benyon was just cordoning off the dangerous area and putting up warning notices. If someone had valuables hidden in the hypocaust, he must have been waiting on thorns for the chance to get his hoard away, and baulked all day by staff and visitors wandering around. He came at dusk, as soon as he dared, when everyone was gone. So did the boy. Maybe he'd already unearthed what was left, and it was too late just to warn him off and hope for the best. X preferred a final solution.'

'Is this a theory?' she asked in horrified fascination. 'Or do you know it?'

'It's a theory. One that fits. In the last days of Aurae Phiala the coinage was shaky in the extreme, a lot of barbarous, debased pieces were being struck everywhere. But this – I'm well briefed on the subject, this isn't my own knowledge – is a fine, full-weight aureus from two hundred years previously, enormously enhanced in value. And the Romans were hoarders. Now supposing some family here had a store of such good gold pieces at the end, when the Welsh attack was threatening, they might very well bury it for safety, in the hope of recovering it later. They seem to have shut their eyes and hoped to the very end.'

'But can one coin prove anything?' she said hesitantly.

'A very special coin. It hadn't lain loose in the soil for centuries, or even for weeks. It's virtually mint-new. That means it's been kept carefully and put away securely, and certainly not alone. In a pottery jar, well sealed. During the slip falling bricks inside the flue may have broken the jar, and rolling earth carried one coin down the slope, for Gerry to find. Not a dull bit of corroded bronze, but fire-new gold. No wonder he went back to look for more.'

'But if someone knew all about it before, this treasure, why hadn't he removed it earlier?'

'It was safe enough where it was, until the river took a bite out of the hypocaust. It's possible the hoard was actually found somewhere else on the site – say the cellar of one of the houses – and put in the flue for safe-keeping, to be drained away gradually. A whole thicket of broom bushes came down in that slip, as you saw. I think there was a way into the flue all along, under cover of those bushes.

Possibly the slip, while it exposed it, also partially filled it in. I think, too, that the find was not merely of coins, but also of small pieces of jewellery and other articles. The indications are that this site may have been exploited for at least a year. You can't dispose of such pieces wholesale. You take one or two, having studied the collectors of the world, and the highly professional fences of the antique market, and place them where they'll bring you in the best and safest return. You lie low for a while, and you disperse a handful of coins, singly, perhaps not to the best advantage, but still it's all clear profit. And when you hit a passionate collector who takes care to ask no questions, then you venture the big deal. But it means dedicated study, exact judgement, and above all, time.'

He could sense, even in the darkness, the enormous wonder of her eyes, fixed unwaveringly upon his face though they saw him only as a bulk solid and still between her and the sky. 'But how do you know all this?' she said. 'About a whole year's robberies from here?'

'I don't yet – not to say know. But for about a year certain pieces of late Roman coinage and art have been cropping up in unexpected places in the international market. Obviously genuine pieces, but of very dubious provenance. Only a few, of course. Collectors are queer fish, you know, liable to banditry without any qualms. But four instances have come to light within the year, through dealers or buyers who did have qualms. And four coming to light argues forty or more in the dark, most likely for good.'

'And there's something to connect these cases with Aurae Phiala?'

'Not until now, not specifically. But period and style are right. You've seen the ones in the museum here, the curvilinear trumpets and dragons, those un-Roman Roman antiquities? Let's say, there was plenty to connect our cases with four or five border sites, of which Aurae Phiala is one. And one such gold coin here, and a cold-blooded killing, are fairly eloquent argument.'

She was shivering slightly but perceptibly, not from cold and not from fear, but with the vibration of some personal and secret tension about which he had, as yet, no right to ask. She might, if he waited, confide in him, but not now; there was no time, if she was to retain her immaculate position in this household. He put a hand upon her shoulder, which was firm and slender, and turned her towards the gate.

'Keep your lips closed and your eyes open, and think about it. And if you want me, I won't be far away.'

'But you won't be here,' she said, not complaining, merely making the position clear to herself, and well aware that her utterance had its ambiguities. 'Not all the time.'

'You won't be entirely unprotected here,' he assured her, 'even when I'm not around. Better get back now, before they come out to look for you.' She sensed that he was smiling again. It wasn't an amused smile, but it was one that sent her away at a brisk and confident walk towards the house, and with a gratifying sense of being respected and appreciated.

The Roman city of Aurae Phiala remained closed to the public next day, and for several days following, an apologetic notice on the gate making known the fact to a largely indifferent general public. The enclosure was never exactly crowded, even in the height of the summer. On the riverside, where the pathway could not be closed, a uniformed policeman paced imperturbably, and occasionally moved people along if they tended to congregate and linger too long. The natives, markedly, did not. They passed, apparently oblivious, intent only on their own business; but hardly a soul in the village failed to pass at some time during that day, and not one missed a detail of what was there to be seen.

Operations had begun early. Breakfast was not yet over at the curator's house when Orrie came to announce that the police were in occupation, and beginning to stake out the ground. Paviour left his coffee without a word, and went rushing away to protect his beloved site, and the two girls followed in slightly apprehensive curiosity. Three uniformed men were there with spades and sieves, and three or four more in plain clothes, with George Felse at the head of operations. More surprising, and to Paviour more confounding and conciliating at the same time, was the presence of Gus Hambro, busy with a large clip-board, charting on squared paper the patch of ground to be taken up, and sketching a hurried but accurately proportioned elevation of the exposed vault of the flue. He had a coloured pencil behind either ear, and a couple more in his breast pocket.

'I knew you wouldn't mind,' said Bill Lawrence, hurrying to account for the phenomenon, a sheaf of plastic sacks and fine brushes under his arm. 'He came along to copy some lettering in the museum, not expecting the place to be closed, of course. When he heard why, naturally he was interested. It was my idea, asking him if he'd like to lend a hand on doing what recording *can* be done on a job like this. He knows his stuff, you know. He jumped at the chance. We shan't be able to do a thorough coverage, I know, but it's a relatively small area, and we may as well keep it under what control we can manage between us. There might be some useful finds.'

'Naturally,' said Gus diplomatically, 'I regard myself as under your orders, sir. If there's any possibility of anything to be gained from this operation – and in the absence of the kind of labour you'd prefer to have on a job like this – I thought an extra pair of hands might be welcome.'

A faint look of baffled pleasure crossed Paviour's harried face and vanished again instantly. However carefully and reverently the job was going to be handled, obviously he expected nothing but disaster. He hovered about the site restlessly, like one barefoot on thorns, all the while they were removing the debris of sagging, uprooted broom bushes, which Orrie phlegmatically loaded into a handcart and wheeled away along the riverside path to be unloaded and burned as far as possible from the sacred precincts. The care with which they examined and photographed those bushes before allowing them to be removed brought Paviour quivering to the spot. With straining eyes he watched small fragments, meaningless to the lay eye, delicately extricated from the tangle of earth about the roots and the soft turf beneath them, cased in plastic, and labelled.

'Not your relics, I'm afraid,' said George, meeting the baffled and frantic gaze. 'Ours.'

He dared not ask, and was not told more. But he could not tear himself away. The operation proceeded methodically once the bushes had been cleared, though the spots where the mysterious fragments had been found were carefully tagged and covered with plastic. The broken fringes of grass were lifted off and stacked well out of the way, the spades began to clear the ground downwards from the arc of russet brickwork, warily because of sinister little trickles of loose earth that drifted down the slope at every movement. Layer by layer the narrow strata of brick and rubble were laid bare. Bill Lawrence, his eyes gleaming with the hunting passion, pounced on the fragments of encrusted ceramic and bone that were left behind in the police sieves, and Gus industriously entered their location in his graph, and sketched in each layer of masonry as it emerged.

Detective-Constable Barnes, large, rustic, intelligent and benign, put down his spade and went to work lovingly with a soft brush on the exposed uprights of the flue, whisking away loose, moist soil that abandoned its hold with revealing readiness. 'Look at that, now! That stuff's only been dropped here a few days. Watch that brickwork dry off in the sun, it'll be as pale as the arch, here, in ten minutes. I reckon there was eighteen inches or so of this passage open till the bank gave way.'

They had just passed that level now, and the darkness that yawned within the flue was black and inviting. Barnes reached a long arm over the ridge of fallen soil that remained in the mouth of the hole, and groped experimentally around within.

'Drops a foot, inside there. The bushes covered it. Nobody walks on a slope like this for choice, only sheep, and they don't let sheep graze this lot. Reasonable folks walk on the level – either up top, or down below.'

'What's it feel like, as far as you can reach?' George asked. 'Still silted over, or any traces of flooring? Tiles? Stone-work?'

'No, rubble. But still dropping. I'd say you'd get clear flooring a yard or two inside there.'

Lesley, watching in fascination from the sidelines, said with conviction: 'You've done this before! I know the signs.'

'Only once, miss.' Detective-Constable Barnes turned his benevolent gaze upon her with pleasure. He liked a pretty girl. 'I went on a dig with a bunch from Birmingham University. They had me brushing out post-holes on some rubbish dump they said was a castle. Not my idea of a castle. We never turned up nothing like this. My dad was a mason – I reckon he'd have been right interested in these bricks.

There's a colour for you! Spot-on what you mean when you say "brick".'

'What's it like above? Never mind further in, how about the first couple of feet?'

'Feels sound as rock. Arched – shallow, like.' His stretched knuckles tapped as far as they could reach. 'Barrel-vaulted, but low. Could be brick, could be stone. But I'd say brick. I can feel the courses.' He withdrew a hand like a shovel, and spread fingers black with the fine dust of centuries and a mere veiling of cobweb. 'Not much for seventeen hundred years, is it?'

The opening loomed before them, sliced into the bank, brushed relatively clean, a narrow, erect oblong of darkness with a rounded roof and pale, red and amber jambs rooted in deep green turf. And within was empty darkness, fenced off by no more than a ridge of soil. George looked round his team, and they were all massive countrymen, well in advance of the minimum police requirements. The slightest person present, leaving out the girls, was Gus Hambro, busy pricking in on his diagram the latest minor find.

'Care to take a look inside for us? You're the ratling.'

'Loan me a torch, and I'll have a go,' said Gus. 'What am I looking for?'

'Whatever you see. Structure, condition – and anything that looks out of place.'

'Right! Hang on to this,' he said to Bill Lawrence, and thrust the clip-board and its records at him. He shed his array of colour pencils, dropping them haphazard into the grass, hesitated whether to shed his tweed jacket, too, and then, considering its worn condition, buttoned it closely for protection instead. The dank darkness had a chill and jagged look.

'Don't go beyond where we can reach you,' George warned him. 'Six feet inside is enough. Just look it over, and memorise whatever there is to be memorised.'

124

'I'll do my endeavour. Right, give us that floodlight of yours.'

He dropped to his knees in the turf, now trampled into glistening, half-dried mud, and plunged head and shoulders under the ochre-tinted lintel. Torso, slim flanks and thighs, thrusting legs, vanished by silent heaves into the hollow under the slope. He was now nothing more than the neatly tapered ends of corduroy slacks, and a pair of well-worn Canadian hide moccasins. And these hung still, though alertly braced, for more than a minute, while the torch he carried ranged round the interior of the passage, and leaked little sparks of muted light into the outer day. He heaved himself six inches forward, and George laid an arresting hand on the remaining available ankle, and held fast.

'All right, you inside there! Leave it at that!'

Indistinct sounds emerged from within the earth, deprived of sense by the complicated acoustics of the soil. There was an interlude of silence, absorbed and intent. Then, without previous movement or sound, only with a sudden gush of closed and graveyard air, the rotten surface above buckled and dimpled, lolling in sagging bubbles of turf, and sending its under-levels of soil cascading down on top of the ancient arc of bricks that upheld it. Those without heard the ceiling yield, with a muffled, sickening grinding of brick against brick and stone upon stone, and the dull, filtering trickle of soil busily winding its way between.

A hollow yell was forced out with the jettisoned air. And George Felse dived forward at the jerking ankles under the archway, felt his way forward towards the knees, and hauled strongly backwards as the roof sagged slowly and ponderously inwards on top of Gus Hambro.

CHAPTER EIGHT

They dug him out with their bare hands, scrabbling like frantic terriers to clear the soil away from his head and shoulders; and within minutes they had him laid out like a stranded fish on one of their plastic sheets in the grass. All the internal filth of generations, cobwebs and dust and soot, had been discharged on top of him as the joints of the roof parted, but an outstretched arm had sheltered his head and face, and he was not only breathing, but spluttering out the dirt that had silted into mouth and nostrils. They had to brush away the layers before they could examine him for worse damage, George on one side of him, Barnes on the other, feeling urgently at a skull that seemed to have escaped all but the loose, light weight of the fall. They drew off his damp, soiled jacket, and felt at shoulders and arms, and could find no breakages. Everyone hovered unhappily. Little rivulets of loose soil trickled capriciously down the slope of raw earth. Somewhere on the sidelines Paviour could be heard protesting that they could not possibly proceed with this excavation in these conditions, that the risks were too great, that someone would be killed.

'No damage,' said Barnes, breathing gusty relief. 'Just knocked silly. He'll be round and as right as rain in five minutes. All that got him was the loose muck, not the bricks.'

'I'll fetch some brandy,' Lesley offered eagerly. 'And take this jacket to sponge and dry, he can't possibly put it on again like this.'

They were two deep round him in any case, nearly a dozen people hanging on the least movement of a finger or an eyelid. She's right, Charlotte thought, watching dubiously but compulsively like all the rest, one grain of sense is worth quite a lot of random sympathy.

'I'll bring one of Stephen's coats,' said Lesley, and set off at a light, long-stepping run for the house.

Charlotte offered tissues to wipe away the trailing threads of glutinous, dirty cobweb from the victim's eyes, for his eyelids were beginning to contract and twitch preparatory to opening. He lay for some minutes before he made the final effort, and then unfurled his improbably luxuriant lashes upon a bright, golden-brown stare of general accusation.

'What in hell do you all think you're doing?' he said, none too distinctly and very ungratefully, and spat out fragments of soil with a startled grimace of distaste. 'What happened?'

It was a fair enough question, considering how abruptly he had been obliterated from the proceedings. His exit had been brief, but absolute, while they, it seemed, were still in possession of their faculties and the facts. He sat up in the circle of George's arm, seemed to become suddenly aware of his shirt-sleeves and the late April chill, and demanded, looking violently round him: 'Where's my jacket?'

'Mrs Paviour's taken it away to clean and dry it out for you. You were taking a look inside there, and half the roof came down on you,' said George patiently. All the victim's limbs seemed to be in full working order, even his memory was only one jump behind.

'Oh, blimey!' he said weakly. 'Was that it?' And he

leaned forward to peer at the spot where two policemen were stolidly clearing away newly-fallen rubble from the mouth of the flue, and a third, well above them on the level ground, was cautiously surveying the crater. 'You'll have to dig for that torch of yours,' he said more strongly, not without a mildly vindictive satisfaction. 'I let go of it when things started dropping on me. That chap up there had better watch his step, there was a gleam of daylight a good two yards forward from where I got to. He didn't put one of those beetle-crushers through there while I was inside, did he?'

'He did not,' said George tolerantly. 'The thing just gave. Mea culpa. I shouldn't have let you do it.'

'The thing just gave. Did it?' He was coming round with remarkable aplomb now, it was with the old, knowledge-able eye that he stared at the ruin of the neat archway which had been their entrance to the flue only ten minutes ago. But all he said was: 'You know what? Either I'm accident-prone, all of a sudden, or else somebody, somewhere, is sticking pins in a wax image of me.'

Some minutes later, when all anxiety on his behalf had ebbed away into renewed interest in the job on hand, when he was sitting hunched with Price's sportscoat draped round his shoulders, and one of George's cigarettes between his lips, and not a soul but George within earshot, he said, softly and with intent: 'Watch it from now on! I'm getting clearer every minute. Somebody'd been hacking at the brickwork inside there. That wasn't any accident.'

'You sure?' asked George in the same tone.

'I'm sure. I lost your torch – and switched on, at that, you won't get much mileage back in that battery! – but I know what I'd already seen. Fresh-broken surfaces, high in the wall. The upstream side was what I noticed. A gash in the brickwork, pale and clean. Even if you have to dig out from on top, now, with care you'll find it. Somebody aimed to bring that flue down.'

'Nobody,' said George, gazing ahead of him at the spot where Price was re-deploying his forces on the level of the caldarium floor, 'can have got into that place ahead of you. Earlier, yes, that I believe. Not since the slip.'

'They wouldn't have to. I told you, at least one gleam of daylight ahead there. More than one hole on top. A crowbar down one of those would be all he needed.' The momentary silence irritated him. He said with asperity, and considering his recent escape with some justification: 'It worked, didn't it?'

'It worked, all right. I'm considering motives. What was the object? To have a second go at you? They couldn't have known you'd even be available, much less put your head in the trap.'

'No, that's out,' admitted Gus generously. 'To seal off the flue, more likely.'

'To hide what's there?'

'Not a chance! There'll be nothing there. To hide the traces of what *was* there.'

Lesley came back from the house with a tweed coat over her arm and a flask in her hand. 'We can also,' she said, looking down at Gus with a slightly quizzical smile, 'offer a bath, if and when you feel equal to it. You can hardly go back to "The Salmon's Return" looking like that.'

He looked down, slightly startled, at the state of his shirt and his hands, and admitted the difficulty.

'And you can't see your face,' said Lesley helpfully, her friendly, candid eyes dwelling upon the spectacle with detached amusement, but not with any apparent repulsion.

'That's immensely kind of you. I'd like to take you up on

it, if Mr Paviour will allow me,' he said, suddenly aware of a little chill in the blood that warned him not to leave out the curator from this or any other exchange on these premises.

'Of course,' Paviour said, with prompt but distant courtesy, 'by all means avail yourself. I can offer you a change of shirt, if the size is right.'

'And as I've got lunch on the way in about three quarters of an hour, hadn't you better take it easy and join us? You'll just have time to make yourself presentable. Bill will be staying, too,' she said, firmly arranging everything to her own satisfaction.

This somewhat drastic rupture in her ordinary routine must in its way, Charlotte thought, be a godsend to Lesley, however deplorable the reason for it. She was also reacting in an understandably female way to having a ready-made casualty of pleasant appearance and attractive manners dropped at her feet. For the second time, too! But on the first occasion, even when deposited half-drowned and battered in the Paviour household, he had belonged by rights to Charlotte, who had pulled him out of the river and demanded shelter for him. This time he was, so to speak, legitimate prey, and Lesley intended to enjoy him.

'If you feel like walking up with me now, I must go back and keep an eye on lunch. Charlotte, will you come and help me?'

The three of them walked back together, Gus steady enough on his legs, and only slightly exercised in mind at leaving the excavation, which had now been transferred of necessity to the higher level. There could be no more attempts to enter the flues from the slope, they were going to have to take up all that island of rotten ground and expose them from above. A more thorough job, and a safer, but infinitely slower. They were staking out the limits of the subsidence now, and Bill Lawrence was clipping a new sheet of graph paper to his board. One of the plainclothes men was busy with a camera. And Paviour, torn between the instinct to follow his wife and the desire to pursue George Felse and renew his protests, hovered in indecision. Charlotte looked back once, and saw him standing motionless, gazing after them, lean and desiccated as a stick insect, but with a face all too human in its tormented anxiety; not all, perhaps, about his beloved and ravaged city.

Lesley could, she thought, do a little more to placate and reassure a husband she knew to be almost pathologically jealous. It was easy to believe that she had no regrets about her bargain, and no intention of backing out of it, but in the circumstances this was a reassurance that needed to be repeated endlessly. And yet everything she did had an open and innocent grace about it. If she devoted herself to her new guest all through lunch, she did so out of a pleasurable sense of duty, and not at all flirtatiously. It was impossible to associate the word with her; there was nothing sidelong or circuitous about the way Lesley approached anyone, man or woman.

As for Gus, bathed and polished and reclothed in his own beautifully pressed sportscoat, he trod delicately, dividing his attention as adroitly as he could between the two of them, repaying Lesley's direct friendliness with wary deference, and turning as often as possible to Paviour with leading remarks on Aurae Phiala, to draw him into eloquence on the subject dearest to his heart.

'I imagine,' said Paviour, regarding him almost with favour over the coffee, 'that you'll be interested in seeing this distasteful invasion limited as much as possible. The damage could be incalculable. I suppose,' he said, almost visibly writhing at coming so near to begging, 'you haven't any influence? The authorities, I believe, do sometimes listen to the opinions of scholars . . .' His thin, fastidious voice faded out bitterly on the admission that he was none.

'I'm afraid,' said Gus ruefully, 'that nobody who won't listen to you, sir, is going to pay the slightest attention to me. But I don't believe, from what I've heard this morning, that the police want to take the dig a yard past where it need go. After all, they do have some evidence, apparently, to connect this boy Boden with the place.' He added deprecatingly: 'I think Chief Inspector Felse means to brief us, as fully as he can, this evening.'

'Will you be staying on to see the job through?' asked Bill Lawrence.

'I'd have liked to, but it doesn't look as if I shall be able to. I got my room at the pub for only two nights. From Friday night on you have to be a fisherman to get in at "The Salmon's Return", even in the close season. I've got to get out today.'

'Oh, no!' said Lesley, aggrieved. 'What a shame, when you're being so helpful. Stephen, don't you think *we* . . .?'

She had rushed in where angels might have hesitated to set foot, and almost instantly she recognised it, and halted in contained but palpable dismay. And Bill Lawrence put in smoothly, as if the tension had never communicated itself to him, but so promptly that Charlotte, for one, knew it had: 'Why don't you move in with me? I've got the whole lodge as bachelor quarters, there's plenty of room for one more, if you don't mind sharing a room? Two beds,' he said cheerfully, 'and acres of storage space. We can run over and pick up your things, if you say the word?'

'Consider it said,' Gus said heartily, 'and thanks! I should have hated to have to go away and miss this chance. I thought I should probably have to go as far as Comerbourne to get a room without notice, and it hardly seemed worth it commuting from that distance.

Especially,' he said, with an engaging smile in Paviour's direction, 'as I more or less invited myself to the dig in the first place.'

Lesley had recovered resiliently from her momentary disarray. She sat serenely silent, apparently well content at having Gus's problem and her own solved so economically. It even entered Charlotte's mind, watching, that there were moments when Lesley deliberately made use of Bill Lawrence to pull chestnuts out of the fire for her.

Afterwards, in the car on the way to 'The Salmon's Return', Bill said, after too patent deliberation and in too world-weary a voice: 'Look, it's easy enough living in this set-up, but you have to know the rules. Be my guest, use my experience and save your own, boy. Rule number one: Never even *seem* to get too close to that lady.' His tone was lightly cynical, and a little rueful; there was no knowing for certain how deeply he felt about what he was saying.

'I wondered,' said Gus, 'why you got off the mark so fast and so smoothly. Apart from having a generous disposition, of course.'

'Don't mistake me, there's nothing wrong with Lesley. She's straight, and she means what she offers. It's her old man. He's mad jealous of her. Oh, he'd have backed up her invitation, all right, if he'd had to. Very correct, very hospitable. But then he'd have made life hell for you, her, and above all himself, by being suspicious of every glance you gave her. It's better to keep a nice safe distance, and be a bit of the landscape, like me.'

'And you've experienced that yourself?' Gus asked mildly.

The voice beside him became even lighter and drier. 'I didn't have to. I've only confirmed it from my own observations since. I was warned off privately, as soon as I came here. By Lesley herself.' There was a brief but weighty pause, and then, as if he had felt oppressed by its suggestive possibilities, he made the mistake of adding, with the same airy intonation: 'Probably she never fancied me, anyhow.'

Gus kept his eyes on the road ahead, and sat stolidly, as though the sharp note of bitterness had passed him by. But from then on he was in no doubt that, whatever this young man felt for Lesley Paviour, it was certainly not indifference.

'In view of all the circumstances,' said George Felse, facing the assembled household in Paviour's study that evening, 'I think it only fair to give you some idea of how this enquiry is progressing. Your professional proceedings are affected, and you have a right to be told why that's inevitable. We want your co-operation. We don't want to upset your routine any longer than we must, or to extend our intrusion a yard beyond what's necessary.'

They were all there, including the young men from the lodge, invited by Lesley to dine at the house. Not an invariable favour, Gus had gathered. Not much doubt that Bill attributed it cynically to his guest's presence.

'Let me substantiate,' said George, 'our claim to move in on your ground. In the first place, the post-mortem on Gerry Boden has shown that he did not drown. There is no penetration of water into his lungs. He died of suffocation, most probably while still stunned by a blow on the head. The time of death, while it's always somewhat more problematical fixing it than is usually supposed, was considerably earlier than the time when, as we have several reasons to believe, he was put into the water. Provisionally, his death occurred somewhere between six and eight in the evening. In other words, about midway between the time when he was last seen, and the time when Mr Hambro was attacked. It's a fair assumption that the attempt on Mr

Hambro's life took place because the murderer believed he had seen the boy's body committed to the river. Seen, or heard, or at any rate become aware of something queer going on, something that might make sense to him and be reported later, even if it made no sense then.'

Paviour licked bluish lips, and ventured hesitantly: 'But if there was such an interval, the boy may have been anywhere during that time, not here in Aurae Phiala at all.'

'Oh, yes, he was here. We know that he hid himself in order to stay here and have the free run of the place when everyone else had gone. We know where he hid. And we know where he was hidden, after his death. From under the clump of broom bushes we removed this morning we recovered, as perhaps you noticed, certain small bits of evidence. One was the broken cap of a red ball-pen, fellow to the black one he still had on him when found. It was trodden into the turf, *underneath* those bushes. They were dragged together and heaped over him after he was killed. Another, from among the broom roots, was a sample of hair, which I think will certainly turn out to be Boden's. He was concealed there on the spot, because at the time of his murder it was barely dusk, and the whole of your river-shore is only too plainly visible from the other side. Therefore, that is where he was killed – right there beside the cave-in.'

'But after you came enquiring for him,' protested Paviour feverishly, 'the enclosure of Aurae Phiala was searched. Surely he would have been found?'

'I'd hardly call it searched. We did walk over the site. It was then dark, perhaps dark enough for the murderer to have risked getting him down to the river, if we hadn't been around. But we were not looking for a body then, at least not on dry land. The fact remains, he was there. Further laboratory work should tell us more. His clothes, for instance. They've already told us something of the first importance, the reason for his hanging around here until after closing-time.'

He looked round them with an equable, unrevealing glance, a pleasant, greying, unobtrusive man at whom you would never look twice in the street.

'Gerry carried a purse for his loose money. Among the coins in it, which the murderer hadn't disturbed, was a gold aureus of the Emperor Commodus, in mint condition. He can only have found it during the school visit. And he can only have found it there, at that broken flue of the hypocaust.'

'That's an impossibility,' said Paviour hoarsely. 'You'll find this is some toy of his own, a fake, a copy . . . How could you account for such a thing? A freshly-minted coin after years in the ground?'

George picked up the cue, and proceeded to account for it bluntly and clearly, as he had done for Charlotte in the night. He sketched in the figure of the murderer, also waiting for dark, to remove his buried treasure from its perilous position, and his unexpected encounter with the inquisitive boy on the same errand; the instant decision that only the boy's total removal could now protect his profitable racket; and the immediate execution. He described the items of Roman jewellery turning up with inadequate pedigrees during the past year, and the peculiarities of style which linked them, if not necessarily to this site, at least to no more than four or five, of which this was one.

'In short, we believe that someone has been systematically milking Aurae Phiala of small pieces, some very valuable indeed, for a year or more.'

There was a long, tight pause, while he eyed them gently again, his glance passing unrevealingly from face to face round the circle. Then Bill Lawrence said, a little too loudly but with admirable bluntness: 'You mean one of us.'

George smiled. 'Not necessarily. There are a good many people in the village who've been here longer than you have, and known this place just as intimately, some of them before it was organised and shown as it is now. The site could hardly be more open. The riverside path makes access easy for everyone who knows this district, and that includes not only the village, but large numbers of fishermen, too.'

'But only somebody with specialist knowledge,' Bill pointed out forcibly, 'would know how to dispose of articles like that to the best advantage.'

'True enough, but gold is gold, and in certain parts of the world it commands far more than its sterling value, even if it's hard to sell in its original form. There may have been other, larger pieces besides the coins, of course, they'd be a problem to an amateur. The helmet, for instance . . .' he said innocently.

Paviour stiffened in his chair, staring. '*Helmet?*'

'The helmet the ghost is said to wear. You remember Mrs Paviour's interesting account of what she and others saw, or thought they saw? That may be no legend, but a chance find, retained as a property to scare off the superstitious, and divert any curiosity about movements here in the night.'

Paviour gathered himself together with a perceptible effort, sitting erect and taut. 'Such a traffic,' he said firmly, 'would require not just some specialist knowledge, but an expert of the first quality as adviser, if it was to escape detection for long.'

'Such as yourself?' said George.

If it was a shock, he was then so inured to shocks that it made no impression. With bitter dignity he said: 'I am a third-rate sub-expert and a fifth-rate scholar, and the real ones know it as well as I do.'

Lesley whispered: 'Stephen, dear!' and laid a hand appealingly on his arm.

Imperturbably George pursued: 'But other authorities have visited Aurae Phiala. There have even been brief and limited digs under some of them.' He was gathering up his few notes, and stowing them away in an inside pocket, preparatory to leaving. He looked up once, briefly, at Charlotte, a glance that told her nothing. 'You might give it some thought. Consider who has visited here, and who has dug, during – say – the past year and a half to two years. No, please don't disturb yourself, I can find my way out.'

He was halfway to the door when he added an afterthought: 'One name we do know, of course. It's just about eighteen months, isn't it, since Doctor Alan Morris left from here on his way to Turkey.'

They were still staring after him, motionless and silent, when the door closed gently; and in a few minutes they heard his car start up on the gravel drive.

The inquest opened formally on Saturday morning, took evidence of identification, and at the police request adjourned for one week. George drove the bewildered but stonily dignified pair who were Gerry Boden's parents back to their home, from which he had also conveyed them earlier, because he was by no means sure that Boden was yet in any case to drive. Not that they were making difficulties or distresses for anyone; their composure was chill and smooth and temporary as ice, but though it might thaw at any moment, it would certainly not be in public. Their disciplines included containing their private sorrows. And in a sense Gerry had always been, if not a sorrow, an ambivalent sort of joy, a perilous possession, capable of piling either delights or dismays into their laps at any moment without warning. Life without him was going to be infinitely more peaceful and inexpressibly dimmer. He could have been anything he had put his mind to, good or bad, and now he was a carefully but impersonally reconstructed body put together by strangers to be presentable enough to be released for burial. Boden had already seen him dead. Mrs Boden had not, but would surely insist on doing so when he was given back to them.

Afterwards, of course, they would take up the business of living again, because they were durable, and in any case had not much choice. And in time they would be comfortable enough, being happily very fond of each other, though they had never in their lives been in love.

George went home to do a little thinking, and take a fresh look at the laboratory reports he'd hardly had time to read that morning. Also to get the taste of despair and disgust out of his mouth and the mildew of misanthropy out of his eyes by looking at Bunty. She was getting a little plumper and a little less sudden now that she was in the middle forties, but her chestnut and hazel colouring was as vivid as ever; and knowing every line of her only made her more of a delightful surprise in everything she said or did. For George had been in love with Bunty ever since he had first heard Bernarda Elliot sing at a concert in Birmingham, while she was still a student, and had never got over her unhesitating choice of marriage with him in preference to a career as a potentially first-class mezzo. Police officers are not considered great catches.

Their only son was busy mending agricultural machinery and driving tractors for an erratic but effective native mission in India, and had just welcomed to the same service his future wife, fresh from an arts degree and a rushed course in nursing. And what Tossa was going to make of the Swami Premanathanand's organisation was anybody's guess, but arguably she would fall completely under the spell of its gentle but jolting founder, as Dominic had done, and lose herself in his hypnotic ambience. George thought of them, and was lifted out of his despond. He withdrew to the study of his morning's professional mail in better heart.

He was halfway through compiling an up-to-date précis when Bunty looked in, unastonished as ever, and announced: 'Miss Rossignol wants to talk to you.' Bunty vanished on the word, and Charlotte, small and trim and magnificently self-possessed, at her most French, came sailing in upon him from the doorway. She looked very determined, and very young.

'Now this,' said George, 'is a pleasure I wasn't expecting. Come and sit down, and tell me what I can do for you.'

'You can tell me,' said Charlotte, looking up intently into his face, 'whether you really meant what you implied last night. Because I've been thinking along the same lines, and not liking it at all. And then, if you don't mind, and it isn't top secret, you can tell me what you know that I don't know about my great-uncle Alan.'

CHAPTER NINE

By late morning the diggers had exposed the broken roof of the flue, and half the arch of its slightly damaged neighbour, for a distance of about six feet, and were setting to work in earnest to remove the shattered brickwork and lay bare the channel below. Since this process involved moving sacred relics, and it was a life-and-death matter to Paviour that they should not be damaged or allowed to fall into disorder, both he and Bill Lawrence were now employed, not so much fully as frantically, in trying to label and number everything that emerged, and laying out the materials of the arch in the grass, aside from the affected area. Barnes, out of pure good-nature and some reviving interest in archaeology, lent a hand under Paviour's irritable and anxious direction, but even with three pairs of hands they had all they could do to keep pace. Gus Hambro had taken over one of the small sheds attached to the museum, where there was a sink and a water tap, and removed himself there with all the minor trophies of the first day's work, and with sleeves rolled up, and an array of small nail-brushes for weapons, was carefully washing off the corrosion of soil and dust from dozens of little objects, most of them derisory: fragments of red glaze, one segment of cloudy glass from the lips of a jug, a plethora of animal bones, two plain bone hair-pins and one with the broken remnants of a carved head, and the single interesting item, a bronze penannular brooch with coiled ends to the ring. A boring job, but a vital one. He had good reason to want to be first in discovering and studying whatever there was to be found, but so far the result was disappointing.

It was a little past noon when the door of his shed opened, and Lesley looked in.

'Lunch prompt at one,' she informed him, and came to his elbow to examine the trifles he had laid out on a board beneath the window. 'Dull,' she said, sadly but truthfully. 'Do you need any help?' There was still a heap of grimy objects awaiting his attentions, their nature almost obscured by layers of soil grown to them like rust.

'I shouldn't. You'll get terribly dirty.' And after a moment's hesitation he asked what he had been wondering all morning. 'What happened to Charlotte? I haven't seen her around at all today.'

'I know. She went off after breakfast in my car. She said she wanted to see somebody in town, but she promised to be back for lunch. I offered to drive her wherever she wanted to go,' said Lesley, frowning thoughtfully down at the little bronze brooch, 'but she wouldn't let me, so I saw she didn't want company. Only two days, and you know, I really miss her. I've just got used to having somebody to chatter to, a rare luxury here. Stephen doesn't chatter, or understand being chattered to. Stephen *converses*. When he isn't being totally taciturn, that is.' She laughed suddenly, recognising how fluently she was illustrating her own theme. 'You see? Failing Charlotte, someone else gets sprayed with words. You don't mind being a stand-in, do you? All the others are far too busy, and you can at least go on brushing bones while you listen.'

'You don't know,' he said, 'where she was going?'

'Charlotte? She didn't say, so naturally I didn't ask her.

Lend me that bigger brush, I can be whisking the top dirt off these things. I'm no use down there, and there's half an hour or so before I need go back to the kitchen.'

She fell in companionably beside him, and went to work removing the worst of the encrustations from still more inevitable bits of bone and animal teeth. 'Graveyard exercise, isn't it? Like Mr Barnes, I dream of digging up another Mildenhall treasure instead of a cow's incisors, but it's never likely to happen to me.'

She had leaned nearer to him, to drop the despised tooth into the sink, and she felt the slight tension that stiffened the arm she brushed against. She drew back a distinct pace, and kept that distance; but he knew that her eyes were on him, in no sidelong glance, but regarding him widely and directly. The challenge to turn and look as straightly at her was irresistible. Greenish-blue like the off-shore sea under sunshine, her disconcerting eyes were laughing at him, though the rest of her face was mild and grave.

'I suppose Bill's been warning you about Stephen and me,' she said quite placidly.

She had set the key, he might as well follow.

'Shouldn't he have done? I understand you warned him yourself.'

She shrugged. 'Just as well to know where you stand, don't you think? I don't suppose it came as any great surprise to you. Only the very unintelligent could help wondering about us. And you're not very unintelligent. Are you?'

'I'm wondering that myself,' he said.

'The door's open,' she said, smiling. 'Anyone's welcome to walk in. And you could walk out any moment you pleased.'

'Quite. But why, if it's like that, did you walk in? And stay in?'

Perhaps by that time he should have been feeling that the

conversation had got out of hand, but he had no such feeling. On the contrary, it was proceeding in perfect control, and not a word had been said on either side without consideration and intent.

'Because I'm a person, too,' she said, sparkling with angry animation. 'He's jealous – all right! But I'm alive and gregarious and talkative, and I'm damned if I'm going to change my nature because he sees more in everything I say or do than I ever put into it. Let him fret that I'm disloyal, if he has to, just as long as I know I'm not. It isn't as if I had any reason to be afraid of him, you know. A gentler, more attentive old idiot never stepped. No, when I went about virtuously warning nice, harmless young men like Bill to keep clear, it was all out of consideration for *his* peace of mind. Now I'm considering mine. I'm what he married. Why should I suppose I'd be doing him a favour by changing into something else? So I've given up the practice. I'm staying the way I am.'

The invitation to equal candour was proffered, palpable on the air. He accepted it. For some reason it would have seemed perverse to refuse it.

'Why he married you,' he said briskly, 'is no mystery to anyone. Given the chance, that is. Why *was* he given the chance? That's the puzzler.'

She had put down the shard of Samian ware she had been brushing, and the brush after it. She leaned with one hip against the edge of the sink, her back half-turned to the window, the better to face him; and even her sea-green eyes had stopped laughing now.

'Because his timing was right. Because he came as such a nice change after the young, handsome, dashing, cold-hearted bastard who'd dropped me into the muck the minute it suited him, and put me off love for life. Or so I thought then. Jilted, I tell you, is no word for what

146

happened to me. And there was Stephen trotting in and out of the office with his little manuscripts, looking rather distinguished and being terribly anxious and patient and kind. So I told him what I hadn't told a soul besides, and he did everything possible to comfort me and make it up to me – as if anyone could! And one of the nice things he thought of was to ask me to marry him. It looked good to me – really, then, it looked like the answer to everything. So I married for what was left, since I'd finished with love. For security, and kindness, for a respectable position, and a crash barrier against all the young, handsome, dashing, frosty-hearted bastards left in the world. The world stopped, and I got off, and that was marriage. And look at me now!'

It was an unnecessary instruction; he was looking at her very intently and steadily, and at a range of scarcely more than a foot. She had turned until she was confronting him squarely, leaning back a little against the stone sink, her hands, grubby from the clinging soil, childishly held up beside her shoulders, with widespread fingers, to avoid dirtying her cashmere sweater. Her short fair hair quivered and seemed to erect itself as if electrically charged, in the small, freakish draught from the window behind her, and through some trick of the fitful sunlight. She had set the pace in all these improbable exchanges, and whether she had now far outdistanced her own intention there was no knowing; but there was no point in trying to turn back, and there might, at least, be something to be gained by following through. For one thing, he doubted very much if she would have revoked on her bargain, even now.

'If it's that bad,' he said deliberately, 'why do you stay with him? The world's still there, if you want to get on again.'

'There's an awful lot of time around, too,' she said. 'I'm waiting. I can afford to wait.'

'For the right moment?'

'Or the right man,' she said.

It was said quite impersonally, almost to herself, but with such abrupt desolation and longing that he was filled with an entirely personal dismay on her account, and instinctively put out his hands to take her by the waist and hold her fast while he found something, however fatuous, however inadequate, to say to her. She was turning slightly away from him when he took her forcibly between his palms. He felt her whole body convulsed by a huge tremor of revulsion and panic, and was distressed into a sharp cry of pity and protest.

'Lesley – don't! My God, I never intended . . .'

She came to life again, her flesh lissom and warm. She twisted to break free, and he held on only to try and reassure her before he let her go, for it was like holding a cat unwilling to be held, the boneless body dissolving between his hands. She reached out to the rim of the sink, to have a purchase for forcing him off, and her fingers missed their grip and slid into the turgid water. She fell against him, drawing breath in deep, transfixing sighs, and suddenly she was silk, clinging with both hands. Her head was against his shoulder, her face upturned close beneath his, with wide-opened eyes and parted lips.

He kissed her, and the passive mouth flowered and burned, in shocked, involuntary acceptance. He felt her hands close on his back, pressing convulsively.

Over her shoulder he saw through the window the whole sweep of grass suddenly inhabited by a single approaching figure, looming large against the driven clouds and gleaming sun, and the distant, skeletal walls. He saw the brisk stride broken and diverted, only a dozen yards away; he saw the long, narrow body lean back, waver and halt. There could be only one reason for such a dislocation. The glass before him had been recently cleaned, and the noon sun shone directly into it. Paviour, coming hopefully up from the dig with a new bouquet of trophies in their plastic sacks, had clearly seen the tableau in the shed.

There was a strange, brief pause, while they hung eye to eye, across all that distance, and perfectly understood that there was now no possibility of disguising their mutual knowledge, that it could only be publicly denied and privately accepted. Then, wheeling to the left with a sudden, jerky movement, Paviour walked away towards the house, still clutching his little plastic sacks. Probably he had forgotten he was holding them.

Gus stood motionless, afraid almost to breathe for fear Lesley should turn away from him in a new access of revulsion, and face the window before that long, stilted, pathetic figure had vanished out of range. It was pure luck that her back had been turned to the light; she had seen nothing. His palms were still clamped with involuntary force on either side of her body, he would have felt any stiffening, any tremor, and she hung fluidly and heavily against him, like draped silk. And Paviour had walked clean out of the frame of the window and out of their sight.

It almost hurt to unclamp his grip on the girl, and separate himself from her, and he did it with infinite care not to offend by the separation as he had offended by first touching her. 'I'm sorry!' he said constrainedly. 'I never meant to scare you.'

She turned aside from him at once, as soon as he released her, reached automatically for her brush and towards the dingy pile of relics awaiting attention. She moved with economy and resignation, and looked curiously calm, as though her recent experience had left her in shock.

'I'm sorry, too. I never thought you did. It simply happens to me. I panic. I can't help it.'

He wondered if he should tell her, if she needed to know. He thought not. She was better off as she was. Her innocence would be impregnable; she had nothing to fear.

'I'd better go,' she said, almost naturally, and put down the brush. 'I've got to see to the lunch.'

She made very little sound, departing, because the door was open, and she moved as lightly as a kitten in her soft walking shoes, so nicely matched to her boyish, slim style in slacks. But he knew the moment when she left, without looking round from his automatic operations on one more fragmentary ivory pin, by the slow, settling tranquillity she left behind her.

Lunch was a minor nightmare only because nothing whatever happened. It cost him an effort to reassemble his stolidly innocent face before he need appear; and then, when he was reasonably assured that his façade was impervious, he had to meet Charlotte head-on at the door.

He had never seen her look quite so un-English or so serenely formidable. There was no wind, and the curled plumes of black hair deployed across her magnolia cheeks might have been lacquered there, they were so steely and perfect. Also he had never realised until that moment how small and slender she was, almost as tiny as Lesley. His mind started involuntarily measuring her waist, and the exercise led on to other highly speculative considerations concerning the resilience of her bones and the scent of her hair, should she ever find herself in his arms, due to an emotional miscalculation on his part and a panic reaction on hers. He failed to imagine it adequately. She didn't look the type. But then, neither did Lesley.

'I missed you,' he said, almost accusingly. 'You've been gone all morning.'

'I had a call to make in town, on personal business,' she

said coolly. 'I hope you managed to divert yourself even without me.' And her thick, genuine, loftily-arched black brows went up, and the eyes beneath them flashed a golden gleam of amusement at his proprietary tone. During the past two days he had given her very little cause to suppose that he attached particular importance to her presence. 'Any interesting discoveries?'

She was referring only to work in progress, and he knew it, and yet every word she said seemed to find a way of probing between the joints of his armour with prophetic force. The defensive reaction she set up in him made him tongue tied when he would most gladly have been fluent; he felt that if he turned his back on her she would see, clean through the tweed of his jacket, the prints of two small, splayed hands, soiled from brushing trivia, clamped against his shoulder-blades.

'If you like,' she said generously, 'I'll be your runner this afternoon, and ferry the bits and pieces up to you.'

'Do,' he said, cheered and astonished. 'I'd like that.' Charlotte darting in and out would be an insurance policy second to none. Against Lesley? When he stood back to consider the incident he couldn't seriously persuade himself that she was likely to come near him again of her own will, however perversely she desired to let off steam. Against himself, then? He flinched from considering it, but it remained a strong possibility.

'We'd better go in,' said Charlotte, only slightly disturbed by his uncharacteristic fervour. 'I'm hungry.'

So they went in. And lunch was the nadir of normality, without an original thought or a perilous suggestion to enliven it. The confrontation through the glass of the window might never have taken place.

By that hour the police had already segregated certain

sections of brick and tile marked with recent scars, a few curved shards of pottery from a jar, and covered from injury a small area of flooring within the flue, with its dust still displaying the faint but positive print of the base of just such a ceramic jar. There had been no gold coins in the detritus. No doubt the last of them had been removed in haste after the murder of Gerry Boden. Only the single one from his purse remained to testify.

On Saturday evenings Bill Lawrence, that ambitious and scholarly young man, had an extra-mural class in Moulden. Which meant that the general invitation to dinner issued at lunch by Lesley raked in only Gus Hambro in addition to the curator's household. Bill had generous licence to come along for coffee afterwards, however late, but his class was timed to finish only at nine-thirty, and since it met in the rear clubroom at 'The Crown' it was long odds against the argumentative local savants consenting to go home before closing time, so that his attendance was at best only hypothetical. Moreover, Bill's own attitude was decidedly ambiguous; nobody had to tell him that his commitments were well known, and invitations issued accordingly. He knew when he was, or was not, wanted.

Not that Bill was missing anything, Gus thought, before the evening was half over. The pretence that everything was normal, that they were a party of congenial people enjoying a social get-together, had become downright oppressive, as if everyone was working a little too hard at it. They had an afternoon of unremitting labour behind them, and perhaps were too tired to make a good job of keeping up appearances. Paviour had grown so brittle that he looked as if the least jolt might send all his joints jangling apart; and though Lesley's extrovert lightness of heart was beyond suspicion, it was rapidly becoming unbearable in this context. All very well for her in her innocence, but Gus was in a very different case. Worst of all, there was no chance whatever of making any real contact with Charlotte, and it was exasperating to have her sitting there opposite him, so near and so inaccessible, watching him with the black, acute gaze of a sceptical cat, pupils high-lighted in gold; a look that asserted nothing, merely observed and analysed, stopping short of judgement only, he was afraid, out of indifference.

As soon as he decently could, and on the plea that they were all tired – to which Lesley frankly assented, eliding a yawn into an apology – he excused himself and withdrew to make his way home. He was glad to be alone, and made the most of the ten-minute walk to his bed, taking it at leisure.

It was a restless, luminous night, the kind that late April sometimes casts up between frosts, mild, starry, with a laggard and minor moon. The shape of Aurae Phiala came into being gradually as he walked, looming largely on his right hand, a series of levels marked out by a series of verticals, standing bones of masonry rearing from long planes of turf.

She came silently out of the unregarded spaces on his left, and stood in his path, a small, compact figure quite still and composed; not making any demands upon him, except by being there. He knew which one she was, though the two of them were very much of a build.

'Lesley . . .'

'It's all right,' she said serenely, still neatly enfolded into her own shadowy silhouette. 'Nobody's going to miss me. Believe it or not, I was so tired I went up to bed the moment you left. You surely don't think I share a room with him, do you? Or with anyone!'

'You shouldn't have come out after me,' he said.

'No, I don't suppose I should. What makes you think it was after you?'

'You do,' he said brutally, and stood fronting her, for want of any way by. 'Who else did you think would be making off this way? Don't pretend you *just happened* to choose this way for your evening constitutional.'

'I never pretend anything,' she said, in the soft, mild voice that seemed to belong so aptly to the dark. 'And I never *just happen* to do anything. In any case, it must be quite plain to you that I ran most of the way from the back gate, or I couldn't have got here before you. I simply felt I wanted to talk to you again. But it wasn't much use my finding out how much I liked you, if all I've done is to make you dislike me.'

'Is that what I'm doing?' he said.

'That's the way it looks from where I'm standing.'

'Maybe you can't see very well from there.'

'I could come closer,' she offered.

It was a highly dangerous gift she had, this one of writing both halves of the dialogue. There never seemed to be any possible answer except the one she wanted. Not that he was trying very hard to deviate from the script.

She took two long, slow steps towards him, her arms at her sides, her head tilted back to look up at him. One more step, and the points of her small, high breasts almost touched him. In the darkness her face was serene and pale, and her dilated eyes huge and fixed. He had the impression that she was smiling.

'Do I look any more friendly from there?' he asked, keeping very still.

She said: 'Gus . . .' experimentally, as if she were memorising and tasting his name; and she laughed, very softly, at its ridiculous brevity and inappropriateness. 'Are you waiting for me to explode when touched? Not this time! Something happened to me this morning that never happened before. Try it. Touch me!'

Her face was very close, turned up to him like a white, wide-open flower; and in obedience to the rules of this game he very nearly did take her at her word. But then he changed his mind, and deliberately held still, even when her warmth leaned and touched him. In a voice he had never heard from her before, whispering, almost fawning, and yet still laughing, she said: 'Gus . . .' again, two or three times over, changing the note as though plucking descending strings. 'It's you,' she said, 'you, you, you're the one . . . It was never like that for me – never – not even with *him* . . .'

She put out her hands, and flattened them gently against his chest; and then suddenly her arms were round him, and her body was pressed hard against his, clinging from shoulder to knee. He returned her embrace partly out of pure astonishment, but kept his close hold of her after that out of heady delight. Her intensity was electrifying. Her body moved against him, tensing and turning fluid again, finding every vulnerable nerve. She freed a hand to tug at the buttons of his jacket, and wound her arms about him within it, manipulating the muscles of his back with fierce, hard fingertips. Her mouth reached up to him hungrily, and fastened on his as he leaned to her, in a kiss that left them both gasping for breath. Her lips, progressing by little, biting caresses along his cheek, whispered dizzily: 'Love me, love me, love . . .' until he found her mouth again with his and silenced her.

They were so wildly engrossed in each other at that moment that they heard nothing outside themselves, only the pounding of their hearts and the gusty breaths they drew. Paviour was within six feet of them before they were aware of him. Gus lifted his head and looked over Lesley's shoulder, and there motionless before him, a lean, angular shape in the darkness, the jealous husband stood waiting with bleak courtesy to be let into their world.

Lesley felt the stiffening jolt that passed through Gus's body, and stirred and turned protestingly to look for its reason. There was one strange moment while they both stared at Paviour, and he at them, rather as though they had no shared language between them, and speech could not help them. Very slowly the two tangled bodies drew apart and stood clear; the most important thing just then seemed to be to accomplish this necessary manoeuvre with a little grace and dignity, not in a humiliating scramble. Even when they were separate, their linked hands parted only gradually and gently.

'I'm sorry!' said Paviour with cold civility. 'I regret forcing this intrusion upon you, but you'll agree it's inevitable.' He looked at Lesley, without any perceptible signs of anger; all that Gus could detect in his voice and his stillness was discouragement and grief. 'Go back to the house, my dear,' he said, 'and go to bed. Leave me to talk to Mr Hambro.'

The most remarkable thing was that she did as she was told, not in a manner that suggested any fear of him, or any great desire to justify herself or placate him. Her shoulders lifted in a small, resigned shrug. She cast a glance at Gus, hesitated no more than a second, and then turned and walked away into the darkness, towards the distant shape of the house within its girdle of trees.

'I have no wish to embarrass you,' said Paviour, when the last faint rustle of her steps in the grass had died away. 'That was not my intention.' There was no dislike in his voice, he stood detached and withdrawn into the night, and the lack of precise vision made this encounter easier than Gus would have believed possible. 'But you see, of course, that I had to intervene.'

'You're being absurdly generous, in fact,' Gus said honestly. 'I'm not going to attempt to justify myself. But I can at least assure you, for what it's worth, that things have gone no further than what you've seen.'

'I'm well aware of that,' said Paviour drily; and though it seemed incredible, there was the suggestion of a sour smile in his voice this time. 'And it won't be necessary to defend yourself. I understand the situation perfectly. I should, I've lived with it for some years now. You mustn't think, my dear Hambro, that you're the first. And I can't hope that you'll be the last.'

'I don't understand you,' said Gus, stiffening.

'You will. Do you mind if I walk with you down to the lodge? It's a little cold for standing around, and we can talk as we go.'

Bemused, Gus fell into step beside him on the path. They walked with a yard or so of the dark between them. And after a moment Paviour resumed gently: 'I take it you'll have heard from Lesley about her earlier love affair, and the way it ended. The way, in fact, that we came to get married. I needn't go into that again. And I needn't tell you what's obvious, that Lesley is a beautiful and charming girl, and highly intelligent. But she has an affliction. Not surprising, in the circumstances. That early shock in love damaged her permanently. She was ill – not physically, but you'll understand me – for some time. On that one subject she will never again be entirely well. What has just happened to you is routine,' he said tiredly. 'I'm sorry, but you'll have to get used to the thought. No doubt she'll have told you that I'm pathologically jealous of every man who so much as comes near her – hasn't she? Well, have I behaved like that? Do you really think I didn't see you with her this morning?'

'I know you did,' said Gus. 'I knew it then. That was not quite what it seemed. It happened almost by accident.'

'You think so?' said Paviour, and the bitter smile in his

voice was clearer than before. 'My dear boy, Lesley has a temperamental disposition to repeat her ruinous love affair with every unwary male who enters her life. Every presentable one, that is. She behaves with every one of them just as she has been behaving with you today. But heaven help any poor fellow who takes her seriously. The game goes only so far. You may even have detected a rather violent reaction on her part, if you ever got so far as taking the initiative?'

Gus walked dourly beside him, and said nothing.

'Yes – I thought so. The signals turn red very abruptly. You'd get no further, I assure you. She would kill you or herself rather than actually surrender. I have good reason to know. She's emotionally crippled for life, and it's my life-work to protect and conceal her disability, and prevent her from doing harm to herself and others. I married her to take care of her. As I have done already through several affairs, all as fictional as this one with you.'

He felt, and misunderstood, or understood only in part, the obstinate silence walking beside him.

'Yes,' he said challengingly, almost as if defending his manhood against some implied accusation, 'I love her as much as that. It was a little late, in any case, for me to marry for any other kind of passion. This does well enough. It's more than anyone else will ever have of her.'

Gus came out of his own private chaos of speculation and enlightenment just in time to capture the implication, and too late to absorb the shock in silence.

'You mean to say that *even you* . . .' He swallowed the rest of the indiscretion with a gulp, and was thankful for the darkness. His mind had been careering along in quite a different direction, it was too much to ask him to assimilate this all in a moment.

'The inference you're drawing,' said Paviour, in a voice thinner and more didactic than Gus had ever yet heard it, 'is a correct one. I knew all about her panic abhorrence before I married her. Sexually, I've never touched her. She is a virgin. She always will be.'

Dignified, pathetic and decent, the man stood there quite obviously telling the simple truth as he saw it, and who was likely to see it more clearly? And it all made sense, or would have done if Gus's blood hadn't still been racing with the remembered persuasion of her body against him, and the ravenous expertise of her mouth, and the ferocity of her nails scoring into his back. That memory confounded the argument considerably. And yet it was true, the initiative had still been hers. All he'd had time to do was go along with her wishes; and if he'd just been reaching the point of having wishes and intentions of his own, he'd been saved by the bell, and she hadn't had to react. Try it! she'd said. Touch me! But deliberately he'd left the next move to her. And now maybe he'd never know which of them was crazy, himself or this elderly masochist – or hero, or whatever he was – who got his satisfaction in cherishing and protecting his wife like a delinquent daughter.

'So you see why it's essential,' said Paviour, gently and firmly, 'that my wife should not see you again. You're not in any illusion that her heart is involved, I hope?'

'No,' said Gus, 'I'm not in any illusion. She won't have any trouble getting over my loss.'

By common consent they had halted well short of the low hedge of the garden at the lodge. The house was in darkness, Bill could not have left the village yet. It would be quite easy, however inconvenient, and there was now no help for it, nothing to be done but what Paviour obviously wanted and expected of him.

'I'll remove myself,' he said, 'totally and immediately. She needn't see me again. I've got my car here, I can pack and get out before Bill comes back, and leave him a note, and my apologies to deliver tomorrow. I shall have had a telephone call. Family business – illness – I'll think of the right thing.'

'I shall be very much obliged,' said Paviour. 'I felt sure I could rely on your good feeling.' And he turned, with no more insistence than that, and no firmer guarantee, and walked away towards his own house, leaving Gus staring after him.

He did exactly what he had promised he would do, and did it in ruthless haste, for fear Bill should come back too soon. True, the same excuse could be offered to him face to face, but there might be some dispute over whether it was strictly necessary to leave before morning, and moreover, in view of Bill's own remarks on the subject of the Paviour marriage, he was not likely to be deceived. Far simpler to leave a few fresh doodles on the telephone pad, and a note propped on the mantelpiece, and get out clean.

'Dear Bill, Client called home, and they ran me to earth here. He wants me to drive over to Colchester and look at a piece he's been offered and has his doubts about. Rush job, because *if* good it's very good, and there's another dealer in the field, so I'm going across overnight. Didn't want to call the house at this hour, please make my apologies to Mr and Mrs Paviour, and thanks to you and them for generous hospitality. I'll be in touch later.'

Probably Bill wouldn't believe any of it, certainly not the last words, but it would do. And Lesley was no doubt used to abrupt diplomatic departures, and would shrug him off and look round for the next entertainment. Perhaps even give a whirl to Bill, whom she hadn't fancied, but who rather more than fancied her, if everyone told the truth. Better not, that might be a collision she wouldn't shrug off so easily.

He needn't go far, of course, but all the same this was a nuisance just at this stage. They might elect to fetch him off the job altogether, and put someone else in in his place. That couldn't be helped. What mattered now was to get out.

He dumped his case in the car, and drove out from the gate of the lodge, and up the gravelled track that ran within the boundary of Aurae Phiala. Bill would be walking home from the village by the riverside path, and the whole expanse of the enclosure and the bulk of the curator's house and garden would be between him and the way out on to the main road. With luck he wouldn't even hear the car. If he did, he would never think of it in connection with a sudden departure until he read his guest's note. All very tidy.

He had to get out and open the gate when he reached the road. He drove the Aston Martin through, and parked it in the grass verge while he went back to close the gate again and make sure it was fast.

He had the stretch of road to himself, and the late moon, at the beginning of its sluggish climb and rimmed with mist, cast only a faint, sidelong light over the standing walls and pillars of Aurae Phiala. Just enough to prick out before his eyes a single curious spark, that moved steadily along within the broken wall of the frigidarium, appearing and disappearing as the height of the standing fragments varied. It proceeded at a measured walking pace, and at the corner it turned, patrolling downhill towards the tepidarium; and for a moment, where the standing masonry dropped to knee-height, he saw the shadowy figure that walked beneath it, and caught the shape of the glowing crest against

161

the sky. The enlarged head, with its jut of brow, was all one metallic mass, hardly glimpsed before it was lost again in the dark. A helmet, with neck-guard, earpieces, he thought even a visor over the face. Dream or substance, the helmeted sentry of Aurae Phiala was making a methodical circuit of the remaining walls by fitful moonlight.

He left the car standing, and let himself in again through the gate; and even then he took the time to snap the lock closed before he set off at a cautious lope across the grass towards the walls of the baths. Once into the complex, he had to slow to a walk, but he made what speed he dared. The night had grown restless with a rising wind; rapid scuds of cloud alternately masked and uncovered the veiled moon, and drifts of mist moved up from the river in soft, recurrent tides along the ground. A night for haunting. He wondered if there was a policeman standing guard overnight, and felt sure there was not; there are never enough men to cover everything that should be covered. He and the sentry had the place to themselves.

The glimpses he got now of the helmet which was his quarry were few and brief, but enough to enable him to gain ground. It had reached the shell of standing walls at the corner of the caldarium. Clearly he saw it glimmer between two broken blocks of masonry, beyond the low rim of the laconicum. Then it vanished. He approached cautiously, and stood by the edge of the shaft in braced silence, preferring to keep his bearings in relation to this potential hazard, while he waited with straining ears and roving eyes for a new lead.

Cloud blew away from the moon's face for a moment, and a spilled pool of light glazed the tops of the broken walls and blackened the shadows; and there suddenly was the helmeted head burning in the brief gleam. As he fixed his eyes upon it, the figure turned, darkness from the shoulders down, bright above, and stood confronting him, and he caught one glimpse of a frozen, splendid, golden face with empty black eye-sockets, under the bronze peak of the helmet.

It was a rapid displacement of air behind him, rather than a sound, that suddenly raised the short hairs on his neck, and caused him to swing round on his heel, too late to save himself. He caught a chaotic glimpse of a looming shape and a raised arm, a violent shifting of shadows and deeper shadows. Then the contours of earth and the complexities of starlight whirled and dissolved about him, as the stone that should have struck him squarely at the base of the skull crashed obliquely against his temple. An arm took him about the thighs and heaved him from the ground; and in some remaining corner of consciousness he knew what was happening to him, and could not utter a sound or lift a finger to fend it off.

He fell, cold, dank air rushing upwards past his face for what seemed an age, and dropped heavily upon some uneven and loosely shifting stuff that rolled at the impact, and bore him helplessly with it.

The breath was knocked out of him, but he never let go of that last glimmer of consciousness. Something rebounded from the wall of the shaft above him, with a heavy thud and a faint ring of metal, and scraped the opposite wall. The light, the only light, was the faint circle of sky now beginning to glow almost with the radiance of day by contrast with this incredible, dead blackness where he was. In the confused panic of shock he prised himself upwards to run, and struck his head sickeningly against an arched ceiling. All over his body the delayed protests of pain began, outraged and insistent. They helped him, too. They made him aware that he was alive, and acutely aware of other things in the same instant: that he was down the shaft of the laconicum, that the wooden cover had been removed in advance to facilitate his disposal, and that the second object tipped down after him must be his suitcase.

He put his head down in his arms for a moment, feeling horribly sick; and before he had gathered his damaged faculties, the thump and reverberation of falling earth and stones began in the shaft, and disturbed dust silted down over him acridly, choking him. He dragged himself frantically forward as stones began to fall about his legs, and holding by the rough bricks of the floor, found the solid wall ahead of him, and groped left-handed along it into the mouth of an open flue.

The rain of stones went on, heavier fragments now, broken masses from the very masonry of Aurae Phiala, or more likely the rim of the laconicum itself, hurled down to lodge awkwardly in the loose rubble, and pile up until they began to climb the walls.

Then he knew that someone was deliberately filling in the shaft. For a long time there followed a staccato rattle of loose brick and tile, and after that there was already so much matter between him and the outer air that the continuing softer fall of earth over all made only a slight, dull sound, receding until he could hardly distinguish it.

The circle of starlight was quenched. Nothing broke the solid perfection of the dark. He was buried alive in the hypocaust, ten feet beneath the innocent green surface of Aurae Phiala.

CHAPTER TEN

For a moment he lay flattened over his folded arms, and let himself sag into a self-pitying fury of bruises and concussion. It was more endurable when he closed his eyes; the darkness was no darker, and infinitely more acceptable, as though he had created it, and could again disperse it. And after a few minutes his mind began to work again inside his aching head, with particular, indignant energy. Because somebody had done a thorough job on getting rid of him – somebody? *Paviour! Who else?* – and circumstances and his own carelessness had played into the enemy's hands. His departure was already accounted for, nobody was going to be starting a hue and cry after him. His suitcase, his clothes, his camera, everything that might have afforded a clue to his whereabouts, lay here under the earth with him. All except the car; and since whoever had followed him and struck him down had brought the suitcase to dispose of along with the body, it didn't need much guessing to decide what was now happening to the Aston Martin. A mobile clue that can be removed from the scene of the crime at seventy miles an hour is no problem. He'd known many a car vanish utterly inside a new paint job and forged plates, within a few hours. By the time someone, somewhere, grew uneasy about his non-appearance, he would be dead. He was meant to be dead already. Only that one lucky movement had saved him.

A movement made a shade too slowly and a fraction of a second too late to show him anything more than a looming shadow, a man-shaped cloud toppling upon him, and a descending arm, before the night exploded in his face. The shadow never had a face. But who but Paviour knew how beautifully his tracks were already covered? Who else had just engineered his elimination from the scene, taking advantage of Lesley's sickness, perhaps even sending her after him deliberately, to ease him out of Aurae Phiala without trace? It couldn't be anyone else!

Or could it? There were two of them, he reminded himself, one to bait the trap for me, and one to spring it. Supposing they – whoever *they* were – had been out in the night on their own furtive occasions, and had to freeze into cover within earshot of that scarifying interview? If they had wanted to get rid of him, and hardly dared to take the risk earlier, what an opportunity!

If he kept his senses, if he let his memory do its own work, there ought to be some detail, even in so brief a glimpse, that would resume recognisable identity. In time he would know his murderer. But time was all too limited unless he gave all his mind to his first and most desperate duty, which was to survive. For after all, he thought savagely, maybe I have got one advantage he doesn't know about: *I'm alive!* Let's see if there's any other asset around. Yes, I've still got a watch with a luminous dial, one little bright eye in all this dark, and it's still going. There may not be any day or night, but there'll still be hours. For God's sake, don't forget to wind it! And there's the suitcase. If I can find it. If it isn't buried ten feet deep under all that lumber. But no, it hit the wall and rebounded, and slid down this side. It's not far. What is there in there that might be useful? There's a pocket torch, though it won't run for long unless I'm sparing with it. And leather gloves. I've got no eyes now but my fingers, and they don't see much in gloves, but I can carry the things, and if I have to dig . . .

That brought him to the real point; for there was no sense in studying how to help himself until he had a possibility in mind. And there was not the slightest possibility of digging his way vertically upwards through that settling mass of earth and stones in the shaft. Try it, if you want to know how peppercorns feel in a peppermill! No way out there. And no way out anywhere else . . .

But there was, of course! There was some seven feet of flue laid open to daylight at the far end of this hypocaust, down by the river. Even the inner end of that was blocked by rubble. Not completely, though. There was room at the top for a cat to wriggle through; and the barrier might be thin, would certainly be loose, since the roof still held up, and no great weight had fallen upon it to pack it hard.

His mind was clearing, he could actually think. With his eyes closed he could even draw himself a diagram of the caldarium, and he had seen for himself, in the one flue they had excavated, how the grid ran, with true Roman regularity.

Consider the landward perimeter, one of the shorter sides of the rectangle, as its base. Then the laconicum is located in the bottom left-hand corner, and that's where I am. And the open flue is very close to the top left-hand corner, the length of the hypocaust away, but on my side. He thought of the huge extent of the caldarium on top of him, and felt sick. My God, it might as well be a hundred miles! Better get moving, Hambro, and just hope, because there isn't for ever, and there isn't all that much air down here, and what there is isn't too good.

Careful, though, don't be in too big a hurry to move until you're sure which way you're going, he reminded himself urgently. And he began to think his way back, with crazily methodical deliberation, to his fall. He had come from the road, towards the river, following the bronze spark; and though he had tried to turn at the last moment, his impression was that in falling he had still been facing fairly directly towards the same point, and had been hoisted over in that direction. When stones began to fall after him he had not turned, simply clawed his way forward until he encountered the wall of the flue, and turned left into its tenuous shelter. Therefore he was now facing towards the left-hand boundary of the rectangle, and no great distance from it. His best line was to crawl ahead until this flue terminated in the blank boundary-wall, then turn right along it, and keep straight ahead, and he would be on the right course for the distant corner where the flue was laid open. If the air held out. If he found the brick passages still intact throughout, or at least passable. If the final barrier – supposing he ever survived to reach it! – didn't prove so thick that he would die miserably, digging his way through it with his finger-nails.

All right, that was settled. Better die trying than just lie here and rot. So before he moved off, he had now to edge his way back a few yards, without turning, for fear of losing that tenuous sense of direction, and feel gingerly among the rubble for his suitcase.

Movement hurt, but goaded instead of discouraging him. The sudden small, hurtling body that went skittering over his feet and away along the route he favoured startled but braced him. The rats got in and out somewhere – probably in a dozen places – and if he could find even a rat-sized hole on starlight he would find a way of enlarging it somehow to let his own body out. If there was a hole there would be air, and he was not going to starve for days, at least.

He was beginning to be aware of the minor horrors that up to now had been obliterated in the single immense horror of being buried alive: the chill, the closeness and earthy heaviness of the air, its graveyard odour, the oppression of the low ceiling over his head, and the soft, settled dirt of centuries cold and thick under his hands, so fine that he sank to the wrist in it in every slight depression where it had silted more thickly, and so filthy that every touch was loathsome, though not so disgusting as the foul drapings of old cobwebs that plastered his head and shoulders from the roof.

His left hand groped among stones and soil, disturbing fresh, rustling falls, but he found the corner of the leather case, and patiently worked it clear. The lock had burst open, clothes spilled from it. He found the torch, small and inadequate but better than nothing, and snapped it on for a second to be sure it still worked. Better conserve that. As long as progress was possible along the outermost flue he could do without light. It took him longer to find the gloves, but he did it finally, and thrust them into his pocket. Now forward, and careful at any offered turning. Far better not risk the interior of the maze. Once reach the outside wall, and all he had to do was keep his left hand on it until he reached the far end. *If* . . . My God, he thought, feeling the cold sweat run down his lips and into his mouth, so many ifs!

He had moved forward only a couple of feet, crawling carefully on hands and knees, when he set his left hand upon something smooth and marble-cold, and feeling over its surface with cautious finger-tips, traced in stupefaction the features of a rigid face, and above the forehead rough, moulded bands, and a shallow, battlemented coronal. He sat back on his heels and dug away silting soil that half-covered it, and his nails rang little, metallic sounds against its rim. It seemed to him then that he remembered the ring of metal as the stones began to fall.

He used the torch for the first time. A bronze face sprang startlingly out of the darkness, a hollow bronze head with chiselled, empty, hieratic features and elongated voids for eyes, with a frieze of fighting figures across its forehead, and curls of formal hair for ear-pieces. The visor had broken away at one hinge from the brow, the crown was dented in its fall, but he knew what he was holding, and even here, in this extremity, it filled him with the exultation of delirious discovery. The thing was a Roman ceremonial helmet, of the kind elaborated not for battle but for formal cavalry exercises, complete with face-mask of chilling beauty. He knew of only one as perfect in existence. Moreover, this one had been carefully cleaned and polished, he thought even subjected to minor repairs, to make it wearable at need. He was holding in his hands the moonlit spark that had been used to lure him back to the laconicum and to his death, only half an hour ago, and had here been jettisoned and buried with him.

The Paviour household was at breakfast when Bill brought the news that his guest had departed overnight. Lesley read the note of explanation and apology with a still, displeased face, and looked up once, very briefly, at her husband, before crumpling the paper in her hand with a gesture which alone betrayed something more than consternation, a flash of hurt, highly personal anger. But she said nothing in reproach against the departed, Charlotte noticed; the anger was not with him, nor did she see any point in expressing it further.

'Nothing I could do about it,' said Bill, hoisting his shoulders in deprecation. 'He was gone when I got back. I shouldn't have thought he need have dashed off overnight, but he knows his markets, I suppose. And if you don't work at it, you don't keep your clients.'

'Mr Hambro has a living to make, like all of us,' said Paviour austerely, 'and no doubt he knows his own business best. But it's a pity he couldn't stay longer. He was a very competent archaeologist, from what I saw of him.'

It was that use of the past tense that crystallised for Charlotte everything that she found out of character in this abrupt departure. She looked from face to face round the table, and all three of them were perfectly comprehensible, both on the surface level and beneath it. She could take the situation at its face value, flatly literal like that note lying beside Lesley's plate, or she could delve beneath the upper layer and recall all yesterday's curious emotional signals, and begin to put together quite a different picture. But in both versions she was negligible, without a part to play. And she was well aware that she had been playing a part, one which had now been written out by some alien hand, and that she was not negligible. He would not go away like this without word or hint to her. Word might, of course, be on its way by a devious route, and she could wait a little; but not long. She was uneasy, and convinced she had grounds for uneasiness. She simply did not believe in what she was witnessing.

She went out with Lesley to the site, but George Felse was not in attendance, only Detective-Sergeant Price superintended the enlargement of the cleared section. It was Sunday morning, and the sound of church bells came pealing with almost shocking clarity through moist, heavy air, and below a ceiling of cloud. It had rained all night since about one o'clock, and the water of the Comer, grown tamed and clearer during the last two days, ran turgid and brown once more. Fitful sunlight glanced across its surface like the thrust of a dagger. The edge of the path, glistening pallidly, already subsided into the river.

'We always go to church for morning service,' said

Lesley, with perfect indifference, merely stating the routine of the day. 'If you'd like to come with us, of course, do, we'd be glad. But I rather thought it might not be the right brand for you, if you know what I mean.'

Charlotte had been brought up in a household cheerfully immune from any sectarian limitations, and not at all addicted to churchgoing of any kind, but the opening offered her was too good to miss. She said the right things, and was tactfully left to her own devices about the house when the Paviour car drove away to Moulden church.

As soon as they were gone she rang up George Felse.

It worried her a little that he didn't seem worried. He listened, he was interested, mildly surprised, but not disturbed at all.

'Or were you expecting this?' she challenged suspiciously.

'No,' he said, 'I wasn't expecting it, and I don't know the reason for it. I don't take this sudden errand very seriously, any more than you do. But there could be a good reason for it, all the same. I think it quite probable that he may have gone off after some lead of his own, something he didn't want to make public.'

'He'd still have found a way of communicating with you,' said Charlotte firmly, 'or with me.' She made no comment on the implications of what she was hearing, because time was too precious, and in any case she had had it in mind all along that Gus Hambro was not quite what he purported to be. Indeed, one of the first things she had ever consciously thought about him when he first accosted her was that a face and manner so candid, and eyes so joltingly innocent, marked him out as a man who needed watching. She didn't attempt to explain or justify her last remark, either, George must take it or leave it. Judging by the brief and thoughtful pause, he took it.

'There may well have been no time for that before he left.

Say, for instance, that he was following somebody. In which case he'll get in touch as soon as he can.'

'And if he can,' she said flatly.

This pause was still briefer. 'All right,' said George. 'No waiting. I'll be over there later on, I've got things to do first. But for public consumption his going is accepted as offered. And in the meantime you can do two things for me. How is it you're calling from the house?'

'There's no one here but me. They've gone to church.'

'Good! Then first, go and tell Detective-Sergeant Price what you've told me, and what I've said. And second – what happened to this note? Is it destroyed?'

'No, I'm sure Lesley just crumpled it up and left it on the table. It's probably been thrown out with the crumbs.'

'Find it if you can, and hang on to it. Would you know his handwriting?'

'I've never even seen it,' she said, surprised at the realisation, 'except a weird scribble on a label tied round the neck of a plastic sack.'

'Then get the note and hold it for me. I'll be over before they come out of church.'

Charlotte hung up, and went to turn out the contents of the blue pedal bin in the kitchen, and there was the loosely-crumpled sheet of Bill's graph paper ready to her hand. Quite certainly nobody was attempting to get rid of the evidence; nor had she really any doubt now that it was Gus who had written this mysterious farewell. Which still left the problem of why.

His senses were beginning to wilt in the earthy, smothering air. Twice in the last hour he had found the passage before him partially blocked, and the outer wall of the flue buckled inwards in a jagged heap of brick and soil, but each time there had been space enough for him to crawl through, with some difficulty and a good deal more terror. The tug of shifting earth at his shoulders brought the sweat trickling down over his closed eyelids, but the clogged space opened again, and brought him sprawling down to the brickwork of the floor, with no more damage than the nausea of fear in his mouth.

But the third time he ran his probing hand against a crumbling wall of earth ahead, there was no way through. The brickwork had been pressed down bodily under the weight of soil, and sealed the flue. His straight run home had been too good to be true from the start. There was nothing to be done but work his way painfully backwards, the flue being too narrow to allow him to turn, until he felt the first cross-flue open at his right elbow. If you can't go through, go round, and get back on course as soon as an open passage offers.

He turned right, and then, with a premonition of worse to come, halted to consider what he was doing. What use was a sense of direction, down here in limbo? His only salvation was the Roman sense of order, that laid out everything at right-angles. Suppose he had to keep going on this new line past several closed flues? Keep count, Hambro, he told himself feverishly. Never mind relying on your memory, for every blind alley you have to pass, pocket a bit of tile – right pocket – every shard means one more you've got to make back to the left.

Into his pocket went one fragment of tile fingered out of the dirt. And at the next left turn another one, because here, too, the wall of earth was solid and impassable. And a third, and a fourth. Then it began to dawn on him that he was beneath the open centre of the caldarium, beneath land which had been cleared of its available masonry for local building purposes centuries ago, and for centuries had been under the plough, with a wagon-road obliquely crossing it.

Constant use and the passing of laden carts had packed down the soil and settled everything into a safe, solid mass. No choice but to go where he still could, crossing the rectangle towards its right-hand boundary, where he had no wish to go, where there was no way out, and hope to God that somewhere one of these flues would have held up, and let him turn towards the river again.

The first that offered he tried, and it took him a few feet only to close up on him from both sides, and force him back. The second helped him to gain a little more ground before stopping him, and he pushed his luck a shade too hard in his hope and desperation, and brought down a slithering fall of bricks over his left arm. When he had extricated himself, with thundering pulse and shaken courage, and opened his eyes momentarily to blink the dust away, he saw that the luminous second hand in the comforting bright eye of his watch hung still, and the glass was broken. There, at eleven-thirteen in the morning of Sunday, went all sense of time; there was no measure to his ordeal any more.

Sometimes he put his head down in his arms and rested for a little while, where the going was better; but that was dangerous, too, because only too easily he could have fallen asleep, and the urgency of movement hung heavy upon him like the malignant, retarding weight of the darkness. He even kept his eyes open now, to ward off sleep the better. His gloves were in tatters, his fingers abraded and bleeding. And he must have been crazy to bring a damned awkward thing like that helmet with him on this marathon crawl, slung round his neck like the Ancient Mariner's albatross, by his tie threaded through its eye-holes; a clumsy lump hampering his movements at every turn, having to be hoisted carefully aside when he lay flat to rest, slowing him up in the bad patches, where it had to be protected from damage even at the cost of knocking a few pieces off his own wincing flesh. Once an archaeologist, always an archaeologist. It was one of the finest things he'd ever seen of its kind, even if it had all but killed him, and he'd be damned if he'd leave without it.

'He wrote it,' said George Felse, smoothing the crumpled note between his hands, 'and he didn't write it under any sort of compulsion, or even stress, as far as I can see. Does that make you feel any better?'

She looked at him intently, the damp wind from the swollen river fluttering the strands of hair on her cheeks, and said firmly: 'No.'

'It should. To some extent, at any rate. But you can be extraordinarily convincing, can't you?' he said, and smiled at her.

'Does that mean we wait for word of him, and do nothing?'

'No, it means I've already done what needs to be done. For good reasons we don't want any public alarm or any visible hunt. But we've sent out a general call on his car, and an immediate on any news of it or him. Orders to approach with discretion, if sighted, but once found, not to lose. By evening we may hear something. Meantime, not a word to anyone else.'

The air was giving out, or else it was he who was weakening. His head swam lightly and dizzily, like a cork on storm-water, and sometimes he came round with a jolt out of spells of semi-consciousness, to find himself still doggedly crawling, and was terrified that in that state he had passed some possible channel riverwards, or left some crossing unrecorded. He had crawled his way clean through the knees of his slacks, and ripped the sole of one shoe open.

There were moments, indeed when he felt as if his knee-joints were bared not to the skin, but to the bone, and suffered the alarming delusion that he was dragging himself forward on skeletal hands stripped of all their padding of flesh.

His mind remained, at least by fits and starts, as clear as ever, aggravatingly clear. He had a surprisingly sharp conception of where, by this time, he was. He had started out to proceed in orderly fashion down the left-hand limit of the caldarium to the river, and thence to the open section. And here he was, God alone knew how many hours or weeks later, forced farther and farther off-course to the right, until he must be within a few yards of the right-hand margin, and no nearer the river than when he had set out. Somewhere at this corner there had been a limited dig, he remembered, about nineteen months ago, but they'd filled in the excavation with very little gained. A disappointing affair. My God, he thought, staggered by the astringent precision of his own thoughts while his body was one blistering pain from cramp, exertion and strain, I'm going quietly crazy. I could recite the text of that article word for word, and I'd never even seen this damned place when I got the magazine as part of my briefing.

I will not go crazy, though, quietly or noisily, so help me! I'll crawl out of this Minoan labyrinth on my own hands and knees, or die trying!

It was nearly half past five that Sunday afternoon when a courting couple in a Mini, returning from a spring jaunt and finding themselves with time for an amorous interlude before they need return to the bosoms of their families, drove off the road on the heath side of Silcaster into a certain old quarry they knew of, and parked the car carefully on the level stretch of grass above the abandoned workings. If the boy had not sensibly elected to back into position and drive out again forwards, and his girl friend had not been well-trained in all their mutual manoeuvres, and hopped out without being asked, to make sure how far back the ground was solid after the rain, a very much longer interval might have passed before George Felse got any information in response to his general call.

'Come on, you're all right,' she called, beckoning him gaily back towards the sheer edge of the quarry, still some eight yards or so behind her, and thinly veiled with low bushes here and there. 'Somebody's been back here before us, it's safe enough.' And she glanced behind her, following the course of the tyre-tracks flattened deep and green into the wet grass, and suddenly flung up a hand in warning and let out a muted shriek: 'My God, no! Stop! Eh, Jimmy, come and have a look at this! Some poor soul's gone clean over the edge.'

The tracks ran straight to the rim, and vanished into the void; a little bush of stunted hawthorn, barely a foot high, was scraped clean of all its twigs and leaves on one side, and dangled broken into the grass. In stunned silence they crept forward to the rim of the cliff, and looked over into the deep, dark eye of the pool which had long since filled the abandoned crater. Rock-based, with only a few years' deposit of gravel and fine matter to cloud it, and almost no weed, it retained its relative clarity even after rain, but it was deep enough to cover what it held with successive levels of darkness. Nevertheless, they could distinguish the shape of the car by the still outline of pallor, light bronze forming an oblong shoal with all its sides sloping gradually away into the blue-green of deeper water.

'Oh, God!' whispered the girl. 'It's true! He went and backed her clean over.'

The boy was sharper-sighted, and bright enough to be

sure of what he saw. 'He never did! That car went in forwards. Look at it! What's more, look at those tracks!'

By instinct they had walked along the wheel-tracks to the edge of the quarry, the grass being longish and very wet, and the flattened channels the smoothest and driest walking. 'Look there, between the wheel-marks!' She looked, and there beyond doubt ran the curious feather-stitch pattern of two human legs wading through grass, midway between the grooves the tyres had laid down. Not merely walking, but thrusting strongly, for the soft turf, though it retained no details, was ground into a hollow at every step. These marks began only about fifteen feet from the edge, and ended in a patch of more trampled grass about six feet from it. Only a few yards of effort. 'You haven't set foot in there,' said the boy, 'and no more have I. Either I'm crazy, or the bloke that did was *shoving* that car. Put her in gear and let her run, and even then, with this growth, downhill and all she'd need a hand to send her over.'

'What, just getting rid of an old crock?' said the girl, relieved of the vision of two young people like themselves slowly drowning as the car filled. 'Is that all? Well, I know they go to some funny shifts to get shot of 'em, I suppose that'd be one way.'

'I don't know! It doesn't look like a job *I'd* throw away,' he said dubiously, peering down at the pale shape below. 'Suppose it was some car pinched for a job, and then dumped? And it's recent – couldn't be longer ago than last night it was put in there.' He made up his mind. 'Come on, we'd better report it. Just in case!'

It was his statement that sent a Silcaster police car out to the quarry less than half an hour later. The colour appeared, the boy had said, to be fawn or light brown. The implications were urgent, with the missing light bronze Aston Martin in mind, and they sent out, after only momentary hesitation, for a skin-diver, to settle the matter as soon as possible, one way or the other. If they were wasting time over an old hulk ditched illegally by its desperate owner, so much the worse. But they couldn't afford to take chances.

The diving unit brought flood-lights and equipment, never being given to do things by halves. The diver went down before the daylight was quite gone, and brought up a report that set the whole circus in motion well into the night.

The first call was put through to George just before seven. 'Got some news of the Aston Martin for you,' said the Silcaster inspector, an old acquaintance. 'Some bad, some good.'

'Let's have the bad first,' said George.

'We've found the car. Dumped in a pool in a deserted quarry up by the heath. Courting couple found the tracks where it had been driven over, and had the sense to report it. We've already had a diver down, and it's the car you want, all right. We're setting up the gear to raise it, but our frogman reckons he could see pretty well into the interior, and –'

'And he isn't in it,' said George, drawing the obvious inference with immense relief. 'That's the good news?'

'That's it. Good as far as it goes, anyhow. No body, no luggage, nothing visible bigger than a rug on the floor. But it leaves you with a problem, all right. Since he isn't there, where is he? Because whoever put his car out of commission down a hole can't have been exactly well-disposed to the owner, can he?'

The air was getting fouler, and he was getting weaker, and he was almost as far away as ever from that unattainable corner where the hypocaust opened one vein to the light of day; though whether it was night or day, and what the hour was, he had now no means of knowing. He had given up hope of

180

finding a way through the centre of the maze. Every hopeful passage he had attempted towards the river had only closed up in front of him and driven him still further to the right, and three times now he had had to turn off to the right even from that line for a short distance, so that he had lost some ground gained earlier. He must now be at the very site, he thought, of that last minor dig, and the one hope he had left was that this right-hand boundary wall might have survived in better case than the opposite one. Since the centre was bedded solid, and the obvious way to his objective had failed him, try the long way round, and pray that it might yet turn out to be the shortest way home. The flues at the rim of the hypocaust had the best chance of surviving, since on one side they backed all the way into solid earth, the brickwork unbroken by cross-passages. And this one towards which he was now crawling, on no remaining fuel but his native obstinacy, would certainly have carried less traffic and less weight during the centuries of cultivation, since the vast bases of the forum pillars alongside it had defied removal even by the ingenious village builders, and baulked all attempts at getting this piece of land under plough. It had always, he remembered from old photographs in the museum, been a scrub hedge between the fields, and a strip of waste ground, good only for blackberrying. This side he might have better luck.

The boundary flue had one other great advantage, considering his present condition of exhaustion and light-headedness. When he came to it, it would be a blank T-crossing, with no way ahead, and could not be mistaken. He had been telling himself as much, and promising that it would come soon, for what seemed hours, which only indicated how tenuous his grasp of time had become, and how slow his progress. But at every move he still reached out a hopeful hand to flatten against the facing wall that still wasn't there – as now.

But this time it was there. His palm encountered the unmistakable rough texture of brickwork, squarely closing the way ahead. He lay still for a few minutes, his head swimming with the weakness of relief, and also with the thick, smothering odour of the air, which had congealed into a peculiar horror of old, cold physical death. He groped out fearfully towards the left, which was now his way, and the flue beside him was open, and clear of rubble as far as he could reach. He fingered the walls, and they were sound; the ceiling above, and it felt firm as rock. He shifted his weight with labour and pain, carefully moving the dangling mask out of harm's way, and reached out towards the right. If that way, too, the flue seemed whole and sturdy, he would begin to believe that his luck was changing at last, and in time. Because either this air was fouler than any he had encountered yet, or he was losing control of his remaining senses.

The vault to the right held up as strongly as on the other side. He felt his way down from ceiling to floor, and his hand touched something which was not mere dust or the ground fragments of brick, or even thick, foul cobweb, but parted beneath his touch in rotting threads, with the unmistakable texture of cloth.

He couldn't believe it, and yet it revived him as nothing else could have done. The helmet was no find of his, but if this was cloth, then this was all his own. His questing fingers felt shudderingly over the scrap he had detected, passed over a few inches of flooring, and recaptured the same evident textile quality in several more tindery rags. And they had this up, he thought, and never found anything better than a few animal bones and pottery, when they couldn't have been more than a few feet away from here. Curiously, though he had no way of verifying his calculations, at this moment he was absolutely sure of them.

And it was at that very moment that his fingers, moving with wincing delicacy where there might be priceless discoveries to be made, encountered what was unquestionably bone, but exceptional in being not fragmentary, but whole, as far as he could reach, without lesion. Stretching, he touched a joint, where the bone homed into the cup of another mass, as naked and as clean. He searched in his blind but acute memory, and brought up vividly the image of a human hip joint, intricate and marvellous.

He was a hundred per cent alive again, and he had to get out of here alive now if it killed him, because he had to know. There was one minor city, not unlike this one in its history, where they found two human skeletons in the hypocaust, some poor souls who had taken refuge in the empty heating system when the place was attacked, and almost certainly suffocated when most of the town was fired over their heads. The same could have happened here. He forgot how nearly dead he was, and how completely and precisely buried, and quickened to sympathy and pity for this poor soul who had died after his burial, so many centuries ago. Very softly he drew his finger-tips down the mass of the femur, stroked over the rounded marble of a knee-joint, and then reached out tentatively where the foot should be. For a leather sandal might have remained embalmed perfectly all this time, as durable almost as the ivory of the wearer's bones. Quite close to his right knee, under the wall of the flue, his knuckles struck against the erected hardness, and the sound was music to him. A solid, thick sole. He felt from heel to toe, and then round to where the straps should be, and the still-articulated bones of instep and toes within. Gently, not to do damage. Also out of some reverence a great deal older than Christian ethics, the universal tenderness towards the dead.

The leather sole was sewn to a leather upper. Clearly his

raw finger-tips relayed to him, with agony, what they found. No straps, no voids between. A very hard, dehydrated shape moulded inwards from the sole, seamed over a smooth vamp, finished at the heel with a hand-stitched band. Above, where the two wings joined over the instep, the small, metallic roundels of eyelets, and the taut cross-threading of laces. The bow he touched parted at the impact, and slid, still formed, after his withdrawing fingers.

Not a fourth-century Roman sandal on this skeleton foot, but a conventional, hand-sewn, custom-made, twentieth-century English shoe.

CHAPTER ELEVEN

It was approaching half past seven that evening when
George Felse made his appearance at the curator's house,
completely shattering Lesley's arrangements for dinner,
and throwing the entire household into confusion. He
delayed saying what he had to say until Bill Lawrence was
summoned from the lodge to join them; and he made no
pretence of maintaining a social relationship with any of
them while they waited. The atmosphere of strain that built
up in the silence might well have been intentional; or he
might, Charlotte acknowledged, simply have shut them out
of his consciousness while he considered more important
things, and the fever might have been their own contribu-
tion, a kind of infection infiltrating from person to person,
guilty and innocent alike, if there were here any guilty creatures, or any totally innocent. George sat contained and
civil and pseudo-simple outside their circle, and waited
patiently until it was completed by the arrival of a
dishevelled and uncertain Bill.

'I'm sorry, I didn't mean to keep you waiting, but I
wasn't even properly dressed . . .'

'That's all right,' said George. 'I regret having to fetch
you over here, but this concerns you as being connected
with this site, and I can't afford to go over the ground twice.
Sit down! You all know, of course, that Mr Hambro left

here last night at very short notice. You know that he left a note stating definite intentions, though in very general terms. I am here to tell you that because of certain discoveries Mr Hambro is now listed as a missing person, and we have reason to suspect that the account given of his departure, whether by himself or others, is so far totally deceptive. No, don't say anything yet, let me outline what we *do* know. He is stated to have left here late in the evening, having received a telephone call asking him to give an opinion on an antique offered for sale on the other side of England. He is understood to have packed all his belongings, loaded his car, left a note to explain his departure and apologise for its suddenness, and driven away at some time prior to half past eleven, when you, Mr Lawrence, arrived home and found his note. Now let me tell you what we also know. His car was driven into a quarry pool on the further side of Silcaster, probably during the night. It is now in process of being recovered, and has already been examined. Mr Hambro was not in it, either dead or alive, nor is there any trace of the suitcase he removed from here last night. We have, so far, no further word of him after he left here. We are treating this as a disappearance with suspicion of foul play.'

The murmurs of protest and horror that went round were muted and died quickly. To exclaim too much is to draw attention upon yourself in such circumstances; not to exclaim at all is as bad, it may look as if you have been aware of the whereabouts of the car all along, and may know, at this moment, where to find the man. Only Charlotte sat quite silent, containing as best she could, like pain suppressed in company, the chill and heaviness of her heart. If she had neither recognised nor even cared to recognise, until now, the extent to which Gus Hambro had wound himself into her thoughts and feelings since he regained his life at her hands, and how simply and with what conviction she had begun to regard him as hers, recognition was forced upon her now. Paviour already looked so sick and old that fresh shocks could hardly make any impression upon his pallor or the sunken, harried desperation of his eyes. Bill sat with his thin, elegantly-shaped, rather grubby hands conscientiously clasped round his knees, carefully posed but not easy. The fingers maintained their careful disposition by a tension as fixed and white-jointed as if they had been clenched in hysteria. Only Lesley, her mouth and eyes wide in consternation, cried out in uninhibited protest: 'Oh, no! But that's monstrous, it makes no sense. Why should anyone want to do him harm? What has *he* ever done . . .'

She broke off there, and very slowly and softly, with infinite care, drew back into a shell of her own, and veiled her eyes. She did not look at her husband; with marked abstention she did not look at anyone directly, even at George Felse.

'I shall be obliged,' said George impersonally, 'if you will all give me statements on the events of yesterday evening, especially where and how you last saw Mr Hambro. I should appreciate it very much, Mr Paviour, if we might make use of the study. And if the rest of you would kindly wait in here?'

Paviour came jerkily to his feet. 'I am quite willing to be the first, Chief Inspector.' Too willing, too eager, in far too big a hurry, in spite of the fastidious shrinking of all his being from the ordeal to which he was so anxious to expose himself. George was interested. Was it as important as all that to him to get his story in before his wife got hers?

'I should like to see Mrs Paviour first, if it isn't inconvenient.'

'But as a matter of fact,' Paviour said desperately, 'I believe I was the last person to see Mr Hambro . . .'

'That will emerge,' George said equably. 'I'll try not to keep any of you very long.'

It was useless to persist. Paviour sank back into his chair with a twitching face, and let her go, since there was now no help for it.

She was quite calm as she sat in the study, her small feet neatly planted side by side, and described in blunt précis, but sufficiently truthfully, how she had slipped out instead of going to bed, and wilfully staged that brief scene with Gus Hambro.

'Not very responsible of me, I know,' she said, gazing sombrely before her. 'But there are times when one feels like being irresponsible, and I did. There was no harm in it, if there was no good. It was a matter of perhaps three or four minutes. Then my husband came.' Her face was composed but very still, in contrast to her usual vivacity. It was the nearest he had ever seen her come to obvious self-censorship. 'My husband,' she said guardedly, 'is rather sensitive about the difference in our ages.'

She had not gone so far as to mention the embrace, but her restraint spoke for itself eloquently enough.

'So he ordered you home,' said George, deliberately obtuse, 'and you obeyed him and left them together.'

Her eyes flared greenly for one instant, and she dimmed their fire almost before it showed. Her shoulders lifted slightly; her face remained motionless. 'I went away and left them together. What was the point of staying? The whole thing was a shambles. *I* wasn't going to pick up the pieces. They could, if they liked.'

'And did they?' George prompted gently. 'You know one of them, at least, very well. The other, perhaps, less well? But you have considerable intuition. What do you suppose passed between them, after you'd gone?'

'Not a stupid physical clash,' she said, flaring, 'if that's what you're thinking.'

'I'm thinking nothing, except what your evidence means, and what follows from it. I'm asking what you think happened between those two men. Of whom one, I would remind you, is now missing in suspicious circumstances.'

She shrank, and took a long moment to consider what she should answer to that. 'Look!' she said almost pleadingly. 'I've been married to an older man a few years, and I know the hazards, but they're illusory. I've known him jealous before, for even less reason, but nothing happened, nothing ever will happen. It's a kind of game – a stimulus. He isn't that kind of man!' she said, in a voice suddenly torn and breaking, and closed her eyes upon frantic tears. They looked astonishingly out of place on her, like emeralds on an innocent, but they were real enough.

'You're very loyal,' said George in the mildest of voices.

Her momentary loss of control was over; she offered him a wry and reluctant smile. 'So is he,' she said, 'when you come to consider it.'

'And your husband joined you – how much later?'

The voice was still as mild and unemphatic, but she froze into alarmed withdrawal again at the question; and after a moment she said with aching care: 'We occupy separate rooms. And we don't trespass.'

'In fact, you didn't see him again until this morning?'

In a voice so low as to be barely audible, she said: 'No.'

'So he left,' said George, 'because you asked him to leave.'

'I didn't have to ask him in so many words,' said Paviour laboriously. 'I made it clear to him that it was highly undesirable that my wife should see him again. He offered

189

to pack up and go at once, and make some excuse to account for his departure. I told you, I make no complaint against Mr Hambro, I bear him no grudge. I'm aware that the initiative came from my wife.'

There was sweat standing in beads on his forehead and lip. He had had no alternative but to tell the truth, since he had no means of knowing how fully Lesley had already told the same story; but his shame and anguish at having to uncover his marital hell, even thus privately, without even the attendance of Reynolds and his notebook, was both moving and convincing. A humiliation is not a humiliation until someone else becomes aware of it.

'And you manage not to hold this propensity against her, either?' George asked mildly.

'I've told you, it's a form of illness. She can't help it. And it can't possibly go beyond a certain point – her own revulsion ensures that.'

'And yet you deliberately kept watch on her last night, and followed her out expressly to break up this scene. You won't try to tell me that it happened quite by chance?'

'It's my duty to protect her,' said Paviour, quivering. 'Even in such quite imaginary affairs, she could get hurt. And she could cause harm to relatively innocent partners, too.'

It was all a little too magnanimous; she had caused plenty of pain, fury and shame to him in her time, by his own account, but apparently he was supposed to be exempt from resenting that.

'Very well, you parted from Mr Hambro close to the lodge, and came back to the house. And that's the last you saw of him?'

'Yes. I had no reason to think he wouldn't keep his word.'

'As apparently he did. We've seen the note he left behind.

You can't shed any light on what may have happened to him afterwards?'

'I'm sorry, I've told you I came straight back to the house, and went to bed.'

'As I understand,' said George gently, 'alone.' There was a brief, bitter silence. 'You realise, of course, that no one can confirm your whereabouts, from the time your wife came back to the house without you?'

'I've been here nearly a year now,' said Bill Lawrence. 'I know the set-up well enough to keep out of trouble. Actually I've known the place, and the Paviours, longer than that, I used to come over occasionally during the vacations, when I was at Silcaster university, and help out as assistant. I had to get a holiday job of some kind, and this was right in my line. I'd started planning my book then. So I know the score. No, he's never actually talked to me about Mrs Paviour, but it's easy to see he's worried every time another man comes near her. Especially a young man. It isn't altogether surprising, is it?'

'And Mrs Paviour *has* talked to you about her husband?'

The young man's long, slightly supercilious face had paled and stiffened into watchfulness. 'She warned me, when I came here officially for this year, that it would be better to keep relations on a very formal basis.'

'She gave you to understand, in fact, that her husband was liable to an almost pathological jealousy, and for the sake of everybody's peace of mind you'd better keep away from her?'

'Something like that – yes.'

'And she acted accordingly?'

'Always. It was possible to get along quite well – one developed the knack, and then enjoyed what companionship was permissible.'

191

That had a marvellously stilted sound, and contrasted strongly with the strained intensity of his face.

'And did she act accordingly with – for example – Mr Hambro?'

Dark red spots burned on the sharp cheekbones. Paviour wasn't the only one who could feel jealousy, and there wouldn't be much room here for elderly magnanimity. Bill clamped his jaw tight shut over anger, swallowed hard, and said at last: 'I'm not in a position to comment on Mrs Paviour's actions. You've had the opportunity of talking to her in person.'

'Very true. Mrs Paviour was admirably frank. All right, you can rejoin the others. No, one moment!' Bill turned and looked back enquiringly and apprehensively from the doorway. 'You say you used to visit here before you came to work here regularly. Did you, by any chance, pay a visit while Doctor Alan Morris was staying here? That was a year ago last October, the beginning of the month.'

'Yes, as a matter of fact, I was invited over to meet him one evening,' said Bill, bewildered but relieved by this turn in the conversation. 'I angled for an invitation when I knew he was coming, and Mr Paviour asked me over for dinner. That's the only time I ever got to talk to a really first-class man on my subject. I was disappointed in his book, though,' he added thoughtfully. 'I got the impression it was rather a dashed-off job. That's the trouble with these commissioned series.'

'Ah, well, you'll be able to offer a more thorough study,' said George with only the mildest irony. 'By the way, you walked to the village and back last night, I believe. So you didn't use the Vespa yesterday? I notice you didn't use it to hop over here tonight.'

'It didn't seem worth getting it out. I'd cleaned and put it away the night before last. It hasn't been out since. Why?'

'How was it for petrol, when you left it?'

'I filled up the day I cleaned it, and it hasn't been anywhere but across here since.' He was frowning now in doubt and uneasiness. 'Why, what about it? What has the Vespa got to do with anything?'

'We borrowed it an hour or so ago, without asking your permission, I'm afraid. You shall have it back as soon as we've been over it. The tank's practically empty, Mr Lawrence. And by the still damp mud samples we're getting from it, it's certainly had a longish run since the rain set in.'

'But I don't understand!' His face had fallen into gaping consternation, for once defenceless and young, without a pose to cover its alarm. 'I haven't had it out, I swear. I haven't touched it. What do you mean?'

'If somebody drove Mr Hambro's car as far as the quarry beyond Silcaster, then – always supposing that somebody belonged here, and had to be seen to be here as usual by morning – he'd need a way of getting back, wouldn't he? Preferably without having to use public transport and rub shoulders with other people. With a little ingenuity a Vespa could be manoeuvred aboard an Aston Martin, don't you think? By the time we've been over your machine properly we may know for certain where it's been overnight. With a lot of luck,' he said, watching the young face blanch and the frightened eyes narrow in calculation, 'we may even know who was riding it.'

He was in the act of crossing to the drawing-room to tell the silent company within that he was leaving them in peace – insofar as there would be any peace for them – for the rest of that night, when there was a loud knock at the side door, along the passage by the garden-room, and without waiting for anyone to open to him, Orrie Benyon leaned in, vast in donkey-jacket and gum-boots.

'Is Mr Paviour there?' He made George his messenger as readily as any other. 'Ask him to come for a minute, eh? I won't traipse this muck inside for the missus.'

His knock had brought them all out: Paviour, Lesley, Charlotte and Bill Lawrence from the drawing-room, instant in alarm because their lives had become a series of alarms, and instant in relief and reassurance when they saw a normal phenomenon of the Aurae Phiala earth leaning in upon them; and Reynolds and Price from the rear premises and the outer twilight respectively, quick to materialise wherever there was action in prospect. Orrie looked round them all with fleeting wonder at their number, and returned to his errand.

'I've just been up as far as the top weir. That path's under water in three places, and the Comer's still rising. She's over to the grass, close by that dig of yours, and fetched down a lot more o' the bank. You're going to have to concrete in all that section and make it safe, after this lot, or we'll be liable for anything that happens to the folks using the path. You'd better come and have a look.'

There was a compulsion about him, whether it arose from his native proprietary rights in this soil or simply from his size and total preoccupation, that drew them all out after him into the semi-darkness of the evening. After the recent heavy rain the sky had cleared magically, and expanded in clear, lambent light after the sunset, so that it was bright for the hour, and after a minute in the open air it seemed still day to them. The morning would be calm, sunny and mild. Only the river, their close neighbour on the right hand as soon as they let themselves out of the garden, denied that the world was bland and friendly. The brown, thrusting force of the water lipping the land had a hypnotic attraction. Charlotte, slipping and recovering in the wet turf in her smooth court shoes, felt herself drawn to it by the very energy of its onward drive, as though all motion must incline and merge into this most vehement of motions. The pale green, glowing innocence of the sky over it was a contradiction and a mockery.

This path was terribly familiar to her, and walking upstream here was like walking back, against her will, to the moment when Gus Hambro had lain at her feet with his face in the river, quietly drowning. Now she did not even know where he was, or whether he was alive or dead. All she knew was that he had not been in his car when it was driven over the edge of the quarry, nor had he been dropped separately into the same deep pool. And therefore there was still hope that he was extant, somewhere in the world, and no great distance from her. It was no secret now that it mattered to her more than anything else in the world, that the life she had held in her hands safely once should not slip through her fingers now.

Orrie stalked ahead like a prehistoric god on his own territory, huge and intent, never deviating from the path even when he waded ankle-deep in turgid water. The rest went round, not being equipped for wading, Paviour scurrying back to Orrie's shoulder round the incursions of the river, anxious and ineffective in this elemental setting, the others strung out in a line that picked its way with deliberation along the foot of the slope, in the wet but thick and springy grass.

Above the glistening dotted line of wet clay that was the path, the bevelled slope of grass rose on their left, and the untidy fall of loose earth had certainly spilled across into the rising water. They came to the place where the first slip had occurred, and where, above them on level ground, the opened flue lay exposed to the sky. It had yielded nothing of value, either to the police or the archaeologists, except the few evidences of wilful damage. Whatever precious thing had ever rested there in hiding, it had certainly been removed in time. Soon the flue would be carefully built up again, if not covered over. But now the expanse of raw, reddish soil was twice as wide, for both shoulders of the original fall had begun to slide away. They stood in a chilly little group at the edge of the torn area, and looked at the slope in concerned silence. The path was still passable here, but by morning, if Orrie was right and the river still rising, it might well be covered.

'If she comes over and starts eating under this bank,' Orrie said with authority, 'all this loose stuff'll wash away like melting snow, and the bank'll go. Ask me, we ought to put up warning notices, both ends of the path. It'll be us for it, if somebody comes along here, not knowing, and goes in the river, or gets buried under that lot when it gives.'

'I should have been glad to have it closed long ago,' Paviour admitted, 'but you know what happens if one tries to close a right-of-way, however inconvenient and dangerous. However little used, for that matter, though this one does get used. You think the river will rise much more? It's some hours now since the rain stopped.'

'Yes, but it takes a couple of days for the main weight to come down out of Wales. I reckon she may come up another two feet yet afore she starts dropping again. What's more, we'll need to do something permanent about it, besides closing it now. That's not going to be safe again unless we firm up this bank with a concrete lining, and lift the path.'

'That would probably be a shared responsibility,' said George Felse, 'with the local council, but Orrie could be right. Is this the only bad place?'

'No, there's a couple more just close to our boundary. But no falls there, so far. This,' said Orrie, jerking his cropped reddish curls at the slope before them, 'is moving now. Look at it!'

As though some infinitesimal tremor of the earth troubled the stability of the whole enclosure, little trickles of soil were starting down from the raw shoulder, a couple of yards to the left of the exposed flue, and running downhill with a tiny, sibilant sound, resting sometimes as they lodged in a momentarily stable hold, then continuing downhill on a changed course; all so quietly, without haste. The disturbed dead, Charlotte thought, trying to get out. If they could remember what it was like to be alive, she thought with a quite unexpected surge of desolation and dismay, they'd let well alone.

A curious effect, this boiling of the earth. When the pool of Bethesda was troubled, it did miracles. She badly needed a miracle, but she doubted if this narrow well into the depths of history, for all its disquiet, could provide one.

'We'd better have a look at this bit upstream,' said George, 'while we're about it. Orrie's right, you may have to put up those notices, for your own protection, as well as other people's.'

Orrie turned willingly, and led the way again, surging through the shallows, and the others strung out behind him on the dry side of the path, gingerly skirting the shifting pile of loose soil. Charlotte was last in the line, since they had to proceed in single file or wade, like their leader. She never knew exactly why she looked back. Perhaps, being the nearest, she heard the slight crescendo of furtive sound that was too small to reach the ears of those in front. The little drifts of earth insisted, and stones began to break free and roll gently and sluggishly downwards. Only small stones, too little to change the world, but they ran, and rolled, and jumped, and the trembling of the well was every moment more urgent with the promise of a miracle; and something prophetic, a small flame of wondering and hoping, kindled in her mind.

So it happened that her chin was still on her shoulder, and she had actually halted and turned in order to watch more attentively, when she saw a sudden small, dark hole burst open in the high mask of earth above her. Not just a hollow, shadowed darker than its surroundings, but a veritable hole upon total blackness. It grew, its rim crumbled away steadily. She saw movement varying its empty blackness, something paler moving within, scraping at the soil. Another biblical image of portent, the cloud, the hole, no bigger than a man's hand, that grew, and grew, like this . . .

It was a man's hand! Feeble, caked with grime, fingers struggled through and clawed at the soil, sending fresh trickles bounding down towards her. A real human hand, alive and demanding, felt its way through into the light with weary exultation.

She was not given to screaming or fainting, and she did neither. She stood stock-still for perhaps ten seconds, her eyes fixed upon that groping, dogged hand, her mind connecting furiously, with a speed and precision she had never yet discovered within herself. The dead were breaking out of their graves with a vengeance. Somebody dumped his car – somebody did this to him – somebody close here, somebody among us. Twenty hours under the earth! He wasn't supposed ever to show up again. Someone is quite confident, quite sure of his work. *I want to know who!* Only one minute, two minutes, she promised silently, and I'll come, I'll get you out of there. But first *I want to know which of them did it! And I want to strike him dead at your feet!*

She turned and called after the dwindling procession winding its way along the riverside: 'Wait! Come back here

a moment, please, come and look! I've found something!'
The right voice, pleasurably excited, urgent enough to halt
them, not agitated enough to give them any warning of
more than some minor discovery, some small find carried
down by the fall, or the vault of another flue broken open.
And that was true, how true, but they wouldn't know the
reason. When they turned to look, she waved them imperi-
ously back to the spot, herself planted immovably. 'Come
here! Come and see! It's important.'

They came, half indulging her and half curious. She
watched their faces as they drew near, and they were all
interested, enquiring and untroubled by any forewarning,
for their eyes were on her, and the hand, grown to a wrist
and forearm now, laboured patiently some feet above her
head. She waited until they were all close, and only then did
she turn and point, ordering sharply: 'Look! Look up
there!'

Two braced arms within the hypocaust thrust at the
thinning barrier of soil at that moment, and sent its rup-
tured fringes scattering. A heaving body, blackened and
encrusted with soil, erupted out of its grave, and with a
staggering jerk, stood erect for one instant on the shifting
slope, before its weight set the whole surface in motion, and
hurled it down upon them in a skier's leaning plunge.

She missed nothing. She even took her eyes from him,
and let the police jump forward to break his fall, in order to
watch all those other faces. There had been a general gasp
of fright and horror; no wonder, there was nothing in that
to incriminate. Bill Lawrence stood with mouth fallen open
in stunned bewilderment, Lesley clapped her hands to her
cheeks and uttered a muted scream. Even Orrie, though he
stood rooted and silent as a rock, stared with eyes for once
dilated and darkened in disbelief. But Paviour gave a high,
moaning shriek, and flung up his hands between himself

and the swooping figure, making an ineffectual gesture of pushing the apparition away. Then, as though he had felt his hands pass clean through its impalpable substance, he plucked them back, and turned blindly to run. Charlotte saw his face stiffen suddenly into blue ice, his eyes roll upwards whitely, and his lips, always bloodless, turn livid. He lifted his hands, spun on his heel in a rigid contortion, and fell face-down on the muddy path like a disjointed puppet.

Gus Hambro reached the grass still upright, in a rushing avalanche of loose soil, and reeled into the arms of George Felse and Detective-Sergeant Price. For a few seconds he stood peering round at them all, and they saw that his eyes were screwed up tightly against the waning twilight as though for protection against a blaze of brightness. He heaved deep breaths into him, dangled his blackened and bloody hands with a huge sigh, and collapsed slowly and quietly between his supporters, to subside into the wet grass beside the enemy Charlotte had terrified herself by striking senseless, if not dead, at his feet.

CHAPTER TWELVE

To Charlotte, in her state of minor shock and illogical guilt, the next twenty minutes resembled one of those ancient comedy films in which sleep-walkers stride confidently about the scaffolding of an unfinished building, converging with hair-raising impetus and missing one another by inches: a purposeful chaos with a logic of its own, and all conducted in comparative silence. After the first stupefying moment, exclamation was pointless. Someone, Charlotte supposed it could only have been George Felse, must have given orders, for the whole group, apart from George and Reynolds, dispersed like a dehiscent fruit bursting, Sergeant Price, with Lesley in anxious ward, to telephone Paviour's doctor, Charlotte to rustle up blankets, Bill Lawrence and Orrie Benyon to fetch the sun-bed stretchers from the garden-room, while George and his constable did what they could, meantime, for the casualties. The principle that victims of sudden collapse and probable acute heart failure should not be moved without medical advice hardly held good on a chilly, wet slope of grass beside a steadily rising river, and with night coming on.

At that hour on a Sunday evening it was hardly surprising that Dr Ross, who had been Paviour's doctor for years, should be away from home. His answering service offered the number of his partner on call, but Price preferred to cut the corners and ring up the police doctor, whom he knew well, and to whom he could indicate – Lesley being temporarily out of the room helping Charlotte to collect rugs and pillows from a cupboard in the hall – what the trouble was likely to be.

'Blue as a prime blue trout, and got all his work cut out to breathe at all. Looks pretty bad to me.'

He hung up as Lesley came in, and hoped she hadn't heard. She had hardly spoken a word throughout, and what she was thinking was more than he could guess. For she could connect as quickly as anyone. Not much doubt of that. And who but the man who had put Gus Hambro underground for good should all but drop dead from shock when the corpse insisted upon rising?

Paviour was laid in blankets on the couch in the sitting-room, livid-faced and pinched, breathing in shallow, rattling snores. She sat beside him, sponging his face and bathing away the sweat that gathered on his forehead and lips. Gus Hambro had been carried straight upstairs to the bathroom to strip him of his wrecked clothes and clean the grime of centuries from his body, and Bill, at his own suggestion, had slipped away to the lodge to bring him some pyjamas and clothes of his own, since the victim's effects were a total loss. Out in the hall by the front door Orrie hovered uneasily, plainly unwilling to leave until he knew what was going on, waiting for the doctor to arrive, and rolling himself one shapeless cigarette after another.

Dr Braby came with an ambulance as escort, having considerable confidence in Price's judgement. The attendant followed him in to await orders, and fetch and carry if required. Lesley relinquished her place by the couch without a word, and stood aside, intently watching, as the doctor turned back the blankets and began a methodical examination. The sight of the sunken, leaden face and the sound of the anguished breathing made him look up at her briefly over his shoulder.

'Will you show Johnson where the telephone is, please? Get the Comerbourne General, and say you're bringing in a congestive heart failure, urgent. I'll give you a note on what he's getting: digoxin, intravenous, fifteen millilitres. We need a quick response, and in his condition I doubt if there'll be any nausea reaction. Hot water, would you mind, Mrs Paviour?'

He spread his bag open beside him, within reach of one freckled, middle-aged hand, and prepared his injection, and very slowly and carefully administered it. For a few minutes afterwards he sat with his fingers on his patient's pulse.

'No history of heart trouble previously?'

'No,' said Lesley, 'he's never complained. He seemed very well, and he didn't bother about regular check-ups, as long as he felt all right.'

'Like most of us. We'll have to send him into hospital, I can't do more for him here. The digoxin will begin to take effect in ten minutes or so, and should reach maximum within a couple of hours. Then he should rally.'

'I'll go along with him,' said Lesley. 'Give me three minutes to put some things together for him.' She looked the doctor squarely in the face. 'You can tell me the truth, you know. Is he going to get over it?'

'No saying yet, I'm afraid. He's bad, but he may pull out of it successfully. Live in hope!'

Was it possible that her hopes inclined the other way? Her voice was so level and her face so still that it was left to the imagination what ambivalent thoughts they covered. If he had really attempted murder, what was there waiting for him if he got over this attack?

'Do you want me to come along with you?' Charlotte asked.

Lesley gave her a faint, brief smile, perhaps detecting the reluctance with which the offer was made. 'No, thanks, you stay here and stand in for me if anyone needs feeding, or coffee, or a drink. I'm going to pack a case for Stephen.' And she went up the stairs at a light and purposeful run, in command of herself and in need of no one to hold her hand, and in a very few minutes was back with her burden. She followed the stretcher-men out through the hall, and there was Orrie still waiting in case he was needed.

He got up when the stretcher came through, his eyes dwelling in fascination upon the swathed body. It looked like a preternaturally long and narrow collection of old bones very imperfectly articulated. There seemed to be virtually nothing under the covering blanket, only two bony feet at one end of it, and a fleshless head with luxuriant grey hair and pointed beard at the other. The face wasn't covered, so he wasn't dead, after all. Just in process of dying. Or pretty near to it, anyhow, touch and go. Orrie looked up at Lesley, and the case in her hand, and understood.

'How you going to get back, then? I tell you what, I'll bring the Morris along to the General after you, and drive you home.'

'Oh, would you, Orrie? It would be a help.' She groped in her handbag and fished out the car keys for him. 'I was going to get a taxi back, but I should be grateful. I'm sorry to spoil your Sunday evening like this.' For ordinarily Orrie would have been in 'The Crown' by this time, or on a fishing day probably in 'The Salmon's Return'. She smiled at him, rather wanly, and went on quickly into the ambulance after her husband; and Orrie went off with the keys in his hand to get the Morris out of the garage.

'Now where's the other one?' Braby demanded briskly, as soon as the ambulance had driven away.

He looked down with astonishment at the slight body in

the bath, newly emerged from its indescribable grime. Gus was covered from head to foot with bruises and abrasions, his knees were rubbed raw, and his hands were a mess, but that appeared to be the sum of what ailed him. His state was something between unconsciousness and sleep, but steadily relaxing into simple sleep. He breathed deeply and evenly.

'Now what in the world,' demanded the doctor, 'has been happening to this one?'

'That,' said George, 'is a long and interesting story, and one I intend to tell you, if you can hang around for a while. Because I think you may very well be useful in more ways than one.'

'Tell me now, it might help. And you may as well finish the job you've started, while you're about it. By the look of him, he won't mind waiting for my services.'

George told him, while they lifted Gus out and wrapped him in a bath-sheet, and patted him dry with gingerly care, for there was hardly a square inch of him without minor lesions. They were still busy when Charlotte tapped at the door.

'I've made up a bed for him,' she reported, when George opened the door to her. 'He's going to be fit to stay here, surely? And Bill's brought him pyjamas, and some clothes of his own. They won't fit too well, but they'll be better than Mr Paviour's. Bill's sleeping here overnight, too. I think Lesley'll feel better with a man in the house. It seemed the best thing to do.'

'You're a treasure,' said George warmly, and came out of the room to her, shutting the others in. 'Which bedroom have you chosen for him? Show me!'

She showed him, saying nothing about the fact that it was next to her own, but it seemed that he had divined as much. He looked at her with a small, approving, almost affectionate smile, and she gazed back at him stubbornly and refused to blush. There were more important considerations.

'I understand your choice,' he said respectfully. 'But for my purposes it might not be a good idea. Would you mind changing to another one? Let's have a look at what's on offer.'

He chose a room as remote from the regularly used ones as the large house permitted, its door solitary on a small cross-landing above the back stairs, which were well carpeted. The window looked out on the shrubberies and orchard at the rear, and was out of sight from the sunny front living-rooms where all the activity of the household centred. The room had a large, walk-in wardrobe which had almost certainly been a powder-closet in Queen Anne's day, when the house was built.

'This,' said George, 'will do fine. You make up the bed, and we'll get him into it.'

'It's too remote,' she said accusingly. 'You can't keep an eye constantly on this room. And supposing he came round and called out? No one would hear him.'

'No,' said George, 'they wouldn't, would they?' He met her eyes and smiled. 'Bring the sheets, and I'll help you make the bed.'

She didn't know why she did what he told her, when she distrusted, or felt she ought to distrust, his proceedings. But she went for the sheets, all the same.

Doctor Braby's report on Gus Hambro was made twice over, once informally upstairs, while he examined the patient, and dressed the abrasions on his hands and knees; and once, with more ceremony, downstairs to the assembled company before he left the house. Gus continued oblivious of both the care lavished on him and the indignities to which he was subjected. The only motion he made was when the doctor, with thumb and finger, delicately parted his eyelids, and then his brows contracted protestingly, and his eyes screwed tight against even this invasion of light.

'Perfectly natural reaction,' said Braby, 'after twenty-odd hours of digging his way out like a mole. As soon as he's released from the necessity of struggle he collapses. There's nothing wrong with him but pure exhaustion, a combination of tension – and that's relaxed now – wear and tear – and that can move into the stage of reparation – and sheer want of sleep. I suppose he hasn't eaten anything all that time, either, but that's a comparatively low priority. After about ten hours' sleep he may wake up enough to want something, but don't worry if he stays out even longer. Pulse is like a rock. He'll do all right.'

The second time – it was considerably later – he phrased it rather differently. He came down the stairs with George just after the Morris had drawn up outside. Lesley was coming in at the door, her face set and pale, with Orrie hesitating half-anxiously and half-truculently on the door-step behind her. But for the master of the household, the cast was complete, for Charlotte and Bill Lawrence were just coming through from the kitchen with coffee and sandwiches, specially prepared against Lesley's return.

'They say,' said Lesley tiredly, in response to enquiries, 'I can telephone early tomorrow, and they'll be able to tell me more then. They said whatever it was you gave him was only just beginning to take effect. I left him looking just the same.' She looked round with slightly dazed tranquillity, seemed faintly surprised to see so many of them, and fixed upon George. 'How is Mr Hambro?'

'I hope you don't mind,' said George. 'We've made free with your house and your bed-linen, and put him into the back bedroom over the shrubbery, where he'll be quiet. He isn't fit to be moved. But we think – we hope – he's going to be all right.'

'Then he's still unconscious?' she said, her eyes widening. 'He hasn't been able to tell you *anything*? About what happened to him? About *who* could have . . . ?' Her voice was carefully hushed and moderate, but she shied away from finishing the sentence. They could almost see the tall, wavering shape of her husband standing behind her, an old man tormented by his inadequacy, and by the youth of every young man who came in sight.

'No,' said George gravely, 'he hasn't come round yet, and he's not likely to before morning. We still don't know whether he ever saw whoever attacked him, or even where and how it happened.'

Bill Lawrence said, with the authority of the half-expert: 'It has to be the laconicum. There isn't any other way he can have got in there. If he'd been exploring from the open flue, he wouldn't have needed to trail around in there for a day and a night. He knew his stuff, he wouldn't lose himself. And there's his car. Whoever made away with that tried to make away with him. Shouldn't we be having a close look at the laconicum right now, whether it's night or not?'

'The laconicum will keep till morning,' said George. 'As for Mr Hambro's actual condition, Doctor Braby can inform you better than I can.'

'Mr Hambro,' said the doctor firmly, 'is suffering from an extreme degree of exhaustion, physical and mental, and however minor his physical injuries may be, they certainly don't help his general condition. At this moment I'd say his nervous collapse has passed into more or less normal sleep, and since his immediate need is for recuperation, I've left him under fairly strong sedation, so that he shall certainly sleep overnight without a break, and probably longer. I realise it's important to get a statement from him – for it seems from his head injury that he certainly was attacked – but from my point of view it's even more important that he should get the long period of total rest which he requires. I'm afraid police enquiries will have to wait until he's fit to deal with them.'

'And will he be fit?' asked Bill. 'I mean eventually? Will he remember, after all this?'

'Remember? Look, we're dealing with a perfectly sound and strong young man, who at this moment happens to be gravely weakened by circumstances strictly temporary. There's no question of serious concussion. Nothing whatever to impair his memory, unless a nervous block occurs, and frankly, I think that very unlikely. Yes, he'll remember. Whether he saw anything of relevance, whether he can identify his assailant, of course, is another matter. But whatever he did record, he'll remember. We may have to wait a day,' he said indifferently, 'to find out what he has to tell, but he'll be perfectly capable of telling it when he does surface.'

He came down the rest of the staircase, passed by Lesley with a sympathetic smile and a general goodnight, and walked out to his car.

'I think,' said George, 'we should all leave you now to get what rest you can. I'm assured that Mr Hambro will be all right until morning, and I'll be in in good time tomorrow to see him.'

'Do you think we should sit up with him?' asked Lesley. 'We would, you know, we'd split the watch. I mean, if he should wake up, and feel lost? After an ordeal like that . . . and in the dark . . .'

George shook his head. 'He won't wake up. The doctor's sunk him for twelve hours or so, I assure you. Sleep is what he needs, and what he's going to get for a while. We shall have to wait. It's only sense, you know.'

He walked out, too, closing the door gently after him. He was not at all surprised to find, before he reached his car, that Charlotte was there in the darkness beside him, though she certainly had not got there by way of the same door.

'You can't do it,' she said in a rapid, indignant whisper in his ear. 'You can't just go away and leave him like this. You've just made it clear that he hasn't said a word yet, but may have plenty to say when he does wake up. Everybody knows it, you've made sure of that. And then you go away and leave him to it!'

'What would you like?' asked George as softly. 'A couple of constables with notebooks sitting by his bed?' He looked at her closely and smiled. 'So you don't accept Paviour's evidence against himself? If the would-be murderer is in hospital at Comerbourne, seriously ill, what is there left to worry about?'

'I don't know! It did look like that. It *does* look like that. All I really know is that Gus is in there asleep, the one person who *may* be able to identify the man who tried to kill him, and everybody knows he hasn't spoken yet, but tomorrow he will. Supposing it wasn't Mr Paviour, after all? People do have heart attacks. I know what I did, I know I meant it, but after all perhaps he was just the most vulnerable. Then there's somebody still around with an interest in seeing that Gus never speaks. That he doesn't live to speak! If it was urgent to kill him last night, it's twice as urgent now.'

The brief and unprotesting silence shook and enlightened her. Dimly as she could see his face, she knew he was looking at her with respect, with affection, certainly with a very gentle and grave measure of amusement.

'That's what you want!' she whispered. 'You've got him all pegged out for bait, like a goat for tigers, waiting for someone to have another attempt.'

'In which case,' said George mildly, 'you may be sure I don't intend the event to go unwitnessed – or uninterrupted.'

'What do you want me to do?' asked Charlotte, charmed into meekness.

'Well, if you insist – it isn't strictly necessary, but it would help. When you're sure everyone else is in bed, you can go quietly down and slip the catch on the back door.'

'I will.' The door at the foot of those well-carpeted back stairs that led to the room where Gus Hambro was asleep; the room, she remembered, with a spacious walk-in wardrobe. 'And what after that?'

'After that,' said George, 'go to bed. And go to sleep.'

'I should have to have a lot of faith in you,' she said, 'to do that.'

'Well?' said George. 'You have a lot of faith in me, haven't you?'

George drove as far as the nearest telephone box that worked, and made two calls, the first being to Barnes, who was standing by for orders, the second to the ward sister in the Comerbourne General Hospital. He was lucky; the night sister on duty was an old friend, and though she was slightly disapproving, she knew him well enough to consent to bend her conscience very delicately to oblige him.

Then he went home to bed.

Barnes let himself in gently by the back door when the house was in complete darkness and silence, eased the catch into place after him without a sound, and made himself reasonably comfortable inside the wardrobe that opened out of Gus's bedroom. Not too comfortable, for fear of drowsiness. He left the door unlatched, but only a hairline open, to admit sound or light should there be either, and adjusted his own line of vision to cover any approach to the bed where the patient still slept, not so much peacefully as rapturously.

He spent a disappointing, even a puzzling night. Nothing whatever was heard or seen to break the serenity. Nothing whatever happened.

Lesley arose very early, to catch the night sister before she handed over duty. She was allowed to ring through to the ward instead of merely making routine enquiries through the office, the case being new and this the first and crucial call.

'Mr Paviour is still unconscious,' said the ward sister, in the carefully bracing voice of one trying to make dismal news sound better than it is, 'but I wouldn't say he's lost ground at all. His breathing is very slightly easier, perhaps, but of course he's very weak. I'm afraid his condition must have been developing for some time without producing warning symptoms. The degeneration is marked. But there's no need to be too discouraged.'

'You mean he isn't really any better?' said Lesley, irritated and demanding. Why must nurses say so much and mean so little?

'Well . . . his condition is much the same. I wouldn't say he's *worse* . . .'

That did convey something, more than it said.

'Do you think . . .' Lesley hesitated. 'Should I visit this afternoon? If he's unconscious, it can't help him . . .'

'Well, I don't think he's going to *know* you, of course . . . I'm afraid he probably won't have regained consciousness. But don't feel discouraged from coming on that account. I think that you'll be glad to feel that you did everything possible . . . In fact, you could arrange to visit briefly at any time that's convenient to you, if you ask at the office. In the circumstances . . .'

'Thank you,' said Lesley, in a small, thoughtful voice, and put down the receiver in its rest.

There was no point now in going back to bed. The morning was bright, clear and still. From the window she could see the river glittering in the first slanting light, like frost-fire. She went down and made coffee, and sat over it for a long time, staring out at the dawn, and going over the telephone conversation word by word, sorting out the grain from the chaff. 'In the circumstances . . .' Visiting hours at the General were generous but fixed; the circumstances that permitted visiting at any time did not need spelling out. But the sister could be wrong, even doctors can be wrong. People confidently expected to die did sometimes turn their backs on probability and decide to come back again, against all the odds. Still . . . ward sisters are very experienced in the prognostication of death. Especially night sisters.

She heard one of her guests stirring overhead in the bathroom, and got up to make fresh coffee and prepare the breakfast. She was busy laying the table, here in the bright, cheerful kitchen instead of the sombre dining-room, when Charlotte came in.

'I'm sorry, I meant to be up before you and start the breakfast, and now you've done everything. I hope you managed to get some sleep?'

'I slept extraordinarily well,' said Lesley, and meant it. 'I don't know how it is. Trust in providence, or what? But I did.'

'You haven't called the hospital yet?'

'I have. I wanted the sister who really knew something, rather than one who'd just come on. She was the one I saw last night, she promised me she'd be standing by for a call from me. His condition is unchanged,' she said, answering Charlotte's unasked question. 'No better. And she insists, no worse. But I'm not sure the lady doesn't protest too much.'

'I'm sorry!' said Charlotte, reading the look more attentively than the words.

'Darling, I married a man nearly forty years older than I am. I've lived all the while with the obvious knowledge that I certainly was going to survive him, probably by many years. All I hope is that I haven't always been awful to him, and he really did get something out of it. While it lasted. It could hardly last all that long, could it? I was grateful, I was contented and happy, and I hope I made all that clear. In love,' she said firmly, 'I never was. Not with him. I don't feel that that was any failure on my part, I never promised it.'

'I don't feel it was, either,' agreed Charlotte, reassured. 'Where do you keep the marmalade?'

They finished the cooking together, just in time for Bill Lawrence's entrance. He was used to breakfasting in pyjamas, unshaven, on the corner of his desk; it did him good to have to face two young women over the breakfast-table. He was scrubbed and immaculate this morning, like the sky, almost arrogantly clean and pure. We must, thought Charlotte, be one of the oddest trios sitting down to coffee in England this morning. How did any of us get here, in Stephen Paviour's house, in this tragic palimpsest of a city without people? And yet everything felt improbably normal and ordinary, like the extraordinary encountered in a dream.

'You didn't look in on Gus?' asked Lesley, looking up at Bill.

'I did, as a matter of fact. I thought maybe I should check. He's still asleep. I'd even say he's snoring now. I hope that's a good sign. I went up to the bed, but he never stirred, so I left him to it. He'll probably sleep until noon.'

It was at that exact moment that the sound exploded above them, somewhere upstairs, remote at the back of the house. A distant, peremptory, wordless bellow of alarm and conflict, curiously like an antique battle-cry. And then a confused thudding and heaving of bodies braced in mute struggle, frightening out of all proportion to its loudness.

They rose as one, strained upright and motionless for the fraction of a second. Then they raced for the doorway, Charlotte first because she had been quivering on the receptive for just such a signal, not only here in the kitchen, but half the night before. They streamed out into the hall and up the stairs in frantic silence.

It was almost over by the time they burst into the rear bedroom where Gus Hambro had been sleeping. Charlotte flung open the door and stood transfixed, a mere witness, with the others brought up short against her braced shoulders.

The sash window stood wide open, the lower half hoisted to its full extent. The top of a ladder projected above the sill; one man was in the act of leaping into the room, a second head loomed just within view behind him. On the bed a large body crouched froglike, leaning with thrusting forearms over an incongruous orange-coloured cushion, which had missed planting itself squarely over Gus Hambro's sleeping face only because, in fact, he had not been sleeping for an hour or more previously, and had hoisted a sharp knee into his aggressor's groin and rolled violently to the right at the moment of impact. He heaved and strained still at this moment, but he was too light a weight to shift that crushing incubus, though nose and mouth were safe from suffocation. It was Detective-Constable Barnes, circling behind him for the right hold, who hooked a steely forearm under the murderer's chin, and hoisted him backwards off his prey with a heave that could well have broken even that bull neck.

The assailant crashed heavily against the wall, and gathered himself as vehemently to battle again; and Barnes and George Felse, one on either side, pinned his arms and wrestled the lunging wrists into handcuffs behind him. He heaved himself to his feet only to find himself bereft of hands. The cushion lay under the chair from which he had lifted it, beside the window; and Constable Collins, climbing in too late to be of more vital assistance, replaced it automatically, and patted it into shape against the wicker back.

'Orlando Benyon,' said George, running rather tiredly through the familiar formula, 'I arrest you on a charge of the attempted murder of Augustus Hambro, and I caution you that you are not obliged to make any statement unless you wish, but that anything you do say will be taken down in writing, and may be used in evidence.'

CHAPTER THIRTEEN

Interrogating Orrie Benyon was a more or less impossible undertaking from the first, because silence was his natural state, and his recoil into it entailed no effort. He was far from unintelligent, or illiterate, or even inarticulate, for he could express himself fluently enough when he found it expedient, but it was in speaking that the labour consisted for him, not in being silent. Here, finding himself already charged with an offence that could hardly be denied, with so many eye-witnesses, but might very well be whittled away to a lesser charge which he could embrace without more than a shrug, with everything to gain and nothing to lose by keeping his mouth shut, he did what all his nature and manner of life urged, closed it implacably, and kept it closed.

They brought him down into the small study, and cautiously let him out of his handcuffs, for he had ceased to struggle or threaten, and had too much sense to try against a small army what had failed in more promising circumstances. It was too late now, in any case, to kill Gus Hambro. That charge he would have to ride; other and worse he might still fend off by saying nothing. And while George put mild, persuasive questions, argued the commonsense course of admitting what could not be denied, wound about him tirelessly with soft, reasonable assumptions and invited him to confirm one by denying another, nothing was exactly what Orrie said. From the moment that he had been overpowered in the bedroom, he did not unclamp his lips.

'Why not tell us about it, Orrie? Six of us saw the attack, and it was pretty determined, wasn't it? You meant killing. Because you'd already made one attempt, and were afraid he could identify you, now that he'd reappeared? What made you choose that particular pool to dump the Aston Martin? And are you sure you wiped all your prints off the Vespa, Orrie? Because you won't have the opportunity now, you know. And nobody else but the police has touched it since. Whatever's there to find we shall find. You might as well make a statement. I'm not holding out any inducements, you know you can't lose by co-operating.'

Orrie sat in a high-backed chair, his spine taut, his head raised, looked through them with his blue, inimical eyes, gathered his wits inside that monumental head of his like the garrison inside a fortress, and said nothing.

'And why did you wait so long, Orrie? All those nice, safe hours of darkness, and never a move from you till broad daylight. What were you waiting for? For something that would make it unnecessary for you to take the risk? What did you hope would happen to let you off the hook? Until you realised it wasn't going to happen, and got desperate.'

Orrie looked through him with eyes like chips of bluestone, and made not a sound.

'This is getting boring, isn't it?' said George amiably. 'Perhaps if we enlarge the cast it may get a bit more interesting.' He turned to Collins, who was sitting unobtrusively beside the door. 'Ask all the others to come in and join us, will you?'

'Since Orrie won't talk about recent events,' said George,

when they were all assembled, 'I suggest we hear what the other interested party has to say about what happened to him on Saturday night. I'm afraid we rather over-stated Mr Hambro's condition, as you may have gathered. It's true he was in an exhausted state, and slept heavily and long, but he was not under drugs, and his memory is not impaired. He did recover enough to talk to me for a few minutes last night, before I left, and he did tell me what I'm now asking him to tell you.'

And Gus told them, beginning tactfully at the point where he had parted from Stephen Paviour and packed his bag to leave Aurae Phiala. He was still slightly grey and drawn, still mildly astonished at being above the ground instead of under it, and his hands were bandaged into white cotton parcels; but otherwise, apart from presenting a mildly odd appearance in Bill Lawrence's clothes, he was himself again. When he reached the apparition of the helmeted sentry there was an uneasy stir of doubt, wonder and sympathy, as if two at least of his hearers were entertaining the suspicion that he might, after all, be incubating delayed symptoms of concussion. He smiled.

'Oh, no, it wasn't any hallucination. I've handled it, it's real enough. And I know exactly where it is, and we shall be recovering it, all in good time.' All the while he talked he had an eye on Orrie, who sat like a stone demigod, apparently oblivious of them all, but so braced in his stillness that it was plain he missed nothing. 'The wearer I didn't see at close quarters. But it wasn't Orrie. Not big enough. And then, the one who came behind and hit me had to be Orrie.'

He told that, too, the blow and the fall, the rattle of stones and metal as the shaft was filled in over him. 'The rest you know. I made for the river as the only other way out I knew. It took me all night and all day, because there were a lot of places where I had to dig my way through.' The details of that marathon crawl were irrelevant at that stage; he left them to the imagination.

'And could you,' asked George, 'identify the man who hit you and tipped you down the shaft? From that one glimpse you had of him? Describe what you did see.'

'It was dark, but there was fitful light. The man I saw was much taller than me – as tall as Orrie – or Mr Paviour. Though his attitude, leaning and striking, with his arm raised, may have made him look even bigger. He was in silhouette, no chance to see if he had a beard or was clean-shaven. His strength didn't suggest an old man. To be honest, that's all I could say.'

'And could you, then, have identified him positively as anyone you know?'

'No,' said Gus with deliberation, his eyes studying Orrie from beneath their long lashes, 'I couldn't.'

The bluestone eyes kindled for one instant with a fierce spark of intelligence, and were dimmed again.

'So that's why we had to proceed with this obvious invitation to the murderer to try again,' said George. 'We had everything to gain, and he couldn't know that he had nothing. Your mistake, Orrie. There are now no less than seven people who *can* identify you as the man who made a murderous attack upon Mr Hambro this morning. You're not asking us to believe, are you, that there are two men around with the same urge – and the same acute need! – to silence Mr Hambro for good?'

Orrie was not asking them to believe anything. By the Comer, with the man he had murdered breaking out of his grave, he had never quivered or uttered a sound. There was nothing worth calling a nerve in his whole great body.

'But I can't believe in all this!' protested Lesley suddenly, pounding her linked hands helplessly against her knee.

'Look, I know it isn't evidence, but I've known Orrie for years, he's worked for us, and I thought I knew him so well. I still think so. He wouldn't hurt a fly. Why should he do a thing like this? Oh, I know I *saw* him! I can't forget it. But to me that means there's more behind this – or else something's happened to him, a brainstorm – he isn't responsible for his actions any more. Why should he want to harm anyone? What motive could he possibly have?'

'The usual motive,' said George. 'Gain. Not, perhaps, to harm *anyone*. But a very solid motive to get rid of Mr Hambro. Who is, I should mention – though of course you already know it, don't you, Orrie? – Detective-Sergeant Hambro of the Art and Antiques Squad at Scotland Yard, an authority on Roman antiquities. He came here in the process of following the back-tracks of certain valuable pieces which have been turning up in suspicious circumstances in several parts of the world, and which can only have come from a handful of border sites, of which Aurae Phiala is one. Someone, in fact, has been secretly milking this place of treasure over a long period. And whoever he is, he was implicated deeply enough to kill unhesitatingly when an inquisitive boy accidentally stumbled on one gold coin from his remaining hoard, and unwisely hung around to hunt for more. His curiosity could have blown the whole racket wide-open. He had to go. Gerry Boden was suffocated; the same handy method – if you happen to be about twice as strong as your victim – that Orrie was using on Mr Hambro upstairs.'

'But you're not charging him with anything like that,' protested Lesley. 'Only with this attack this morning. How could he know anything about what Mr Hambro was doing here? None of us knew. He never told us anything. It seems you can't even be sure these things came from here. If he'd been helping himself to valuable things like that, and turning them into money, why would he go on working hard for what we pay him here? It doesn't make sense.'

'It makes perfect sense,' George pointed out, 'as long as he still had treasures to dispose of, and kept them hidden here. Things like that can't be unloaded on the market wholesale, like potatoes. It has to be done gradually and cautiously, with long intervals between.'

'I see that,' she admitted unhappily. 'But in that case, what on earth has he done with the money he's already made? He doesn't spend much, that's certain. And personally, I simply don't believe he *has* much. He doesn't own a thing but his small-holding, not so much as a second-hand car. He hasn't even got a bank account. Stephen and I have sometimes changed cheques for him, if he got paid that way for some of the odd jobs he did in the village.'

It was at this point that Charlotte got up from her place and walked out of the room. In the curious peace of having Gus alive again, and his assailant in custody, she had been sitting back and letting these exchanges pass by her as impartially as she might have watched the Comer flowing by, until a few chance words pricked out of the back of her mind a small memory, a minute thing that fitted like a key into the whole complex of this mystery, and caused it to open like the door of a safe. She closed the door after her, and went purposefully up the stairs to Lesley's room.

When she came back into the study, as calmly as she had left it, and as quietly, Lesley was still warmly arguing the case for Orrie. And Orrie, though he had not turned his head, now and again turned his stony eyes and let them rest upon her.

'But you see how Orrie's behaved throughout, not at all suspiciously, quite the opposite. You agree he told you all about the Boden boy hiding in his shed all that time . . .'

'That was a very intelligent move,' agreed George, 'and

he could well afford it. It didn't implicate him in the least – quite the opposite – and it did underline his co-operative zeal. It cost him nothing, and made him look good.'

'And last night,' she pressed on, 'Orrie was urging us to have all that slope concreted up, to make it safe. Would he do that, if he had valuables hidden there?'

'By now,' said George, 'he has nothing hidden there. What was left was almost certainly removed on Wednesday night, immediately after the boy was killed.'

'Then where is it now? If you could find some of these coins and things in his possession, that would go far towards proving it. But I don't believe in it. I'm certain Orrie wouldn't at all mind having his cottage searched, but I'm even more certain you wouldn't find anything guilty there.'

Charlotte leaned forward, and held out in her open palm the smallest of Lesley's keys.

'And I'm sure,' she said, 'that you'd be equally willing to open your safe-deposit box at the bank, where we went to put in a package last Thursday. A small package, but very heavy. For Orrie!'

They had all turned to stare at her, Lesley wide-eyed and mute, her kitten-face pale and bright in wonder. Charlotte had half-expected to have the key indignantly snatched from her, but Lesley hardly glanced at it, only once in a puzzled way, as if she was too stunned at this moment to connect with her usual aplomb. Her smooth brows contracted painfully, frowning back into past occasions, for the first time with doubt and dread. She looked from Charlotte to Orrie, a blank, bewildered question, more than half afraid of encountering an answer. Then at George, as being in authority here, and deserving some part of her attention.

'Yes, that's true, Charlotte and I did go to the bank in Comerbourne. I did have a little box to put in my safe-deposit, Orrie asked me to keep it for him. We've done it before, you know – I don't remember how often, but several times. He lives in rather a lonely place, and these days one hears such . . . We never thought anything about it, why should we? Just keeping things for him a little while, until he needed them and asked for them out. I know he put an old brooch of his mother's in there once, when someone told him it might be valuable, and he was thinking of selling it. They didn't usually stay in long . . .'

She looked at Orrie again, briefly, and the monolith had certainly stirred, and the blue eyes quickened uneasily for an instant. She looked at George, and her own green eyes were wide and gleaming with realisation and disquiet.

'Now I don't know where I am! I don't know anything! *Can it have been that?*'

'If you have no objection to my taking charge temporarily of your key,' said George, 'and if you'll agree to accompany me to your bank and open your safe-deposit, that can be answered, can't it?'

'Yes,' she said in a whisper. And even lower, almost to herself: 'I didn't know! *I didn't know!*'

The key passed into George's hand. The granite monolith had perceptibly moved, heaving its great head round to stare at the small thing changing hands. If stone can shudder, the brief convulsion that shook Orlando Benyon was just such a movement. But his mouth stayed shut; only now tightly, violently shut, as if at any moment it might break open and breathe fire.

'Of course,' said George reasonably, 'there are difficulties in this theory. Orrie has never in his life been out of England, seldom, I imagine, out of Midshire. Two of the objects recovered in this case surfaced in Italy and Turkey respectively. I don't doubt even Orrie could sell or pawn a gold coin in a good many places here in England, and get away with it, but he'd hardly have the knowledge or the address to work the trade on a big scale. This is a difficult, specialised market – unscrupulous enough if you know where the fences are, and which collectors don't care whether they can ever show their collections, but otherwise rather dangerous. There are plenty of enthusiasts who are quite satisfied with gloating in secret. But you have to know where to find them. Somehow it seems to me that Orrie is hardly in that league.'

Orrie's eyes swivelled again, silently signalling his awareness of every move for and against him, and still reserving his own defence in this defenceless position.

Lesley sat back with a sharp, defeated sigh, seeming for a moment to have relinquished a field that was out of her control. She pondered for a moment in depressed silence, and then suddenly her slight body arched and stiffened, like a cat sighting a quarry or a foe. She seemed to be in two minds whether to speak or hold her peace. Her rounded eyelids, delicately veined like alabaster, rolled back from an emerald stare.

'Chief Inspector, a day or so ago you said there must be an expert involved. I didn't believe in it then, now I begin to see what you mean. You even mentioned a name – Doctor Morris. He was here just before he went abroad for this Turkish year of his. He brought the text of his book about this place. We were just about closing up the small dig we had that autumn, it was October already, but it had been a good season. And you know something? I'd never known Doctor Morris to speak disparagingly of Aurae Phiala until then, never. And yet he went away from here, and spent three weeks on that text in Turkey before he posted it to the publishers. And you know what the finished book is like.

Deliberately playing down this site! I can't call it anything but deliberate. Why? *Why?* There has to be a reason! And that dig – it never produced much – not to our knowledge, that is! – it was still open when he was here. Bill will tell you. He visited then, he knows. Wouldn't it account for everything, if Alan Morris stumbled on a really rich discovery while he was here, and kept it dark? If he was tempted, if he moved his finds, put them in a secret place, and left them hidden until he could get them away? He went straight from here to Turkey. And Charlotte tells me nobody's heard from him since.'

She looked at Gus, who was watching her with a guarded face. 'It's your case, you know more about this than I do. If you've been working in contact with all these other countries, and thinking on these lines – I mean about the need for an expert to run the show – then I can't believe that you've never matched up these times, and considered the possibility of a connection between Doctor Morris's exit from England and the beginning of these deals in Roman valuables. I say considered the possibility, that's all.'

'The police of several countries have made the connection,' said Gus drily. 'They could hardly avoid it.' He carefully refrained from looking at Charlotte.

'Then you didn't come here just to look at one of several places that might have been looted – you came here because the connection with Doctor Morris made this the most probable. And you weren't likely to lose interest and go away again,' she added, 'when you ran head-on into Charlotte on the premises, and found out who she was.'

This time Gus did look at Charlotte, fleetingly and rather apprehensively, and even at this crisis he had not lost his engaging ability to produce a blush at will.

'But will someone tell me,' said Charlotte, ignoring the phenomenon, 'why, if my great-uncle found a valuable hoard here and kept his mouth shut about it, he didn't simply pack the lot up and take it abroad with him then?'

'It wouldn't be a practical proposition,' said Gus simply. 'He was booked by air, which means a limit on weight, and too much excess baggage might arouse curiosity. Also some of the things – if there were others like the helmet, for instance – might be quite bulky and very fragile, and need careful transportation. But mostly just plain caution. Someone who knew the ropes would also know the risks. He wouldn't try to smuggle out too much in one go. I don't doubt some of the most precious and most portable things were taken out straight away and disposed of. The rest, we think, were taken from wherever they were found, and hidden in the broken flue of the hypocaust, which seems to have been completely concealed then by the clump of broom bushes. The art of hiding something is to do it decisively, and then go about your business without ever glancing in that direction, as if it wasn't there. The cache was safe enough until the river rose and brought the bank down.'

'There's still another question,' Charlotte pursued. 'Being an expert on antiquities come by honestly isn't the same thing as being expert in disposing of them dishonestly. Would my uncle have had the first idea how to set about it?'

'One evening while he was staying here,' said Lesley, 'we were talking about the shady side of the business. About cases he'd known, and how people went about getting rid of rather specialist stolen property. It was the evening you were here, Bill, do you remember?'

'I do,' said Bill unhappily, from the corner where he had sat silent all this time. 'He seemed to know a good deal about it, he went into a lot of detail. Even names. I didn't think anything about it then, after all it was interesting, and we were all asking him questions.'

Charlotte looked enquiringly at Gus, and waited.

'I'm afraid he did know,' said Gus regretfully. 'He acted as consultant for us occasionally, and he probably picked up a good deal about the top fences in the business. The problem collectors he knew already. And then, you see, he had the top-weight to work the racket in a big way, as an amateur couldn't do. His name and reputation would count for as much underground as in the daylight. Collectors would take his word and pay his price.'

'Well, all right!' She had a curious feeling that she ought to be experiencing and showing more indignation, that it was all part of some devious and elaborate charade, of which she understood something, but not enough. She had probably made one mistake in timing already, with that key. Writing her part as she went along was not so easy. But at least her voice had the right edge of irritation and challenge. 'But all you're describing is an absent master-mind in voluntary exile – or sanctuary – somewhere in Turkey. Whoever prowled about the riverside all day on thorns, waiting for everybody to go home and night to fall, so that he could salvage his last instalment of gold, whoever found that poor, silly boy rifling his cache, and killed him and hid his body until night, it certainly wasn't Great-Uncle Alan by remote control from Aphrodisias. *If* he's at the bottom of this affair, then he had an agent here on the spot to keep an eye on the place and feed the remaining stuff out to him gradually – either to him, or wherever he directed. Somebody well-paid and unscrupulous, and once recruited, in for good. They *had* to trust each other, either one of them could destroy the other. So even the assistant was deep enough in to have to kill the boy who blundered into the secret, and try to kill the detective who was getting too close to the truth. Well, at least we all know who made that last murderous attack on Mr Hambro. Do we therefore know who this local agent was? Is that what you're saying?'

There was a brief, expectant silence, in which everyone looked at Orrie; but he maintained his silence as though nothing that had been said bore any reference to him. However delicate your fingering, it's difficult to find a sensitive spot in a being who has no nerves.

'Yes,' said Lesley, slowly and clearly, 'we do know. At least, *I* know.'

She had their attention at once, but more, she had Orrie's. For the first time he turned his whole body, and fixed the sharpening stare of his blue eyes on her, and though the crudely splendid lines of his face never quivered, it was plainly a live human creature who peered through the slits of the mask. She looked back at him for a long moment, steadily and squarely, and it was as if her look was a reflection of his, for her face, too, was motionless and tranquil in its bright purity, but her eyes were alert, uneasy and agitated.

'There's something that happened just over a month ago.' She turned to face George, and addressed herself resolutely to him throughout. 'I never wondered much about it then, I had no reason to, and until now I'd forgotten it. But I can't tell you about it without telling you how I came to be . . . where it happened . . . where I saw it. And if this case is going to come to court, ever,' she said, clasping her hands tightly on her knee, 'this would have to come out in evidence. I can't even ask you to keep it in confidence.'

'I can't promise anything,' said George. 'It may not be necessary to make anything public that would hurt or embarrass you, but I can promise nothing.'

'I know. I'm not asking you to. It's Stephen who would be hurt, and *he* doesn't deserve it.' And after a deeply-drawn breath she said, clearly and steadily: 'I've been Orrie's mistress for eighteen months. I was actually in love with him. There wasn't anything he could have asked of me that I wouldn't have done for him. It was like a disease that turns you blind. I never saw, even for a moment, that he was making a convenience of me, using me as cover while he bled all that gold and treasure out of Aurae Phiala. I didn't believe it even when you charged him. Now I know it's true.'

Even then, it was not the bonds of silence that Orrie Benyon broke. They had all been watching Lesley in such fascination that for an instant no one was watching him. It was like the almost silent explosion of a leopard out of its cover, so sudden and so violent that his great hands were not an inch from her throat when Barnes and Collins pinioned both arms and dragged him off, and even then the blunt nails of his left hand drew a thin red thread down the creamy smoothness of her neck, and a drop of blood gathered and spread in the roll collar of her white sweater. But the most impressive thing was that Lesley never shrank or blinked, only turned a blazing, defiant face and stared him out at close quarters until he was hauled off her and thrust back into his chair. She did not even lift a hand to touch the scratch. There was something superb about her confidence that they would not let him harm her.

Then she sat silent, still fronting him unflinchingly, while he broke his silence at last for want of being able to express himself with his hands, which were always more fluent. Wide-eyed, long-suffering, with all the distaste she felt for him and for her own infatuation in her set face, she listened to the names he found for her, and never tried to stem the flood. Neither did anyone else. It would have been useless. He had been containing it in doubt and patience for so long that no banks could have held it now it was loose.

'Damn you to hell for a lying, swindling whore! Don't

listen to her, she's lying, she's nothing but lies right through. Ditch me now, would you, like you ditched him after he'd served your turn? Drop the whole load on me to carry, and you stroll out of it as pure as a lily, you dirty, cheating devil! But it isn't going to work! Not with me! Deeper than the sea, I tell you, this bitch – look at her, with her saint's face! And *she* began it, *she* called the tune – not only about the bloody gold, but the sex kick, too. You think she ever wanted that old man of hers, except for cover and an easy meal-ticket? Winding herself round him with that tale about being let down, and her life ruined – poor bloody misused innocent, needing his pity! But she didn't want any of *his* bed, bargain or no. Kidded him she was a sex-nut-case, a virgin nympho who couldn't stand being mauled but couldn't help asking for it! But it didn't take her long to pick up the clues with a real man, I tell you! With me she was all nympho! You wouldn't credit all the games that one knows. You think she intended to stick it out here with that old fool for life? Not a chance! We were going to clear up the lot, and then take the money and get out together – the cheating sow, *I thought we were!* – No hurry, we'd got our ways of passing the time while we waited. Every time her old man's back was turned – in her bed and mine, in the shed, in the orchard, down in the hollow where the bloody Roman jakes was, and that was hell on them stones, but she liked it to be hell sometimes, she'd think up ways to make it hell, ways you'd never dream of. Nails, teeth and all, she knows the lot! Six more weeks, and we'd have been ready for off, somewhere safe and soft for life. And then that bloody river had to come up and start the damned bank slipping . . . !'

His voice, even in murderous rage, was a deep, melodious thunder, the singing western cadences like a furious wind in strings. Although no one was holding him now, he heaved and strained against his own grip on the arms of the chair, as though he were chained. 'I'll fix her, though! I'm going to make a statement that'll see her off, the dirty, cheating bitch, the way she's trying to see me. There's nothing in her but lies, and lies, and lies. You can't twist fast enough to have her. You can only kill her! I *will* kill her! I'll . . .'

The pealing thunder snapped off into abrupt silence. He shut his mouth with a snap, biting off words too dangerous to utter. For he was charged only with the attempt as yet, not the achievement.

'You shall have your chance to make a statement, all in good time,' said George, to all appearances unstartled and unmoved. 'Go on, Mrs Paviour. Say what you were going to say.' She would not be interrupted again; Orrie had made his point and could bide his time.

'I realise,' said Lesley quietly, 'that it's my word against his. I realise that my recoil from him now makes him want to drag me down as low as he can. I can only tell the truth. I never knew anything about any thefts from the site, but I do admit the affair with him. I wish I needn't. It wasn't even a happiness while it lasted – not for long. My own fault! Yes, I was going to tell you . . . We did meet in his cottage sometimes. That was what I had to explain, how I came to be there in his bedroom.' She took a moment to breathe; she was quite calm, even relaxed, perhaps in resignation now that the worst was over. 'The last time was about a month ago. I don't remember the exact date, but it was in the last few days of March. He had a letter with a foreign stamp on the table by the bed, and I was surprised and picked it up to look at the stamp, out of curiosity. I didn't know he knew anyone abroad. It was a Turkish stamp, and the postmark was the twentieth of March. When he saw me looking at it he took it out of my hand and dropped it into a drawer. But afterwards I kept thinking I knew the hand-writing, and couldn't place it. It was addressed in English style, the lay-out and the hand. I had the feeling that it was familiar in some special way, that some time or other I'd copy-typed from a hand like that. I had. I know now. I happened to turn out some notes I typed up for him while he was staying here. It was Doctor Morris's handwriting.'

'She lies!' said Orrie, shortly and splendidly, without weakening emphasis. 'There never was any such letter.'

'A month ago?' said George sharply. 'Dated the twen-tieth of March? You're sure it wasn't old? From a previous year?'

'Quite sure. The date was plain. It was March of this year.'

'Then about six weeks ago Doctor Morris was unques-tionably alive and well, and still in Turkey?'

'He must have been. He addressed that envelope, I'm certain of that.'

'Where in Turkey? Could you read the postmark? Was there anything to give you a clue to where he could be found now?'

She shook her head. 'I can't remember anything more. It was the date I noticed – ' She turned and looked full at Orrie. 'But *he* can tell you. He must know where Doctor Morris is. He's always known.'

The briefest of glances passed between George Felse and Gus Hambro; and Gus, who had been silent during all these last exchanges, said suddenly, briskly and forcibly:

'I doubt if he does. *But we do*. We know exactly where Doctor Morris is. He's down in the flues of the hypocaust, luggage, briefcase, typewriter and all, and he's been there ever since he left your house to catch his plane, nineteen months ago.'

She had had no warning, none at all; for once her sixth

sense had failed her. She came out of her chair with a thin, angry sound, quivering like a plucked bow-string, torn between panic acceptance and the lightning reassertion of her terrible intelligence; and in the instant while the two clashed, she shrieked at him: 'You're lying! You can't have been near where we put hi . . .'

The aspirate hissed and died on her lip, and that was all, but it was fierce and clear, and just two words too many. She stood rigid, chilled into ice.

'He wasn't on the direct route, no,' agreed Gus softly, 'but my route was a good deal less than direct. There's hardly a yard of flue passable in that hypocaust where I haven't been. Including the near corner where – "*we*" – put him. I left your bronze helmet with him for safekeeping. As soon as you're in custody we're going to set about resurrecting them both.'

The deafening silence was shattered suddenly by a great, gusty, vengeful sound, and that was Orrie Benyon laughing. And in a moment, melting, surrendering, genuinely and terrifyingly amused by her own lapse, Lesley Paviour dropped back into her chair and laughed with him, exactly like a sporting loser in a trivial quizz-game.

CHAPTER FOURTEEN

She laughed again, when she was alone with George in his office at C.I.D. headquarters in Comerbourne, with no shorthand writer at hand and no witnesses, and he asked her, with genuine and unindignant curiosity – since indignation was quite irrelevant in any dealings with Lesley – : 'Do you always contrive to have not merely one fall guy on hand in case of need, but at least two? And doesn't it sometimes make things risky when you decide to change horses in midstream?'

'I never plan,' she said with disarming candour, 'not consciously. I just do what seems the clever thing at the moment.'

All too often, he reflected, it not only seemed clever, but was. She had matched every twist until the last, the one she hadn't foreseen even as a possibility. For some built-in instinct certainly acted to provide her with escape hatches and can-carriers well in advance of need. Why, otherwise, had she gone out of her way to let Charlotte not only see but handle the package still waiting to be reclaimed from the bank? And to tell her guilelessly that it was Orrie's, and not the first time he had put similar small items into safe-keeping? Thus underlining for future reference his involvement and her own naïve innocence. She had even scattered a few seeds, according to Charlotte, concerning Bill

Lawrence's solitary and furtive prowlings about the site, in case she should ever need yet another string to her bow. Lesley collected potentially useful people, and used and disposed of them like tissues, without a qualm.

'I'm not sure,' he said, 'it was so clever to write off Orrie. I wonder at what stage you made up your mind to throw him to the lions? You did allow him the chance to drive you back from the hospital last night. Hadn't you decided then? He'd been waiting on hot coals for a chance to talk to you alone. He wanted you to do your share, didn't he? You were in the house, it was your turn to do the necessary killing. Even a delicate little woman could press a cushion over the face of a man fast asleep under drugs after an exhausting ordeal. But you never intended sticking your neck out for him. Why didn't you tell him so? Obviously you didn't, or he wouldn't have left his own attempt so late. He waited all night, hoping you'd do the job for him. And I don't doubt you slept soundly.'

'Never better,' she said.

'Was it more fun letting him sweat? Was it just to make sure he *would* mistime it and be caught? Or were you afraid you wouldn't get back alive from the hospital with him if you pushed him too far?'

'I'm never afraid,' she said, and smiled. 'I don't drive through red lights, but I'm not afraid.' He believed that, too.

'And of course,' he said, 'it was only going to be your word against his, since your husband was going to die. And if you were winding up the operation and getting out with the proceeds, Orrie was going to be a liability as well as an expense, wasn't he? But what would you have done if he'd refused to put his neck in the noose, and decided to take a chance on Gus, and sit it out?'

'I'd have thought of something,' said Lesley confidently.

'In the end even you had to make one slip.'

'I shan't make another. I knew your thumbs were pricking about me,' she said without animosity, 'when you encouraged me to do poor old Stephen out of his alibi for the night. I could hardly do that without pointing out that I hadn't got one myself, could I? But even now, what are you going to charge me with?'

'Concealing a death will do to begin with.'

Lesley laughed aloud. 'You'll never make even that one stick. Not without Stephen's evidence, and you're going to have to go rather a long way to get that, aren't you?'

'Just as far,' said George, 'as the General. It's a mistake to be too clever at reading between the lines. Neither Doctor Braby nor Sister Bruce told you any lies, they just didn't tell you the whole truth. Sister told you repeatedly he wasn't any worse. She didn't say he wasn't any better. He is, very much. Digitalisation is taking effect excellently. He's out of danger.'

'But she told me,' said Lesley, genuinely indignant at such duplicity, 'that he was dying!'

'She did nothing of the sort. She told you simply that you could visit any time, even out of visiting hours. What you read into that is your worry. So you can visit, if you'd like to – under escort, of course.'

She made a small, bitter kitten-face, wrinkling her nose. The jolt was shrugged off in a moment; she adapted to this as nimbly as she did to everything. 'Thanks, but in the circumstances perhaps it wouldn't be tactful. It certainly wouldn't be amusing. But even if you do get to talk to him,' she said, strongly recovering, 'he won't say a word against me, you know.'

'You may,' said George, rising, 'find you've overestimated even his tolerance. How will you get round it then?'

'I'll think of something,' said Lesley.

It was two days before Stephen Paviour was sufficiently recovered to be visited briefly in hospital, and even then George put off what he really had to tell and ask him for two days more, and consulted his doctors before taking the risk of administering a new shock. By Thursday evening his condition was so far satisfactory as to allow the interview.

In all his life of half-fulfilment, of disappointments and deprivations, of loving without being loved, he had perhaps become accustomed to the fact that no one ever came to break good news. It was better to hear the whole story at once than to put it off, since his forebodings were almost always worse than the reality. And with long experience he had acquired a degree of durability against which even this might break itself and leave him unbroken. All the same, George approached the telling very gently and very simply. Flourishes would only have made sympathy intolerable.

Paviour lay and listened without exclamation or protest. There was offence and pain in it for him, but beneath the surface there was no surprise. When it was over he lay and digested it for a minute or two, and strangely he seemed to lie more easily and breathe more deeply, as though a tension and a load had been lifted from him.

'They both admit this? It's been going on – how long?'

'Since before Doctor Morris's visit. Perhaps two years. Perhaps even more.'

'I was rejected,' he said slowly. 'I had to respect her morbid sensitivity, and cherish her all the same, and I did it. That I could bear. And all the time she was wallowing with that beautiful draught-horse, that piece of border earth. While she fended me off with those elaborate lies, because I was too dull, too civilised, too old to serve her turn.' He thought for a moment, and there was colour in his grey face, and a spark in his normally haggard and anxious eyes. 'I'll tell you,' he said, 'exactly what happened, though I see now that it was not what happened at all, since there's no truth in her. This propensity of hers – to provoke men and then recoil from them – this feigned propensity . . . She used it on Alan Morris, too. You know he was a ladies' man? But a gentleman, and experienced enough to be able to deal with her. I was not worried at all.'

It was a bad moment to interrupt, but George had thought of one thing he needed to ask. 'Do you remember one evening during his visit, when young Lawrence came to dinner? Was there a conversation then about the criminal side of the archaeological interest? About how to market stolen antiques?'

Paviour looked faintly surprised, but the intervention did him good by diverting his own too fixed bitterness.

'I do remember it. I couldn't understand then why she should be so interested in such things. I understand now. She was picking his brains. I took it simply as her way of engaging his attention. I'm sure it was she who began the discussion.'

She had, George thought, such a housewifely sense of economy. She never threw away a solitary detail that might some day, suitably perverted, turn out to be useful.

'I'm sorry, I put you off. Please go on.'

'The last night of Morris's stay I had a lecture in the village, one of a series the county education office was putting on. When I came back I found Lesley sitting on the steps of the garden-room, in a hysterical condition. She was wet and cold and crying.'

No doubt, thought George, she can cry at will. God help the jury that has to deal with her!

'She said,' went on Paviour in a level, low voice, drawing up the words out of a well of anguish, 'that she had gone out for a walk with Alan by the river, and he had attacked and tried to rape her. And she had fought him off and pushed him into the Comer. It was credible, you understand, I had experience of the violence of her revulsion. She was very convincing in my case! And I loved her, and let her be. With someone who didn't understand – yes, there could be a tragedy. I didn't question it. She said she had got him out, but he was dead. She swims very well, you know, she was born by the river. I coaxed her to take me where he was. He was dead. There was no mistake. I knew – *then*, of course! – that exposure of such an affair, however accidental it might be, however innocent she might be, would destroy her totally. Her balance was already so precarious, you see. So I hid his body in the hypocaust. We were in process of closing the small dig we'd managed to finance that year, at the corner of the caldarium. It was pitifully small, and we got almost nothing from it. But it did afford a grave. I did it all myself, by night. I'd kept back his typewriter, and all his documents, and a suit of his that fitted me best. There was nothing to be done but take his place, his flight was booked, and it would account for his leaving. We were much the same build, and of course the same age. That goes a long way towards making a passport photograph acceptable, unless the officers have reason to suspect something, and they had none. I had to shave off my beard, but he wore a moustache, that was a help. He was not really very like me in the face, but the same general type, I suppose. And I was wearing his clothes, his hat, his glasses. It worked quite smoothly. We'd talked about his plans, I knew what was needed. And if I'd forgotten anything, I realise now, she would have prompted me. She did prompt me, many times. I took up his air reservation, his hotel reservation in Istanbul. And I worked over his text there, on his typewriter, and made sure that the manuscript he sent to his publishers on Aurae Phiala should put off all enquirers thereafter. It had to. There must never be a full-scale dig here, never.'

'The purpose was not, in fact, to conceal any valuable find,' said George. 'Just a body.'

'I never knew of any valuable find until now. No . . . I was hiding poor Morris. It wasn't a grave he would have rejected, you know.'

'We've found him,' said George. 'The pathologists may still be able to tell us how he died. I very much doubt if it was by drowning. I should guess he walked slap into one of their meetings, and found out what they were doing. In the circumstances, I doubt if he'd hold anything against you.'

'I hope you're right. I always envied him, but we were good friends. After I'd posted his book – yes, that he *would* hold against me, wouldn't he? That must be put right! – I telephoned his friend at Aphrodisias, and apologised for a change of plans, and paid my bill and went to the railway station. I changed to my own clothes in the baths there, and then flew home on my own passport. We'd left the last segment of the hypocaust open on purpose. I put all his other effects underground with him, and covered him in again with my own hands. It was not easy. None of it was easy.'

Very gently and reasonably George asked: 'Will you, if the issues we have in hand come to trial, testify against your wife? I promise you shall be fully informed of the weight of evidence against her with regard to any charges we prefer.'

'I'll testify to the truth, as far as I know it,' said Paviour, 'whether it destroys her or no. I realise that I myself am open to certain charges, graver charges than I understood at the time. Don't hesitate to make them. I have a debt, too. I made her possible.'

'No wonder the poor soul nearly dropped dead with shock when you came heaving out of the earth,' said George, two days later, in a corner of the bar at 'The Salmon's Return', with a pint in front of him, and Charlotte and Gus tucked comfortably into the settle opposite him. 'He took you for his own dead man rising. You'd hardly credit the difference in him now it's all over, now he doesn't have to live with his solitary nightmare, and there's no hope and no horror from her any more. The tension's snapped. Either he'll collapse altogether for want of the frictions that have kept him on edge, or else he'll look round and rediscover an ordinary world, and start living again. Just now I'd say all the odds are in favour of the second, thank God!'

'Do you think he'll really testify against her?' Charlotte wondered. 'He may feel bitter against her now, but what about when it comes to the point?'

'He'll testify,' said George with certainty. 'You can't love anyone that much, and be betrayed as callously as that, and not find out how to hate every bit as fiercely. Not that we know yet who did kill Doctor Morris. If those two decide to talk, of course, *she*'ll say *he* did it, and forced her to trick her husband into covering up for him. What he'll say I wouldn't bet on, except that it's more likely to be true than anything we get out of Lesley.'

'Who do *you* think actually did it?' asked Gus.

'Ordinarily she was the teller and he was the doer. But supposing Doctor Morris really did drown, in this case she may very well have done it herself. If he started taking a suspicious interest because of all her leading questions, *she*'s the one he'd be watching and following. There's a skull fracture, not enough to have killed him, probably, but it does bring Orrie into the picture. We may get a conviction for murder against both, but at least we can fix her as an accessory. Paviour will see to that.'

'Did you know when you set your trap,' asked Charlotte, 'that it was Orrie you were setting it for?'

'It wasn't for him,' said George simply. 'It was for *her*. I had a queer hunch about her, even before Gus came round and told me what he could. Two people were involved. And the cast wasn't all that big, even if I did make soothing noises about the village and the fishermen not being ruled out. And all of them male but Mrs Paviour, and all, somehow, so accurately deployed all round her, like pawns round a queen. If Gus was being stage-managed out of the world, who was more likely to be the stage-manager, the one who initiated that scene in the night, or the one who interrupted it? And if she had an accomplice, who was it likely to be but a lover? I did toy with the idea of young Lawrence. He was obviously jealous, though that could be regarded as evidence either for or against. And the Vespa was his, but his consternation when he heard about it being used rang true. And then, which of them was Lesley more likely to choose? The nice, dull, civilised scholar, her husband in embryo? Not on your life! So I was betting on Orrie, yes, but I didn't *know*! I was beginning to feel we might make a respectable case against him for Gerry Boden, though it would be mostly circumstantial. The boy had inhaled fibres from a thick, felted woollen fabric. I hope we'll be able to identify them as coming from Orrie's old donkey-jacket. His brand of wood-dust, fertiliser and vegetable debris should be pretty unique. And so's he, in his way. He must have slipped back from the vicarage garden as soon as it began to get dusk, caught the boy grubbing in the hypocaust, killed him and hid his body until it should be dark enough to get it down to the water, collected his aurei, and gone calmly back to his work. He almost certainly had the gold pieces in his pocket when Price called on him at home around nine o'clock to ask about Gerry's disappearance. And even after that he was cool enough to call in at "The Crown" before he went back to Aurae Phiala to send the body down the river. Not a nerve anywhere in him.'

'So you were following up his movements all the time,'

said Charlotte, 'while you hardly ever seemed to look in his direction.'

'Never let wild creatures know you're watching them. They tend to go to earth. If you carry on as if you haven't even noticed them they may emerge and go about their business. Not that it paid off with Orrie. There'd have been gaps in his time-table, if we'd had to proceed on the evidence, but we couldn't have proved how they were spent. Still, I'd have taken the risk of charging Orrie. On her I had nothing. I hoped – so did Orrie! – that she'd attempt the job herself. Then we'd have had her red-handed. *I* hoped she'd be frightened enough. *He* hoped – he *believed* – she cared enough. But we were both wrong. So I had to bluff it out the hard way, and hope to get through her guard somehow.'

'And I thought I'd wrecked it,' Charlotte said ruefully, 'going off at half-cock like that over her key. I'd only just realised what was going on. I wasn't very clever.'

'Not a bit of it! Once I had that key she had her back to the wall. Oh, she could have stuck to her story that she knew nothing about the coins. But she'd have had hard work accounting for the rest of the deposit.'

Stephen Paviour had authorised the opening of the box two days previously, and it had yielded, in addition to the coins, a highly interesting collection of documents concerning Lesley's buoyant financial situation, though without a word to explain it. She must have made good use of her holidays abroad with her husband, and the few occasions when she had accompanied him to digs in other countries. Nor is it always necessary to go abroad to find the kind of collector who asks no questions, and doesn't mind keeping his acquisitions to himself, well out of sight.

Charlotte thought of those tormented and tormenting lovers, so unevenly matched except in beauty, who now stood charged jointly with the murder of her kinsman.

244

'Would she ever really have gone away with him, as he thought? If their plans had gone on working out, right to the end?'

'Not a chance!' said George. 'Not with a crude, handsome, lumpish piece of earth like Orrie. She had all the money at her disposal, she could vanish and be rich. He'd helped her to put away plenty, mostly in banks in Switzerland. And what a trusting soul he was, everything was in her name! No, he'd given her a lot of pleasure, and been a lot of fun, but she'd have sloughed him off without a qualm. The world is full of men!'

'Not,' said Charlotte, torn between satisfaction and unwilling pity, 'the world where she's going.'

'Don't be too sure!' warned Gus feelingly, thinking with almost superstitious dread of the kitten's emerald eyes and sharp, insidious claws. 'Even if we do fix her, come eight years or so, and she'll be out on the world again – sooner if the charge is reduced. She isn't going to deteriorate, she isn't going to forget anything, only learn new tricks, and never in this world is she going to change. She'll come out ripe and ready for mischief. Give her half a chance, and she'll be popping up in another mask to lure another poor sucker to his death. No, my girl, you save your sympathy for me and the world that has to cope with her.'

George finished his beer, collected their glasses, and brought them another round. They had been installed here with Mrs Lane all the week, and they seemed, he thought, to be getting on very satisfactorily together. Gus was involved in the documentation of the case from two angles, and could also claim to be a convalescent, entitled to take his duties at a rather leisurely pace, but it was questionable whether he would have strung out his work locally quite so long if Charlotte had not been still at 'The Salmon's Return'. Tomorrow Gus was leaving for London and duty at last; and it could hardly be coincidence that Charlotte was going to town by the same train, to confer with her solicitor and make preparations for the reburial of her great-uncle. He had known even stranger circumstances bring people together. In a sense, Gus Hambro had been a dead duck from the moment he drew Charlotte after him on his nocturnal rush to have one more look for a missing boy. When you have given someone his life back, it may be magnanimous to give it wholly and go right away and forget the benefit, but it's very human to keep a thin, strong string attached, and retain a proprietary interest.

'I'll leave you to it,' said George. And he looked at Charlotte with the private look that had somehow developed between them. 'It's a big step, you know. I'd sleep on it, if I were you.'

'Your wife didn't,' said Charlotte.

They halted at the crest of the bowl to look back over the shallow, undulating expanse of Aurae Phiala. The flood water had passed, the weather was settling into the pure spring-like hush that sometimes comes before a turbulent May. The river ran deeply green and tranquil under its shelving banks. Away to their right, round one corner of the caldarium, tarpaulin screens fenced off the enclosure where the police had dug Doctor Alan Morris out of his grave. The inquest had not yet opened. But there would be no problem of identification there, with all his belongings securely buried round him, like a pharaoh.

'I wish he could have come out of it alive,' said Charlotte. 'But I'm glad he comes out of it with credit. In a sense he was defending the ethics of the profession, if he died because he suspected their thefts and tried to prevent them. For a time you thought I might be here as his agent, didn't you?'

'And for a time,' he said, 'you thought I might be behind

the racket myself, didn't you?'

'You knew so much about it, too much. How was I to know which side you were on? I always knew you weren't what you seemed. And I knew you'd latched on to me after you found out my name, not for my charm.'

'Only half true,' he said. 'I don't believe you were ever in doubt for a moment how I felt about you.'

Their voices were as tranquil as the evening sky, and they were standing hand in hand.

'There was a time,' she owned serenely, 'a very brief time, though, when I did wonder just what you were feeling for Lesley.'

'I'd never given her a thought of any kind,' he said firmly, 'until she began to make a dead set at me, after she'd whisked my jacket away to dry and brush it, when I got buried that time. She'd begun to have suspicions already, because she seized that opportunity like a pro. And I was fool enough to carry stuff on me that I shouldn't have done – my passport with the bill from that Istanbul hotel still in it, and some notes, and even a drawing of that gold triskele brooch from Italy, the one that started me on the case. She couldn't very well mistake it. She sold the thing in Livorno. After that it was all "do stay to lunch", and "move in with us, we've got plenty of room". You she wanted under her eye to find out what you were up to, me to dispose of permanently. Not that I realised it then. I just played her shots back to her, to find out what the game was. She'd made up her mind I had to go for good. Underground. I was getting a lot too near to what I was after.'

He remembered with a convulsion of painful rapture and guilt the clinging frenzy of that small body, which this one beside him must some day wipe out of mind. Aloud he said: 'Those scenes with me were staged for him. She could manipulate him like modelling clay. His job was to interrupt us and very politely, very considerately, ask me to leave. So that she and Orrie could entice me back to the caldarium and dispose of me, with everything accounted for, a farewell note waiting, and no questions asked.'

The moon, a filigree wafer of silver foil, was rising, and the Welsh shore had dimmed into a deep, twilit blue of folded hills. Aurae Phiala was as beautiful as ever, and as pure. No part of this greed, violence and deceit had done more than glance from its present-day surface, which was only illusory. It had outlived all its own tragedies long ago.

'I went to see Mr Felse at his home on Saturday morning,' said Charlotte, 'after he flew that kite about Great-Uncle Alan, and started Lesley thinking what a convenient scapegoat he'd make. And he told me about the Yard enquiries, though not about you, and said they'd led inevitably to considering my uncle as one possibility. And then I asked him again if *he* believed in it. And he said, personally, no. He said scholars are seldom rich, but no matter how great the temptation to personal gain, if a find of that magnitude did turn up, the strongest temptation of all would be the innocent one, to the excitement and glory and public admiration. I loved him for that. Because, you see, until then I hadn't been quite so sure myself. But he was right. And because I wanted him to be right, I began to take his word for everything.'

'So that was when you met his wife,' said Gus, remembering George's enigmatic valediction. 'What was that all about, anyhow? What was it his wife didn't do?'

They had begun to walk back, turning away from the crude tarpaulin shape and the scarred ground. And they forgot all the dead of Aurae Phiala in the blessed conviction of being themselves rather more than usually alive.

'She didn't back away and demand time to sleep on it,' said Charlotte, 'when she was asked if she'd consider marrying a policeman.'

ELLIS PETERS

The author of the bestselling *Brother Cadfael* novels

MOURNING RAGA

AN INDIAN WHODUNNIT

As a favour to his girlfriend Tossa's beautiful but erratic filmstar mother, Dominic Felse agrees to escort a teenage heiress back to her father in India. But travelling with the spoilt, precocious Anjli is no sinecure – and the task of delivering her to her family proves even less easy.

Dominic and Tossa find themselves embroiled in a mystery that swiftly and shockingly becomes a murder investigation. For behind the colourful, smiling mask of India that the tourist sees is another country – remote, mysterious – and often shatteringly brutal . . .

'Strongly plotted story of kidnapping and murder in a well-observed Delhi. Exciting and humane.'
H. R. F. Keating, The Times

FICTION/CRIME   0 7472 3121 4

A selection of bestsellers from Headline

FICTION

GASLIGHT IN PAGE STREET	Harry Bowling	£4.99 □
LOVE SONG	Katherine Stone	£4.99 □
WULF	Steve Harris	£4.99 □
COLD FIRE	Dean R Koontz	£4.99 □
ROSE'S GIRLS	Merle Jones	£4.99 □
LIVES OF VALUE	Sharleen Cooper Cohen	£4.99 □
THE STEEL ALBATROSS	Scott Carpenter	£4.99 □
THE OLD FOX DECEIV'D	Martha Grimes	£4.50 □

NON-FICTION

THE SUNDAY TIMES SLIM PLAN	Prue Leith	£5.99 □
MICHAEL JACKSON The Magic and the Madness	J Randy Taraborrelli	£5.99 □

SCIENCE FICTION AND FANTASY

SORCERY IN SHAD	Brian Lumley	£4.50 □
THE EDGE OF VENGEANCE	Jenny Jones	£5.99 □
ENCHANTMENTS END Wells of Ythan 4	Marc Alexander	£4.99 □

All Headline books are available at your local bookshop or newsagent, or can be ordered direct from the publisher. Just tick the titles you want and fill in the form below. Prices and availability subject to change without notice.

Headline Book Publishing PLC, Cash Sales Department, PO Box 11, Falmouth, Cornwall, TR10 9EN, England.

Please enclose a cheque or postal order to the value of the cover price and allow the following for postage and packing:
UK & BFPO: £1.00 for the first book, 50p for the second book and 30p for each additional book ordered up to a maximum charge of £3.00.
OVERSEAS & EIRE: £2.00 for the first book, £1.00 for the second book and 50p for each additional book.

Name ....

Address ....

....

....